the sugar baron's daughter

Loveleen Kacker is a member of the Madhya Pradesh cadre of the Indian Administrative Service. She is the author of a novel on the Naxalite movement called *Terror in the Jungle* and has also written several books for children, including the popular *Saloni* series. At present she is Joint Secretary (Child Welfare) in the ministry of Women and Child Development.

the sugar baron's daughter

loveleen kacker

HarperCollins *Publishers* India

First published in India in 2007 by
HarperCollins *Publishers* India

Building 10, Tower A, 4th Floor, DLF Cyber City, Phase II,
Gurugram Haryana – 122002, India
www.harpercollins.co.in

ISBN 13: 978-81-7223-462-1

ISBN 10: 81-7223-462-7

Typeset in 12/14 Lapidary
Nikita Overseas Pvt. Ltd.

Printed and bound at
MicroPrints India, New Delhi

To my friends in the sugar industry,
and with special thanks to Sewak Grewal

anmol

I opened my eyes and scratched the back of my neck. It was wet with perspiration. It was an effort to lift my head and look out of the window. All I saw was the leaden sky and the criss-cross of electrical wires. I closed my eyes in disgust. Another muggy day, still and oppressive as Delhi always is in the monsoon. Next year, next year, I promised myself, I would have the money to buy air-conditioners both for the bedroom and the car. No more freezing in winter and boiling in the summer for me. Next year I was going to hit the big time. It was bound to come, considering the things I had in hand. A clear twenty-lakh package was forthcoming, ten for me and ten for Bhaskar. Then there were the other two deals that were almost through. They would also bring us about ten lakhs together. Quickly I joined my hands towards the picture of Ma Durga. It would be sacrilege to even say the amount in my thoughts. The moment I had all that lovely cash I would leave this middle-class refugee colony and its middle-class values forever.

I looked at my watch and was surprised to find that it was only seven-thirty – much too early to get up. The children would be creating a ruckus downstairs and Mataji and Vidya would be too busy preparing breakfasts and lunches to make my coffee. Best to simply lie in bed and wait for Vidya to bring it to me. Where were my cigarettes? I grinned even as I lit up. Why was I feeling so happy? Right. Kulbhushan's phone call. Kulbhushan Singh, scion of the oldest and most respected business family in western Uttar Pradesh, had called me up. *Me*. Anmol. Son of the loyal family retainer.

And the funniest thing was Kulbhushan requesting me for a meeting. 'Anmol Bhai,' he had begun. The bastard! He added and dropped his bhais to suit his purpose. There had to be an angle to it, or why would he have remembered Anmol Bhai after fourteen years? 'How are you, Anmol Bhai? How are Bhabhi and the children? Um, you have two sons, don't you?'

'A son and a daughter.'

'Of course,' Kulbhushan allowed himself a tiny embarrassed laugh. 'Well –' he began and stopped.

I was silent. There was no way that I was going to make things easy for him.

'– I was in town and I thought why don't I call up Anmol Bhai and catch up on the news? How about lunch tomorrow?' The second part was delivered in a rush, as though he needed to get it over with.

'Tomorrow? Let me see.' I put my hand over the mouthpiece and snorted as I looked out of the window at the rather sad papaya tree that drooped in the heat. I had no diary to consult and was totally free, but I wanted him to wait. 'Why this sudden love for me, Kulbhushan?' I asked finally, my curiosity getting the better of me.

'Really, Anmol, does there have to be a reason?' His voice cooled a little and acquired a master's tone. 'But if you are really busy –' he let that sound detached and businesslike.

Naturally I panicked. 'No, Kulbhushan. I'll make myself free for you,' I said quickly. Kulbhushan was not a man to call without reason. And besides, what was the sense in fooling myself? I needed to know about the welfare of Hukam Singh Mills, and about Nagina. *Nagina.* All of a sudden there was a tightness in my chest. Thinking of Nagina always did that to me.

'Good. Then shall we first meet at the bar at the Oberoi? We can choose the restaurant later.' Kulbhushan put down the phone without waiting for me to respond.

Hukam Singh Mills and Majhauli. Majhauli and Hukam Singh Mills. Magical words that transported me back to my childhood. Rai Sahab Hukam Singh had established the sugar mill in Majhauli forty years ago, soon after Independence. Actually he'd bought the house first. The house, built by an Englishman who had spent a lifetime studying the flora and fauna of the Terai region, was stately and elegant. The Englishman, Sebastian Hopkins, was a bachelor who had come to India to visit his brother who was a major in the British army, a pale ginger-haired man, bravely shouldering the white man's burden in savage India and hating every minute of it. But Sebastian fell in love with India and didn't mind the mosquitoes and the heat and the native population. What he didn't care for was the local architecture and so he created, in the heart of Uttar Pradesh, at a point where the foothills of the Himalayas began, a huge and perfectly English home replete with a ballroom, a breakfast room, a dining room, two drawing rooms, eight bedrooms, a library and a music room. And every stick of furniture in the house was imported from good olde England.

Hukam Singh bought Green Paths, as the house was called, almost, but not quite, translating its original name, with the gold and jewellery that he had brought from Pakistan after Partition. He is reported to have paid ten lakh rupees for it, a fantastic sum at that time. It was not a bad bargain though, for the furniture came with the house, as did fifty acres of prime land. Of course there were others who said that Hukam Singh didn't pay a paisa for it. They claimed that he just annexed it after Sebastian left and then had the revenue records adjusted in his favour. Hukam Singh was twenty-three years old at the time.

The day Hukam Singh moved into the house he stood on his doorstep and watched the sun set. Everything in his life had changed. His father had refused to leave Pakistan and there was no one to guide him, no one to share his responsibilities. As the setting sun cast a red glow on his face, Hukam Singh vowed to reclaim the former glory and prestige of his father Rai Sahab Izzat Singh. Then he turned his eyes heavenward and took an even more difficult vow – not to marry till he had made as much money as he had spent purchasing the property. It was a tough vow but he never wavered from it. It took him ten years to build the sugar mill and the godowns and the colony of houses for his workers and officers, ten years for his balance sheet to show a profit of ten lakhs. The day that happened he went to his mother. 'Beeji,' he said. 'Where's the girl you keep talking about? It's time I got married.'

Beeji was overjoyed and immediately set off for Haridwar where an old school friend of hers lived. When their children had been born the two women had decided to marry them to each other when they grew up. Beeji's friend had stuck to her side of the bargain and kept her daughter unmarried though she was only a year younger than Hukam Singh and disgracefully old for a bride. Hukam Singh could have had the pick of the youngest and loveliest virgins available, but he was a dutiful son, and when Beeji came back with the bride and forty of her relatives he kept his peace. Hukam Singh and Vimla were married by Arya Samaj rites on the night of Kartik Poornima, and two days later he sent all forty of her relatives back to Haridwar.

Everyone remarked on the extraordinary love that Hukam Singh bore for his old wife – with the emphasis on 'old' – but they didn't say that for long. Vimla Singh was the perfect partner for Hukam Singh. She was a strong, capable and hardworking woman. In fact, the staff and workers of Rai Bahadur Hukam Singh Sugar Mills probably feared her more than they feared her husband. Vimla Singh bore two children and then settled down to run Hariyali and the workers' colony for her husband. It was Vimla who got the sewage lines laid in the workers' colony and the gutters lined with cement. It was she who taught the workers' wives about hygiene and family planning and opened a school for the workers' children. It was to this school that I, Anmol, son of Durga Das Malhotra, manager of the mills, first went.

I was still thinking of the Rai Bahadurs of Majhauli when Vidya came in with the coffee, newspaper and bad news. 'The prime minister has announced the government's decision to implement the Mandal Commission's Report. We missed the TV news yesterday thanks to the children's party.'

'Brats gone? Guddu gone?' I asked.

'All gone, thank god.' Vidya sat down on the chair and poured out two cups of strong, sweet coffee. Her long thick hair was plaited tightly and fell across one shoulder like a snake. I wondered if there was time for a quickie but knew that Vidya would never agree. My wife was the most inhibited woman in the whole country. She might have had outlandish political opinions but when it came to sex she was a bore. She even wore salwar suits to bed like Mataji did.

Vidya looked at me with knitted brows, 'What does it mean, Anmol?'

'What?' I asked absently.

'This Mandal business. People kept saying that V.P. Singh wasn't serious about it and now, out of the blue, he has gone and announced the implementation of the Mandal Commission Report.'

'Forget it. In this country politicians will do everything and anything for votes. It's another vote stunt to win the backwards.'

'But don't they already have reservation?'

'They do. Actually, I don't know too much about Mandal. These guys will keep coming up with bizarre ideas. This time it's probably reservation for the backwards, though don't ask me who the backwards are.'

'Anmol, did you talk to Bhaskar?'

I was pouring my second cup of coffee. 'Bhaskar?'

'Ya, Bhaskar. About my job in *The Times of India*?' Vidya started pulling off my sheet. 'Get up, I've got to make the bed.'

I stood up reluctantly and sat with the newspaper on the easy chair folding my legs beneath me. The cane bottom of the chair sagged dangerously but held somehow.

'This chair is a symbol of my patience,' said Vidya. 'The day the cane breaks and your bottom touches the floor, I will blow a fuse.'

'Bofors. Punjab militants.' I threw down the paper. 'The news is depressing. Is there more coffee?'

Vidya had taken up the duster and was struggling to remove a patch of glue in the corner of the mirror, a dirty brown residue left behind by innumerable bindis. The sticky mess would not get cleaned. 'Imagine the damage to our skins,' she fumed. Her forehead was creased with concentration, her mouth pressed in a tiny moue that was typical of her. Vidya in the mornings was a Vidya charged with tasks to do and best avoided because, given the slightest chance, she would embark on a tirade on the plight of women – she looked upon herself as a champion of women's rights. I think, in moments of self-reflection, Vidya imagined herself leading a march for women and shouting: *Nahin chalega, nahin chalega, auraton par atyachar nahin chalega!* She was wiping bottles of cologne and aftershave and muttering to herself. Now was the time to speak. 'I'm going out to lunch today.'

'No!' Vidya exclaimed in disbelief. 'Goodwork Consultants is *actually* entertaining a client?'

'Actually the client is entertaining me.' Even to myself I sounded a bit elated. 'I'm lunching with Kulbhushan Singh at the Oberoi Hotel.'

'Can he get me a job?'

'What?'

'Never mind. Who's this big shot?'

Was there really someone who didn't know the Singhs of Majhauli? 'He's the son of Rai Sahab Hukam Singh of the sugar mill in Majhauli, who else?' I was short with her.

'Achha. Okay.'

Vidya's indifference annoyed me. But then she wasn't born and brought up in Majhauli. Poor Vidya, she was one of those lakhs born in middle-class homes in Delhi and doomed to spend a lifetime commuting on DTC buses, breathing exhaust fumes and munching peanuts. What did she know of green mountains and fields of thick sugar cane and air imbued with the smell of fermenting sugar cane juice? Perhaps it was best she didn't know about Majhauli, for my memories were precious, too precious to be shared. I stood up and stretched my arms. It was time to shake off my lassitude and go for a haircut. It wouldn't do to give Kulbhushan the slightest hint of shabbiness.

In my nervousness I was the first to reach the bar at the hotel. All the stools and the deep sofas were empty – even the bartender wasn't prepared for guests, it seemed. I went in search of the men's room and spent five minutes examining my face in the mirror and generally admiring myself. This was one area where no one could fault me for I was the prototype of the handsome tall Punjabi male and looked as though I had been brought up on a diet of milk and apples.

The bar was still deserted when I returned. The thing to do is to look calm and in command of the situation, I told myself. So I sat down and ordered a gin and lime. I was on my second drink and debating whether I should pay for the drinks and go to Pandara Road for a cheaper meal when Kulbhushan walked in. Immediately I felt inferior and gauche. In spite of the hot weather Kulbhushan wore a long-sleeved silk shirt with cream-coloured trousers and matching brown shoes. He was of medium height, slim and clean-shaven with soft, manicured hands that were virtually lost in my huge grip. I looked at my crumpled cotton shirt with printed black and red dogs and was disgusted with myself. I looked like a sales rep. I ran my fingers through my short hair and wished I had not had it cut. It was because of the pressure from Vidya, I told myself. It makes your head look twice its size, she had said. Long hair did no such thing for Kulbhushan. He looked sophisticated and suave as he sat on the sofa and carelessly snapped his finger at the bartender. 'One gimlet.'

'Yes, Sir.' The waiter sprang to get his drink.

'Well, Kulbhushan,' I said, trying to be hearty. 'You look good.'

The Rai Sahab family always did this to me. They reduced me to a gibbering idiot with ten thumbs and zero self-confidence. I thought only Hukam Singh, his wife and Beeji had this effect on me, but now Kulbhushan, who was a full four years younger than me, was making me feel like a country bumpkin. I tried to think of the time I had challenged him to climb the tamarind tree and rubbed his nose in the dust for not being able to. But even then Kulbhushan had maintained his dignity, taking his punishment manfully and not running off to his mother like a sissy. You had to admire the boy. He only shrivelled when Nagina was around, for she treated him like an errand-boy.

'How's Nagina?' I asked, desperate to know yet afraid to ask. It was better, far better, if Nagina remained a memory.

'Fine, just fine. She does all the blimp's work and looks after his house in Delhi now.'

'Blimp?'

'Her husband. Satya Pal Aggarwal. Mr Bania with the moneybags. He sits back while Nagina runs around in circles.' He saw the bewildered expression on my face and waved his hand in a gesture of dismissal. 'Forget Nagina.'

I nodded, taken aback by the way he referred to his brother-in-law. 'Well,' I said, taking command of myself. 'Since the pleasantries seem to be over, perhaps you could tell me the reason for this invitation.'

Kulbhushan lifted a finger in admonishment. 'Not before lunch.' He signed the check carelessly and we walked to the lift and rode up to the Chinese restaurant on the top floor. I was at least five inches taller than him and twenty kilos heavier, but it was to him that the maître d'hôtel rushed and it was with him that the menu was discussed in knowledgeable whispers while I looked at the tops of the trees of the golf course and smoked in an attempt to appear nonchalant. Kulbhushan didn't ask me what I would like to eat, which was just as well because I would have ordered chicken corn soup and chilli chicken without even reading the menu. Instead we had some exotic clear soup followed by a variety of steamed appetizers and then the main course, which was duck in god-knows-what. We drank a bottle of white wine with our food. By now I was drunk and bored, a dangerous combination.

'Anmol Bhai,' began Kulbhushan, and I shook my head to clear the somnolence that threatened to take over. It was coming finally, the reason for all this bhai-bhai business. 'Don't you ever think about Majhauli and the mill?'

I tried staring at Kulbhushan in an attempt to intimidate him. 'What do you mean, "think about Majhauli"? Why do you want me to "think about Majhauli"?'

'Don't you want to know how we are doing and whether things are well with the mill? After all, you grew up there.'

'Get to the point.'

'Okay,' he said, suddenly sitting up and looking me straight in the eye. 'You know about the way a sugar mill functions so I don't have to explain too much to you. Recollect, if you will, that we have to pay cane prices to the farmers through the cane societies. This year the government of UP has raised the state-advised cane price to thirty-eight rupees a quintal! Almost double the cane price announced by the Government of India. Naturally, we have cane payment arrears – so does every other sugar mill in UP. There's no way we can pay all the money we owe to the farmers. And what we owe them is considerable – almost five crore rupees. We have tried to get a larger quota of free sale sugar released, but no luck. You know how the government works. Nothing gets done.' A frown marred the smooth whiteness of his brow as he dug into his pocket to find his cigarettes. 'We are in a mess in Majhauli these days. Five crores to pay and that bastard Bihari creating trouble everyday. Mind you, we are not the only ones with cane payment arrears. All over UP the sugar factories are feeling the pinch. In fact, we are not facing as big a cash crunch as some of the others.' He put his hand inside his pocket again and this time pulled out a spotless white hanky and proceeded to dab his brow. I smiled to myself. Serves him right, wearing silk in summer. The gigolo! 'This fellow Som Dutt Bihari is advising the farmers not to give us cane till the earlier payments are cleared. With the kind of influence this guy has in the neighbourhood, it won't be long before they start listening to him. Then we will truly be in a soup! We can't pay them unless we run the factory, and if they don't give us cane the factory doesn't run!' He ground out his cigarette in the ashtray. 'Bihari is a troublemaker and the only way to settle this problem is to work out some settlement with him.'

'Interesting,' I said. 'But what does it have to do with me?'

'You could do something for us.'

'I could?'

'Yes. Speak to Bihari. You know Som Dutt very well. You are probably the only person, apart from Imtiaz Khan, who can influence him.'

'I knew Somu, but that was years ago,' I protested. 'And who's Imtiaz Khan? I don't know him.'

'You may not know Imtiaz Khan – the MLA – but you were Som Dutt's closest pal. And you belong to Majhauli.'

'I belonged to Majhauli years ago. Why will Somu or this Khan, whoever he is, listen to me?'

'He will listen to you. You are – were – his friend. You have the welfare of the mill in your heart. Of course he'll listen to you.'

'You're crazy,' I shook my head. Did this cocksure young man really think that I would talk to Somu or Imtiaz Khan on behalf of the mill? Didn't he know the circumstances in which I had left Hukam Singh Mills? I recalled his father's expression when he'd found out what I had done. Rai Sahab had said very little, but his face had turned black with anger and a thick vein had bulged in his forehead. I remembered how the blood rushed into the whites of his eyes as he'd raised one shaking finger at me and said in an awful voice, 'Get out, and stay out.' I had not gone back to Majhauli since. Never. Not in fourteen years.

I looked at Kulbhushan again, struck by how similar and yet how different he was from his father. He definitely had Rai Sahab's good looks, the high patrician nose with the pinched nostrils and the thin lips. He also had Rai Sahab's slim physique, the narrow shoulders and the non-existent buttocks. But the whole picture was wrong. Kulbhushan's lips were sensuous, not stern, his eyes almost coquettish, his skin too smooth and rosy. Something about him disturbed me, but I couldn't put my finger on it.

'Have you asked your father?' I asked finally, when it seemed that Kulbhushan wasn't going to break the silence.

'What?'

'Does your father know that you have come to me for help?'

'Yes. Do you want him to talk to you?'

No, I didn't wish to talk to him. Nagina was the only one who could. Kulbhushan was much too scared of him and Vimla

Singh wouldn't dream of it. 'No, no, of course not,' I answered, 'but the fact is I can't come to Majhauli. I'm too busy.'

'Busy? Playing politics? Perfecting the role of Delhi's smartest Mr Fixit? Oh, I know all about Goodwork Consultants, and let me assure you that I don't expect you to work for nothing. You will be more than compensated for your troubles. All I want you to do is to buy us some time, say three months, and make Som Dutt Bihari promise that he will continue to supply cane during that time – that's all. Between you and me, we are expecting a recovery of more than eleven per cent this year, almost twelve per cent in fact. We'll be able to catch up with our payments. I understand that bastard Bihari's game very well. He wants that the factory should stop crushing cane altogether, so that he can create a big hue and cry about the rich owners and the poor starving farmers. That will bring the chief minister running pell-mell to Majhauli. And who gets the most mileage out of this whole show? Bihari and Imtiaz, who else? He's a smart crook, that guy. I tell you, he's fooling both us and the farmers. I've tried talking to him, but he behaves like we are filmi-style zamindars who dance on the corpses of workers and he is Datta Samant! We are in a mess, we need your help, Anmol Bhai.'

'That means the factory won't start this year?'

'It will start! Don't forget we have some cane of our own. We can begin with that. Besides, as I said, I don't want Bihari to tell the chief minister that we haven't started crushing. But if he prevents the farmers from giving us cane, the factory will come to a halt very soon.'

'When do you plan to start crushing?'

'First of October. There isn't much time left. You have to come and speak to Bihari.'

'But I told you I can't come. I'm busy.'

'Didn't you hear what I said? Bihari won't let us run the factory!'

'I did hear you, Kulbhushan. But it's your problem, not mine.' I said this softly, almost to myself. Kulbhushan didn't appear to have heard me.

Kulbhushan's face was flushed with wine and anger. He banged his fist into his palm and roundly abused Somu and Imtiaz. He raved about what selfish bastards they both were. They were on his payroll. They took his money every month yet refused to cooperate when he needed help. I watched the performance with amusement. Rai Sahab would never have shown such an unseemly love for money. If Rai Sahab had been handling this situation he would have spoken of cane driage, loss of weight and loss to the farmers. He would have pooh-poohed profit and spoken of workers' welfare. But then he belonged to a different generation. He might have lived like a maharaja but he never discussed money or showed an interest in it.

I got up to leave. I knew what Kulbhushan wanted from me and I wasn't going to do it. 'Okay, Kulbhushan,' I stuck out my hand. 'Nice lunch and nice chitchat. Keep in touch.'

'But, Anmol Bhai, what about Bihari?' Kulbhushan stood up suddenly and knocked over a glass. His carefully cultivated poise was shaken. I, the paid servant, couldn't possibly be refusing him!

'I told you I'm busy.'

'You bastard!'

'No foul language, Kulbhushan, please. If I get down to it your vocabulary would never be able to compete. You requested me to do something and I can't do it. That's no reason to call me names. Find another chamcha. The Rai Sahabs don't own me or my father.' I turned my back on him and walked out of the restaurant.

In the great plains of northern India there is little physical beauty. You can travel for miles and all you will see is the great, flat, dusty countryside with no hills or valleys and very few trees to break the monotony. The villages are collections of thatched brown hovels with narrow twisting paths between them that turn into rivers of slush in the monsoon and remain coated with the slimy waste of animals during the rest of the year. You have only to see these villages to realize how disorderly and impractical the Indian mind is. If it hadn't been for the British we would never have understood the value of straight roads, parallel intersections and sewage lines.

When the factory began crushing in mid-October the factory gate was open day and night. The cane managers and their staff sat at rickety tables issuing parchis to the farmers who brought in their cane for crushing. The line was unending; the trucks, tractor-trailers and bullock carts just kept coming, night and day, piled high with cut sugar cane. The turbaned farmers would park their vehicles outside and wait patiently, seated on top of their load of cane, wrapped in heavy, chequered blankets. They had to be equipped for every kind of weather, for the business of getting a parchi, weighing the cane, and the unloading, took anything from two hours to three days. Often in December, when the early morning sun rose from behind the haze of hundreds of cooking fires, you could still see the patient farmer sitting still as a statue on the top of his cane, only the occasional curl of beedi smoke an indication that the man had survived near-zero degree temperatures in the open all night. Keeping vigil with him were his bulls, those great ponderous beasts that seemed never to complain of hunger or thirst, cold or even weariness, plodding on and on till one day they just dropped dead in harness.

The road through the other gate lead to neat rows of houses in the workers' colony, past two cooperative stores, the schools, the senior manager's bungalow and then a long stretch of leafy avenue that brought you to the lawns of Hariyali. There were two gates set into the wall, one for the factory and the other for the colony. A huge black-and-white painted sign, with letters more than two feet high, stretched across both the gates – Rai Sahab Hukam Singh Sugar Mills Pvt. Ltd. Both the gates were manned by burly uniformed guards from Haryana.

As you entered the gates you saw the brilliant beds of seasonal flowers, then the house itself, set against the purple foothills of the Himalayas, like a picture-postcard. There were always flowers in Hariyali, no matter what the season. Though there was a hothouse tended by an army of gardeners, what I really loved were the scented local flowers like the desi roses, the raat ki rani, the marigolds and the mogra. The house itself was painted white and had long, narrow windows aligned geometrically on each of its three storeys, with all its shutters painted green. The entrance was dominated by four tall columns, fluted at the top. Behind them was a deep veranda with white cane furniture and lots of plants, big-leafed and deep green in colour. The green and white colour scheme was repeated in the entire house and gave it a character that was cool, aloof and pristine. Or at least that was my memory of it.

Back then I had been a constant fixture in Hariyali for I grew up with Nagina and Kulbhushan and I loved the house like it was my own. If you have lived in a house like Hariyali you can never live anywhere else and think of it as home. Its beauty ran in my veins. Though I grew up with the children of the malik-log, I always remained the son of the manager – ultimately an inferior. Though I could romp through the gardens and steal guavas and mangoes, my permissible limits inside the house were defined by the staircase. I could never go up to the bedrooms. I had hundreds of meals with Kulbhushan and Nagina, but not one with Hukam Singh and his wife. When the servants served us, the children, I was served last and rarely got the leg piece in the chicken because the baba-log wanted it. Nagina and Kulbhushan sensed the difference in social status between themselves and me, and there was always that slight uppishness in their behaviour. So, even though we fought like equals and clawed at each other, I always reined in before my bigger fists and tougher muscles inflicted real damage on either of them, and I did so instinctively. I notice today the same slightly superior and commanding tone that my own children adopt with the children of the maid. No matter how clean and well-dressed the help's children are, class differences creep in. And because I grew up with the owner's children for companions, I knew well the reflex that made me lower the volume of my voice in their presence and change its timbre till it sounded appropriately deferential.

It was 1972 and the war with Pakistan was on. It was time for admission to intermediate after high school and there was serious concern in our extended family about What Anmol Should Do. We sat huddled in the drawing room of our house with its ugly dark furniture and drapes; nobody spent money on interior decoration in the Seventies. Even though I was the subject of this big family debate, nobody expected me to be there and if I insisted on being present, Mataji said, I should sit inconspicuously in the corner and not speak unless spoken to.

Mataji sat demurely behind Pitaji though nobody was fooled by this show of humility. My mother was a strong-willed lady who took hard decisions with great ease, but she suggested them in such a clever way that Pitaji always felt that the brilliant idea was his. Father, as befitted a good RSS man, sat erect in his pajama-kurta with his hands folded on his flat stomach. Next to Mataji sat my grandmother, blind but in possession of all her mental faculties; she had her own ideas about what Anmol beta should become. And on the other side of Pitaji sat my uncles – nondescript non-entities each one of them, but as their status demanded deference, they sat around and pretended to give the matter serious thought.

'Maji,' Pitaji addressed my grandmother. 'The issue really is very simple. The National Sugar Institute in Kanpur is an old and prestigious institution. It has courses in sugar technology and engineering, in fact in all aspects covering the manufacture of sugar. Anmol should study there and eventually take my place in the mill.'

'But he should go to college first,' protested my grandmother.

'For what? To get a useless BA degree that will prepare him for nothing and will not even guarantee him a job as a clerk in an office? Is that what you want Maji, a babu for a grandson?'

'Of course not! My grandson will become an officer.' Maji spoke with pride and conviction.

'Nobody is going to make your precious grandson an officer, Maji. Look at the interest he shows in studies. It's only because he is my son that they have been passing him to the next class every year. Left to himself he would still be in the eighth.'

My blood boiled at this unfair comment but I was quiet. Mataji had warned me to remain so, promising that no matter what Pitaji said she would send me to college. My father always ran me down. I may not have been the world's smartest student but I certainly wasn't given the passing grade because of my father. Besides, who was he to suggest that I was a dud? He himself was only a high-school pass.

'We have to think about a career for him, one that is guaranteed and that will ensure that we are looked after in our old age – not left to take on the burden of his wife and children!'

I had barely finished high school and here my father had not only decided my life's course, he had also written me off. I opened my mouth to tell him that I was never going to marry and certainly not the girl of his choice, when I caught Mataji's's eye. She shook her head at me and smiled the special smile that she kept only for me. I took a deep breath and tried to calm myself.

'It has to be the mill for him,' repeated Pitaji.

'What is the guarantee that Rai Sahab will take him?' asked my grandmother.

'Guarantee? What guarantee do you want? When we came from Pakistan what did we have apart from the clothes on our backs? It was Rai Sahab who took care of us. He paid me the manager's salary for one whole year before I actually worked as a manager.'

'True. Then we shall continue to live here and serve Rai Sahab,' said my mother with a finality that sounded like the death knell to me.

I had never expected Mataji to let me down so blatantly after assuring me that she would send me to college. I jumped up and shouted, 'Have you people gone completely crazy? I'm not joining any sugar technology course and I'm not going to work for a sugar mill. Never! I'm going in for Economics or Accounts. The future is with one who knows his numbers.'

'Hat moya!' said my grandmother.

'Not going to join the mill?' yelled Pitaji in utter amazement.

'No, I'm not going to join the mill and rot in this place for the rest of my life. I hate it and I hate the smell of cane juice! You can't force me to join the mill. I'll run away!' I didn't hate the mill as much as I hated the idea of remaining with them forever.

'Not going to join the mill, hain? Going to run away, hain? Well, you are not that old that I cannot take my shoe to you and flay the skin off your back!' Pitaji threatened. 'You are incapable of taking decisions, so you listen to me. You are right in so far as you say that this is an era of specialization. There is hardly anybody who has studied sugar technology. Even Rai Sahab himself has learned only through experience. You do this course and you will get double my salary.' He leaned forward and spoke with glittering eyes, 'Double, I tell you. And who knows, you might be managing the mill alone one day, as the general manager! Rai Sahab is very disappointed in his son Kulbhushan, you know.' Mataji and the uncles nodded their agreement throughout this performance.

'No, never! I'd rather die!' I shouted, tears starting in my sixteen-year-old eyes. Subconsciously I realized that this was the time to take a stand or I would forever live in the shadow of my father, just like my uncles had. But I was still a child and had a child's fears and exaggerations.

Pitaji bent down, picked up his chappal and threw it straight at me. It caught me on the left shoulder. Such a red-hot fury broke inside me then that I was shocked at its intensity. I lunged at Pitaji, screaming as I moved, 'All your bloody life you have licked the soles of your precious Rai Sahab! But I'm not going to do that. I'm going away to live my own life. I won't give you vultures the right to decide my life for me. I'm going away, I'm not going to stay here one moment!' I was shouting and kicking in impotent rage, for the two uncles were hanging on to my arms. I don't know what I would have done if they hadn't held on to me. 'And don't you dare raise a finger at me again! You hit me again and you face the consequences!'

There, opposite me, Mataji and Maji hung on to Pitaji, who was shouting and calling me names. 'Dog! Kamina! Get out of my house immediately! Ungrateful wretch! I should have taken the lathi to you some time back and beaten sense into you while there was time. Bloody modern generation! You will eat up your mother and father and won't even belch!'

With supreme effort I pulled myself free of my uncles and straightened the sleeves of my too-short shirt. 'I'm not going to study sugar technology, Pitaji. You can convince Guddu to do so when he is old enough!'

I was smouldering with rage as I left the room. How dare Pitaji treat me like a demented child! Imagine spending a lifetime in some mofussil town and convincing myself that life didn't exist beyond its boundaries. Slowly my anger dissipated and a deep grief enveloped me. I was only sixteen and I didn't want to spend my life in a stupid place like Majhauli. I wanted to live, to see the world. Feeling hot tears gather behind my eyes I walked straight out of the house to my misery seat.

Behind Hariyali, well away from the house and almost touching the boundary wall, was an old mango tree. It hardly bore any fruit, but it was large, leafy and embracing. Halfway up the tree and well hidden by the leaves, was a fork in the branches where one branch grew upward and one grew parallel to the ground. In the horizontal branch was a broad, bottom-shaped indent that made a perfect seat totally hidden from the world, private and secure. I had found the seat a year ago when I had climbed the tree in search of green mangoes. It was my misery seat away from the eyes of the world.

That day I climbed the tree and scrambled up to my seat only to find Nagina there. She was sitting on my misery seat and reading a book. She had probably had another run-in with her mother. Finding no place to sit I planted my foot on an untried branch and went crashing to the damp earth. Nagina's trilling laughter followed me. Angered, I jumped up and without waiting to check my bruises climbed up the tree again.

Her bottom in the bucket, her back against the trunk and her feet planted before me, she looked at me and smiled maliciously. 'You didn't break a leg? Not even an arm! Tut-tut-tut,' Nagina jeered.

'This is my tree.'

'Not true, I'm afraid. This is my tree.'

'I discovered it.'

'So what? It's my property, so it's my tree.'

'Huh! Property doesn't belong to girls, it belongs to boys.'

Nagina's feet came down sharply and she sat up and glowered at me. 'You are just like Mummy! Madam Perfect Singh! Girls don't get the property! Girls have to abide by a strict moral code! Girls have to be perfect to ensure them wealthy husbands! And you! You foolish, uneducated Punjabi MCP, with your lassi muscles and soggy brain! Girls don't inherit property, my ass.'

Nagina was eighteen, two years older than me, and I hadn't a clue what she meant. What was an MCP and how did lassi make muscles? She was furious, and I wasn't sure why. I gaped at her stupidly. Though my mind had begun to rebel at my father's ideas, my world was still restricted to the one described by the school at the district headquarters where I studied. I was really no match for a smart girl like Nagina with her highly westernized upbringing.

'You are a fool and I have no time for fools,' she said, and climbed down the tree with lithe grace. Just before she actually stepped down, she looked up at me, her face framed by a halo of mango leaves. 'Don't you ever forget that this tree is mine,' she said in anger, and was gone.

I shall never forget the way Nagina had looked that day. She wore dark blue jeans and a canary yellow T-shirt. Her strong muscular neck was like a stately column supporting her head. When she looked up at me her face formed a perfect oval in which her coal black eyes burned in anger. Her shoulder-length hair, very wavy and thick, fell around her face in tangled curls. To my untrained eye it made her look very exotic, and very bold, for girls in my circle didn't cut their hair. But then she was the owner's daughter and had her own code. Her bobbed hair and yellow T-shirt and jutting breasts with no dupatta to cover them, were seared on my brain, and the image was to trouble my dreams for years to come.

I left Majhauli that night and went to Allahabad. I stole money from Mataji's purse and didn't tell anyone where I was going. An aunt of mine lived in Allahabad, in Katra, and she greeted me with lamentations and resignation. I soon found myself enrolled in the Government Intermediate College with Mathematics, Statistics and English as my subjects. When my father heard of my choice of subjects he exploded with frustrated rage. 'Bloody fellow will end up as a munshi in some Delhi firm talking *git pit* in English and thinking he owns the world. The English have gone but they have left their dirty spawn behind. They even shit in English.' But I was happy – I had got away from the oppressive atmosphere of my home.

When I came back to Majhauli a year later, I was two inches taller and wore my hair long. I hummed songs by the Beatles and Elvis Presley like they were temple hymns. I must have looked awful with my long hair and those loud, printed shirts that were all the rage at that time, but in Majhauli I was a hero. The colony kids followed me around, staring at me and listening to me talk. Father scoffed at my accomplishments and refused to speak directly to me. Whenever I was in earshot, he would ask my mother what she thought her precious son hoped to do in life. Did he want to become mirasi, a singer? Maybe if he stood at the crossing and sang with one hand clapped to his ear, people might take pity on him and throw him a few coins.

How those remarks of my father had hurt. But the more he hurt me the more defiant I became, as though I wanted to hurt him back – hurt him till he knew the pain that I felt. When I organized all the kids and staged a rather banal play about a lovelorn pair who commit suicide in the end, Pitaji was disgusted. He shouted at Mataji, wanting to know whose son I was that I had dreams of becoming a Rajesh Khanna.

The later generations may not realize this, but they owe those of us who grew up in the Seventies a real debt of gratitude. This was the generation that broke all taboos and defied their parents, that sought new vocations, that married out of caste and class and that faced all parental and societal pressures. The funniest things used to be considered bad – watching movies with friends, talking to the opposite sex, sitting down if your father was standing, choosing your own career, speaking without being spoken to. The list was endless. I pursued a BA with Economics Honours in Delhi after completing my intermediate. Father stopped talking to me altogether. And finally I became part of the 'in' crowd. But that was then, and much after I fell hopelessly in love with Nagina and was ordered out of Majhauli forever. I couldn't tell Kulbhushan anything about that.

After I walked out on Kulbhushan at the Taipan in the Oberoi I drove home. Kulbhushan had succeeded in upsetting me so much that I couldn't go back to the office. It was three in the afternoon. I opened the door and walked into the house. Mataji and Pitaji were dozing in the veranda. The moment they saw me they jumped up, expecting the worst.

'What's the matter, beta?'

'Why have you come home so early?'

'Are you okay?'

I was already angry and their queries irritated me no end. 'I'm not a government servant and I have not been suspended. Neither am I a servant of Hukam Singh. I come and go as I please. I am the master of my time.'

Pitaji's face, that wore an expression of one expecting the worst, arranged itself back into its habitual long-suffering look and he sat down again with his hands fisted together and placed against his mouth. But Mataji persisted. 'It's only three in the afternoon!'

'I know. I own a watch.' I stormed up the stairs. What a family – suspecting the worst of you just because you come home early! I did my best towards Mataji and Pitaji but I couldn't love them. Maybe if I escaped them I could learn to love them, I thought.

Upstairs, the children were bent over their books and Vidya was asleep. I sat down heavily on the bed and began removing my socks.

'Anmol? What's the matter?' Vidya woke up with a start and looked at her watch and then back at my face. 'You didn't go to office today.' The tone was accusing. 'Bhaskar telephoned. He said something important had come up.'

'Hang Bhaskar,' I said getting into bed with her. All that unaccustomed drinking in the afternoon was making me sleepy.

'Listen to me, Anmol. He said it's important. He had fixed an appointment for you with some joint secretary somewhere. Get up, Anmol, and talk to him.'

'What ministry?' I was almost asleep.

'I don't know. No wait, Food Processing.'

I sat up and clutched my aching head. All this drinking in the afternoon just didn't suit me. Why on earth did Bhaskar have to fix the appointment today? I dialled his number but the line was busy. It's no use fighting fate, I thought, as I lay back. Bhaskar would have to get another appointment.

I'd barely dozed off when I woke to the sound of loud shouting and screaming. It was Father and Guddu again. I pulled a pillow over my head and tried to muffle the sounds. God, this was a madhouse. When was I going to get away from it all? If only the fool had made something of his life. As the intensity of the fight increased I sat up and lit a cigarette. There was nothing to do but wait for it to get over. If I intervened I would have to take sides and then I was sunk no matter whose side I took.

'Get in here, you fool, and stop crying!' Fifteen minutes into the fight, Vidya pushed open the bedroom door and dragged Guddu inside. 'Stop blubbering like a baby. Be a man, Guddu.' She wiped my brother's face and his eyes with her dupatta and stroked his hair till he quietened down, sending me desperate signals with her eyes which I refused to acknowledge. Vidya was a crusader who needed causes to fight and 'The Rehabilitation of Guddu' was one of her favourites. She turned to me, as I knew she would, and said, 'Anmol, you have to do something for Guddu. What is the use of your knowing all these secretaries and ministers if you can't get your own brother a job?'

I knew I should have kept quiet and remained hidden beneath the sheet, but like someone who cannot resist scratching a healing wound, I said, 'Get Guddu a job. Get you a job. Do you think I run an employment agency? Or do you think I am the president of India that I can get him a job where and when he wants?'

I looked at Guddu's gaunt face with irritation. He was unshaven and his crumpled kurta-pajama was dirty. He looked like a person who had suffered immense tragedy. But I knew that it was an act. Guddu was one of those people who wallowed in self-pity and blamed the whole world for his problems.

'First of all, ask him what he wants to do. I'm even willing to give him some capital to start a business – but does he know what business he wants to do?' I stubbed out my cigarette and impatiently lit another.

'I went for an interview today,' said Guddu sitting up with a nervous jerk, his voice trembling. 'And they said you have so many degrees but no experience. Now how can I have experience if no one gives me a job?' His voice rose in self-pity and showed signs of breaking again.

'But I got you a job as a salesman for Tata's. And your lordship thought that the job was below your dignity.'

'I can't sell what I don't believe in,' Guddu cried passionately.

'Okay. But then I asked you to work for me in Goodwork Consultants and you thought that was also beneath you,' I shouted, my impatience mounting.

'Goodwork Consultants is a big fraud! You only bribe officers and get wrong things done!' Guddu declared with passion. 'I'm not willing to be part of it.'

'What is right and what is wrong? Has anyone been able to define that? I help people to get their work done and I charge a fee for it. Is that so wrong? You might take a taxi and go and murder your aunt. Does it matter to the taxi-driver that he is ferrying a murderer to his destination? He's only doing his job – he's not the keeper of the murderer's conscience, is he?' I was smoking furiously.

'Of course he's responsible!' shouted Guddu. 'I hate the work that you do! You have no sense of what is morally right and wrong. It is not all right to make money by any means – it is not!'

'And it's morally right to live off your brother – ?'

'I'm leaving this house this minute!' shouted Guddu. He stood up and pointed a trembling finger at me. 'I'm going. Nobody understands me here.' His painfully thin frame swayed.

'Guddu,' said Vidya, totally unaffected by his histrionics, 'did you go to the interview looking like this?' She pointed to his unshaven chin and unironed clothes.

'What's wrong with my looks, hain? Are they hiring my looks or my brains? This was the country of Mahatma Gandhi. It has now become a country where we can only appreciate wealth and looks. Look at him,' Guddu indicated me. 'Should I have gone looking like him?'

I rolled my eyes heavenward and slumped back on the bed. Guddu was impossible.

'If you want to live in the world you have to do as everyone else does, Guddu,' said Vidya. 'You look like a vagabond. No one will give you a job like this.'

'He looks like a hippie – a junkie,' I muttered.

'Nobody understands me,' said the twenty-six-year-old baby and ran out of the room.

'What on earth is the matter with this boy?' Vidya sounded worried. 'I wish I could do something to help him.'

'What he needs is a sound beating! I'm warning you, Vidya. I have had enough of his foolishness and the day he tries my patience too much I'm going to throw him out. Perhaps I should have done it long ago. He will remain a burden on me all my life.' I got out of bed and went to the bathroom. 'Father was so busy making a man out of me, he forgot about Guddu!' I banged the bathroom door shut.

I was disgusted. I had come home hoping for some peace and quiet and all I had done was get trapped in an old family dispute for which there was no solution. I was sick of my family. Sick. I should have gone for the appointment in the food processing ministry. That would have helped to clear an important case, which would have got me a great deal of money. Money spelled freedom. What I wanted was real money, solid money, money to be a gentleman of leisure. But to be in that category of people you had to be born into that class. I was doomed to remain working class, slogging my arse off and supporting the entire family.

Life was most unfair.

Kulbhushan was one of those who never took no for an answer. Never having had his wishes denied, he did not know how to handle refusal. So I was not entirely surprised to get a phone call and an invitation to dine at Nagina's residence a few days later. What was surprising was that he invited me to her home and that he invited Vidya too. Vidya took the invitation calmly. And why not? Kulbhushan was just a name to her. After all, she had never seen the set-up at Majhauli. Besides, she herself was moving in exalted company these days. She had recently become part of an intellectual forum called 'Awaken the Country'. They thought the intellectuals of the country were not doing enough to educate the people. They believed newspapers warped the news to suit their purpose and there was nobody to tell the readers what was true and what was a distortion. Their group had begun its campaign by a visit to the office of the former prime minister. Rajiv Gandhi, at a loose end with time to spare, launched their booklet with great fanfare, ranted against the press of the country for not presenting him in the correct light and told them to start a campaign against V.P. Singh. Focus on the Mandal issue, he said. It was the bounden duty of the press to expose V.P. Singh for what he was and if the press had become so lily-livered and craven that they dared not speak against the prime minister then their group should tell the people that V.P. Singh was working for the disintegration of the country and its division along caste lines. You have to unite and fight this malaise, urged Rajiv Gandhi, otherwise it will ruin the country. The Mandal Commission Report was going to be implemented because of the obstinacy of one man and his fear of the political challenge raised by the rally organized by Devi Lal. Instead of worrying about real issues like poverty eradication or education, the PM was worrying about caste! Rajiv Gandhi had stood up in anger, said Vidya, and thundered: Are there no backwards among the Muslims, Christians, Sikhs? Why is the National Front government looking at caste backwardness and not at economic backwardness? Very impressed, the group had expressed confidence in Rajiv Gandhi as a person and urged him to lay bare the facts of the Bofors controversy and throw himself at the mercy of the people's court. He would then come back, they assured him, in the next elections after being forgiven by the people, and he would emerge stronger and more capable of leading this miserable country into the twenty-first century. Rajiv Gandhi had been moved by their sentiments and shaken hands with everyone. Vidya hadn't exactly held on to his hand (the way I had done when, years ago as a child, I shook hands with Richard Nixon on his visit to India), but she would clearly have liked to.

'Vidya, you are quite confused about Rajiv Gandhi,' I said. 'Sometimes you accuse him of corruption and sometimes you think of him as, quote, "The Hope of India" unquote. He is just an impostor who is balding and getting quite jowly. There is no one capable of leading this miserable country into the twenty-first century.' I was frowning over my wardrobe and wondering what to wear for Kulbhushan's dinner party. It was only the end of August and the choice was limited to bush-shirts. I chose a bright canary yellow one and examining my ruddy face in the mirror decided I looked fine. In fact, I looked like a handsome bodybuilder, with solid biceps and shoulders. In the mirror I could see Vidya standing in her petticoat and blouse and staring at V.P. Singh as he spouted some nonsense on TV.

'Perhaps you think this oily character, who can't even look you in the eye, is capable of it?' she said, pointing to the TV screen.

'I never said that. And you had better hurry.' I slicked my hair down with Brylcreem. Did it look better plastered down or all curly and falling over my forehead?

Vidya began pleating a white cotton sari with a gold border and gold motifs on it. 'I hate these formal parties of yours, Anmol, and I'm always dressed wrong for them.'

'That makes two of us,' I said, giving my hair a final pat. Vidya nearly always dressed in white and in cotton. It went well with her image as a social crusader and I cannot deny that it lent her a certain dignity. Still, I often wished she would wear bright colours like I did, or at least silk even if she had to wear white. But she would not agree. The result was that we looked like a pair of peacocks, me all colourful and flamboyant and she, crumpled and dowdy as a peahen. Which was sad because in women beauty is after all more desirable than dignity.

'In a country where you have to pay money to file an FIR, he promised progress, technology, a corruption-free government...' said Vidya still staring at the TV screen. She had finished brushing her hair and now reached up to plait it.

'Who? V.P. Singh?'

'Of course not. Rajiv Gandhi.'

'Corruption-free? And Rajiv Gandhi?'

'When he first came he did promise to make the country strong, self-reliant, modern and clean.'

'Till he began to let us down.'

'Till he began to let us down,' repeated Vidya, sighing and letting her plait snake down her back. She wore a big red sindoor bindi and little else by way of make-up. Somehow she looked good, like Jaya Bhaduri. Vidya was an attractive woman, and even though she cultivated the simple bharatiya nari look, believe me, she was not one to take things lying down. 'Perhaps it was not him but the people who surrounded him who let us down,' she added.

'Perhaps. Are you ready?'

'Yes,' said Vidya pinning her sari. 'But Mataji was making a face. This, mind you, when I have fed the children. Or at least tried to. How do you make kids eat when they are not hungry? Every day they eat dinner after the nine o'clock serial and today Mataji says feed them and go.'

We left without saying goodbye to anybody.

Nagina lived in a quiet lane in Sunder Nagar. The door was opened by a liveried servant and we followed him in, our footsteps muffled by the thick-pile carpet. I looked around in awe. The house was lavishly ostentatious. All the furniture was silver-plated. The chairs' arm-rests had silver heads of ferocious lions, the legs were wonderfully crafted lion paws and there were tails, too, artfully entwined round the back legs of the chairs. Kulbhushan welcomed us and immediately took Vidya and me off for a tour of the house pointing out the main attractions – the stools made of real stuffed elephants' feet and a centre table of silver fishes with eyes studded with precious stones. I could see Vidya shuddering in distaste. Kulbhushan knew little about Vidya, otherwise he wouldn't have said too much about the animal heads that adorned the walls of the house. In one of her many self-appointed roles, Vidya was a conservationist and a defender of the rights of animals. But Kulbhushan seemed to enjoy Vidya's pithy comments and took them laughingly. Even when she said that he was a pretty boy and his head would look wonderful on the wall at the top of the staircase, Kulbhushan held his smile. I sat on one of the lion chairs and let her harangue him. Thank god I wasn't getting the lecture. I had just taken the first sip of my drink when Nagina entered. About a dozen people were in the room laughing and chattering but everyone turned to look at her. There was a second of complete silence, or did I imagine it?

Nagina, my Nagina. My first and only love. I was looking at her after fourteen years and I was smitten once again. My god, I loved this woman. How had I survived without her? The intensity of my reaction frightened me. I looked around in desperation, afraid of giving myself away. But I couldn't look away for long. I was mesmerized by her almond-white skin and the sweep of her hair, which rose in a mysterious peak at her forehead and made her face look longer than I remembered. Her eyes were all made up, like an actress', with the eyelids painted a peculiar ash-pink to match her lips. Her lips were outlined a shade darker. It gave her a curiously artificial yet provocative look. When I tore my gaze away from her mouth, I was caught by her eyes. And when I escaped the eyes, I was caught by the specks of gold in her hair. Her clothes added to the feeling of otherworldliness. She wore black trousers and a blouse with a black and gold panther print, her wrists and ankles were adorned with heavy gold links. Nagina glided through the room, lighting it up with her presence. Her face was gorgeous and she knew exactly the effect that she was having on everyone and played it to the maximum, flaunting her sexuality. She was more beautiful than ever.

'Hello, Anmol,' said Nagina in her deep husky voice as she finally came up to me. 'Meet my husband, SP.'

I stared at her.

'Anmol...?' she repeated uncertainly.

'Anmol Bhai, be a good chap and say hello to Nagina,' said Kulbhushan, sidling up beside her. 'And this is my brother-in-law, SP Aggarwal.'

It was only then that I noticed the man who was with Nagina. He looked like a career diplomat, an ambassador, with his thick snow-white hair and smooth, clean-shaven face. He shook hands with me and briefly nodded by way of greeting.

I was the tallest and the broadest man in the room, but I was all wrong – my clothes, my hair, my style. I was sure that Nagina was amused by me and not in the least bit impressed. The silence extended as I shuffled awkwardly, not knowing what to say. Nagina's husband stood calmly by – like royalty – waiting for me to present myself, while I thrust my hands deeper inside my pockets and clenched my fists. I wanted to say something, remark lightly on this and that, but for the life of me I couldn't think of anything to say. I could only stare at Nagina's prominent collarbones and the heavy gold half-moons that she wore in her ears. Eventually, Nagina took pity on me and asked if I wanted a drink. I nodded even though I already clutched a half-full glass.

Then I remembered I hadn't introduced Vidya. 'This is my wife, Vidya,' I said grabbing hold of her arm and caught the look in Nagina's eyes as she took in her dowdy white cotton sari and her small serious face, rather like that of an idealistic student's.

Our last day together had been spent in the cane fields of Majhauli. That evening we both had sugar in our hair and heat in our bodies. I remembered the intense excitement of her full-bodied ardour, the passionate, hot embrace of a girl who had clung to me after biting me on my arm. She had fought me, bit me, kissed me, raced me, loved me and finally forgotten me...

'What do you do, Mr – ?' Nagina's husband finally deigned to ask.

'Malhotra, Anmol Malhotra,' I blurted. 'I have my own business, my own company, Goodwork Consultants.'

'Is that so?' He already sounded bored. *Blimp* – I suddenly remembered the name given to him by Kulbhushan.

'Anmol is the dada of Delhi,' said Kulbhushan, finally dropping the 'bhai' and ending all pretence. 'He is a one-man show. Anything you want done in Delhi, catch hold of him. From airline bookings to the transfer of an officer, from drug licences to defence deals, from the collection of election money to the swearing in of chief ministers – Anmol is into everything.'

'Only he doesn't work for anyone unless it suits him,' said Nagina, draining her glass and putting it down. 'Isn't that so, Anmol?'

'All I know is that this brother and sister are out to ruin my reputation. I only wish I was one-tenth as capable as Kulbhushan is making me out to be,' I said trying to be flip.

'Very interesting,' said the blimp. 'But how do you know the brother and sister so well?'

'We grew up together,' said Nagina. 'Didn't we, Anmol?' She put a hand lightly on my forearm and I felt a sudden rush of blood to my loins.

'Yes,' I breathed, my throat suddenly constricted with intense emotion as the look in her eyes took me back to Majhauli. To that day fourteen years ago when my life changed forever.

It was the first day of cane crushing and the second day of October. Traditionally, a day for celebration and worship. Hundreds of seasonal workers and their families visited temples in thanksgiving. The good times had returned. There was an air of festivity all over Majhauli. In the evening the boilers were fully fired and glowing orange. As was custom, the first cane was ceremonially fed into the crushers by Rai Sahab. The town was celebrating with glasses of cane juice, and the farmers had begun to line up outside the gates with cartloads of cut cane.

Inside the factory the boiling pans were bubbling with sugar cane juice and the engineers had begun to take samples to check its colour and consistency before adding the chemicals. The chief engineer scooped up a glass of thick dark brown syrup which contained millions of tiny crystals of sugar, held it against the light and checked the sugar formation. Satisfied, he gave the signal and the entire lot was poured into huge, round, drum-like structures which were then rotated at high speed. The sugar crystals were separated by centrifugal force and whirled around until they flew out of the chute, all white and transparent and hot. The taste of that first batch of hot sugar was simply divine; the taste of it lingers in my mouth to this day. Like the workers, we too scooped out the warm sugar and rolled it into huge laddoos before eating it. As a boy I could easily eat half a kilo of pure sugar this way. The quantities eaten by the workers were larger. The factory would write off at least one to two per cent of the production as incidental losses, all which was actually eaten on the premises!

That day it was late in the evening by the time the first sugar began to pour out of the chute. Rai Sahab and Pitaji had already left but Nagina, Kulbhushan and I hung on, waiting to sample the first hot sugar. I was nineteen years old, on holiday from college in Delhi, supremely cocky and confident. Nagina was twenty-one, two years older than me and gorgeous with a beautiful face and the body of a siren. Kulbhushan was about fifteen, gangly, pimply and forgettable. Luckily for us, as the future Rai Sahab, the workers paid him more attention and didn't notice the silent fight that Nagina and I had for the first laddoo of sugar.

Our squabble began unexpectedly and escalated fast, becoming savage, like a power game that had to be won. As the warm sugar flowed out of the chute, I elbowed Nagina aside and grabbed the first handful. My mouth was already watering in anticipation of the taste when Nagina caught my hand with both of hers and pulled. She wanted the first laddoo. Though caught off-guard, I wasn't going to let my prize go so easily. I shook off her hand and opened my mouth to stuff in the sugar when Nagina attacked. I was already well over six feet tall and very strong, but Nagina fought with great strength and landed quick sharp blows on my torso and upper arms, blows that hurt me enough to lunge against her in a flash of anger and push her back. Nagina fell heavily against the iron railing and I fell too. The sugar laddoos, that I held in both my hands, were crushed and the white sugar flew out and fell over both of us like a shower of rice, getting into our hair and faces and our necks and clothes and clinging everywhere in hot sweet blobs.

The breaking of the laddoos enraged both of us and we went for each other like a couple of jungle cats. Nagina was in a murderous fury and when it was clear that she couldn't fight me, she put her head down and sank her teeth into my forearm with all her strength. My mouth opened in a yell of pain and I jerked my arm back. She had drawn blood and the droplets of blood fell into the new batch of sugar staining it red and then pink. I stared with surprise at the welling blood on my arm and, taking advantage of this, Nagina went flying down the stairs and out of the factory. It took me only a minute to regain my balance and taking the stairs three at a time, I went after her.

Nagina ran fast and I raced to catch up with her. She was out of the factory premises and already in the fields. Her long hair flew behind her and her legs pumped strong and sure. It was a while before I caught up with her and swung her down. She fell heavily on her back and took at least twenty canes down with her. I fell on top of her. She grabbed my hair and was ready with her arsenal of teeth and nails. But this time I was prepared and with one hand caught both her hands while with the other I tried to push back her head. Both of us struggled and wrestled, twisting and turning and suddenly my hand found one of her round, heaving breasts. I was in the midst of a fight and I must have hurt her for she cried out. I looked in surprise at my hand, which she did not push away, and the fight went out of both of us. Slowly my fingers curled around her breast again and I squeezed hard till she again let out a cry. But she didn't protest and when I bent my head to kiss her she opened her mouth wide and almost swallowed me.

The clamp of her wet open mouth on my lips disgusted and excited me beyond measure. I clutched both her breasts and in desperation ground my body into hers. Nagina responded with equal ferocity, moaning with desire as she lifted her legs and arms and clamped me hard. My fumbling fingers struggled with zips and buttons and hooks till Nagina took over. In a minute she was lying on the sugar cane naked and open to me and the skies. Gasping in fear and ecstasy I put a hand on her sex and almost seared my hand with the pulsating heat of it. I had no time to savour the soft wetness for I could not wait any longer and pushed myself into her. Our excitement and desperation was such that we both lost our virginity with minimal fuss. I was still lying on top of her, our breath coming in harsh gasps, when I was again aroused by her softness beneath me. I pulled myself up and straddled her, running my hands over her taut breasts and erect nipples till I could hold myself no longer and once again plunged deep, drawing a scream of pain from her. My inexpert movements and uncontrollable passion must have hurt her but she wasn't complaining.

Hours later, or was it aeons, we awoke to the world and laughed at our sugar-filled hair and scratched bodies and torn clothes. We lay in the sugar cane field, our arms entwined around each other, our bodies tired and bruised, satiated but only for the moment. The wound in my arm was beginning to throb but I was hardly aware of it. I could only look at her in awe, my mind refusing to accept the fact that I was touching Nagina and that she was asking me to be her lover again. Once more we melted into one another, driven by a tidal wave of passion which we didn't know how to control. Finally we rose self-consciously and dusted our clothes and hair. Then we clung to each other and declared everlasting, undying love. We held one another and dreamt of a life filled with love and happiness. We foresaw no difficulties, we saw no ugly differences of class and we entirely forgot the world in which we lived. We stayed out till dawn, walking among the cane fields, chewing the cane and drinking the juice from each other's lips. I couldn't keep my hands off her. Every now and then we clung to each other and I kissed every part of her body, stroking her again and again with my huge hands. It was the happiest time in my life – unreal, beautiful and transient.

The bubble didn't last long. Within minutes of reaching home I was filled with shame, guilt and despair at what I had done, for the first person I saw when I came home was Pitaji. I had only to see the look on Pitaji's face for reality to hit. Pitaji was in the garden exercising, as he did every morning of his life. He wore loose khaki shorts and a sleeveless vest even though the morning was cold. I knew the sequence of his regimen and when I saw him swinging the wooden weights I knew that he had just finished a hundred push-ups. With the ease of practice, Pitaji swung the weights around his head first with one hand and then the other, up and down, up and down, the muscles of his chest and shoulders rippling smoothly. That's when I felt the first prick of real fear. Father was an RSS man, committed to old values and unwavering in his loyalties and principles. He was also a tall and big man. I saw him take in my torn dishevelled appearance. My hair was wild and sticky with sugar. Bits of leaves and grass and muck clung to my clothes and I had the look and smell of sex about me. He looked at me in wordless contempt. I couldn't stand it. I turned tail and ran into the house into the sanctuary of my room.

Quickly I stripped my clothes and had a bath in freezing cold water. As yet Pitaji didn't know who the girl was. The day he knew he would kill me. I trembled in fear. What had I done? Oh god, what had I done? Then I brushed the tears from my eyes. I loved Nagina and I would marry her today if I had to. I would give up college and join the factory if that was what she wanted. I was in love and I would do anything for my beloved, anything. Still I trembled.The shivers seemed to begin somewhere inside me so I sat gripping my arms in a vice-like hug repeating the name of Nagina to myself while I waited for the axe to fall. I sat like that for an hour unable to calm down, fuelling my fear and love in alternate strokes. I made wild schemes of running away to America and striking it rich there. Or maybe going together to the mountains and living in an idyllic cottage beside a bubbling stream where Nagina would cook and I would hunt for food. Our parents would look for us everywhere, sorry for having lost their tempers. One day we would read a newspaper appeal – 'Son come home. Mother serious. We agree to everything.'

'*Anmol!*' Pitaji's voice thundered. Fear clawed at my vitals. The time for reckoning had come. I was so frightened, I couldn't move my limbs. But I knew I if I didn't make an immediate appearance, Pitaji would drag me down in front of everyone. Taking a long, trembling breath, I stood up and went out onto the veranda.

The first thing I saw was Rai Sahab's jeep. The second thing I saw was Rai Sahab himself. And the third thing I saw was the gun he held in his hands. He stood frozen with his foot on the jeep's fender, dressed in a kurta-pajama. He wasn't looking at me or at Pitaji, who stood in the veranda, looking shell-shocked. He seemed to be staring at the jeep's number plate with great concentration. For a minute I stood still, waiting. Nobody spoke, nothing happened.

'Namaste, Rai Sahab,' I squeaked when it seemed as though everyone had been struck with paralysis and then Rai Sahab turned to face me.

I think my heart didn't beat for a full minute as I looked upon his red face and eyes in terror. He had the look of a deranged man's last struggle with sanity. Slowly he raised the twelve-bore rifle and aimed it straight at my chest. Still nobody spoke. I could hear Pitaji's laboured breathing behind me as he too realized that Rai Sahab wasn't in a sane frame of mind. As for me, I was turned to stone. I looked into Rai Sahab's wild eyes, and then at the gun. I was dead sure it was my last day on earth. Finally, after a long struggle, sanity won, but the icy tone of Rai Sahab's voice was more frightening than death. 'Get out at once, and stay out,' he rasped hoarsely.

And I got out.

Not just me, Pitaji got out too. He resigned the same day and left Majhauli for Delhi. Rai Sahab didn't stop him.

*

That had been fourteen years ago, and I hadn't seen the Rai Sahab family since. In all those years I hadn't so much as uttered Nagina's name. And now here she was before me, trailing a husband and speaking in a husky voice that she hadn't had before. Somehow, and I don't know how, the group had broken up and I found myself alone with Nagina clutching an empty glass. She took the glass away from me gently and handed me a full one.

'Anmol!' Nagina put out a hand to touch my arm and moved again by the evidence of a long-forgotten emotion, I sucked in my breath involuntarily, afraid that the others would notice the electricity between us. But Satya Pal was busy talking to a sultry siren in a backless choli and Vidya was talking very earnestly to an intellectual type with a long salt-and-pepper beard. It was as though all those years in between had never happened.

'Nagina,' my voice was hoarse with emotion.

'Anmol, I have to talk to you alone,' she said urgently. 'Where can we meet?'

'What?'

'In the Lodhi Gardens' restaurant. At seven o'clock. Tomorrow morning,' she said quickly as I saw Kulbhushan signal to her from across the room.

My heart swelled with a sudden rush of blood. What a girl! She wanted to meet me again. Surely it meant that she loved and desired me.

For the rest of the evening I behaved like a lovelorn youth. I stood in the corner and drank steadily following her panther figure with my eyes wherever she went. I was thirty-three years old and she was thirty-five, but between us there were no barriers, not of age, not of class. My heart was thumping like a twenty-year-old's and I couldn't wait for tomorrow.

The next morning I parked my blue Maruti outside Lodhi Gardens half an hour early and hurried inside. The restaurant was on the first floor of an old building that had stood there so long that the trees and their branches had all but covered it. It was the hallowed rendezvous point for desperate drinkers and desperate lovers. But at this hour it was deserted. I bounded up the stairs two at a time, impatient to see Nagina, wondering if my face was still flushed from last night's excesses. Vidya had been remarking on that flush since the last night and wondering if I was ill. I wasn't physically ill, but I was bitten by the love bug, which in Urdu poetry is equivalent to being terminally ill. I was sure Nagina wouldn't be there yet but I was prepared to wait. I burst into the restaurant, panting a little with the exertion and there she was, dressed in a jogging suit of white and yellow, her hair tied in a high ponytail, drinking black coffee.

'Hello, Nagina,' I said, my heart in my mouth.

'Hello, Anmol,' she smiled, and we shook hands like Europeans.

The restaurant was dark and deserted. The light of the early morning barely entered the room. After the initial handshake she sat silent, eyes fixed on the table, fingers fiddling with the coffee cup. I stared at her downcast eyes in awe. What was she doing here, waiting for me, old lassi muscles? Nagina's slim, beautiful hand was on the table and I covered it with mine. Her hand trembled and she made an attempt to withdraw it but I was beyond control, beyond reason. She was there to meet me and I loved her. Nothing else mattered in the world. I held her cool hand against my hot cheek, my breath coming faster. 'Do you remember, Nagina, the fight we had over the sugar laddoos? I still have the mark of your teeth on my arm.' I rolled up the sleeve of my shirt and showed it to her.

She put her smooth, manicured hand over the old scar and shook her head. 'I should never have done that. But you provoked me. You thought no end of yourself in those days, you know. And that made me angry.' She smiled at me and I smiled back, foolishly happy.

'I have never been able to forget you or Hukam Singh Mills. All these years have passed but even now, if I hear the name of Majhauli, I get emotional.'

'But you don't want to help us?'

'Help you?' For a moment I was at sea. 'Oh, you mean about what Kulbhushan said. He'll sort it out, I'm sure, and without my help.' I dismissed Kulbhushan. 'Do you think life could have turned out differently? For us, I mean? If Rai Sahab and my father hadn't got to know? Do you think we could have got married?' My heart was beating rather painfully and I was shocked at saying what I did to a married woman. But I couldn't help it. Nagina had unleashed a storm in my heart.

'I don't think you should say all this to me, Anmol,' Nagina sounded breathless too.

'But you remember, don't you?'

'I remember.'

'Nagina, I've missed you,' I said. She did not reply. But at least she didn't withdraw her hand.

I looked at her heartbreaking beauty with longing and despair. In hindsight, I would realize that I was the besotted one and Nagina only an unhappy woman – attracted to me, of course – but looking more for emotional and mental support than declarations of undying love. So, though we responded to each other, we were actually on different wavelengths. But at that moment in the dark restaurant in Lodhi Gardens with the whispering trees all around, love was in the air and, eternal dreamer that I was, I was already imagining a situation in which I came home from office to find a beautiful Nagina waiting for me at the door. (In this dream scenario what happened to Vidya and the blimp is unclear.)

'Anmol, listen to me. Please help Kulbhushan. He's in trouble. We don't have five crore rupees to pay the farmers and we can't afford to close the factory. That Som Dutt Bihari is indulging in double talk. He says if we don't pay the farmers they will stop supplying the cane. But he is also saying that if the factory stops he will set fire to it, because it is a bumper year and the farmers are flooded with cane. If the factory doesn't crush, their cane will rot in the fields itself. Bihari understands the Catch-22 situation in which we are but he won't listen to any one of us.'

'But why is all this worrying you? Let Kulbhushan worry about it. In fact, let him go to hell!'

'But it's my factory too!'

I looked at Nagina in anger. She was ruining the dream. I let go of her hand and spoke with a frown, 'What about your husband? He has sackfuls of money. Why doesn't he help out?'

'The whole thing is too complicated. I can't explain now. He's... he's tight-fisted, but that's not the problem. Papa doesn't want to ask him.' She sounded flustered and waved her hands around. 'Besides, nobody has that kind of money in cash. We need five crores in cash, for god's sake!'

'Hmm,' I said disbelievingly, and was horrified to find her beautiful eyes fill with tears. 'Nagina, don't cry. Listen to me.'

She took out a hanky and dabbed her eyes. 'Think of me, Nagina. I mean, what will Rai Sahab say if I land up in Majhauli and start interfering in the mill's affairs? He'll have a heart attack. Worse, he might even call the police and have me locked in jail!' I shuddered at my last memory of Rai Sahab. 'He might even shoot me!'

'He wants you to come too.'

'But why me? I don't want to be involved in the mill's affairs.'

'But you *are* involved in the mill's affairs. Because you were born in Majhauli and you grew up there. Because you are emotionally attached to the mill. Because you love me!' The words were out before she could stop them and she clapped her hand to her mouth in horror.

'I'm glad you said it, Nagina. It's out in the open now. I do love you. I've loved you all along and I have lived in a vacuum all this while. Now that you are back in my life, I've come alive. I love you, Nagina.' I spoke like a besotted sixteen-year-old who has to repeat his words to hear the sound and rejoice in them.

'Anmol, please don't say that.' Nagina removed her hands from her face and clutched my forearm, right where she had bitten me. Her eyes implored me to help, or maybe my feverish imagination thought so. But at least one thing was clear, I wasn't immune to the appeal in those eyes and I was human enough to cover her hand with mine and nod consolingly. She dropped the subject then and we talked about Majhauli and the happy times we had shared there. As we spoke I realized she was right. I was involved with the mill's affairs. In the same way that I was involved with her.

'Madam!' The restaurant owner came up. 'Someone's coming. I have a veranda at the back.' Quickly we went to the back veranda and sat side by side on a sagging diwan. We were so close that we touched each other from shoulder to thigh. Thick, leafy trees screened us from curious eyes and the singing of hundreds of birds played their melody only for us. Nagina smelt of roses and cloves and my heart was racing. With every beat it it sang out her name. Unable to control myself, I pulled her roughly to myself and kissed her. Suddenly she was sitting on my lap, legs on both sides, and I was hugging her to my heart. We kissed deeply, our mouths open and urgent. We had found each other after such a long time. I was practically chewing her face, excited beyond control. Then I pushed my hand between her thighs and she immediately recoiled and stood up. I knew I had gone too far but there were no recriminations.

'Anmol, you will help Kulbhushan, won't you?' Nagina said as I stood up to face her. She slid a slim hand around my neck and playing with the strands of hair visible below my collar, said, 'Please help him.' She bent suddenly and bit my lower lip hard. A cry rose in my throat. 'For my sake, Anmol. Because if you help him, I'll get what I want.'

'What do you mean?' I pushed her away a little, wishing she would stop talking about the mill and concentrate on us.

'The factory, Anmol. We need your help, please. For my sake.' This time she brought her mouth lightly on mine, like a hovering butterly, then she turned abruptly and was gone. I touched my lip with my finger and found a drop of blood on it.

C.V. Bhaskar was my partner, friend, mentor and guide. A good Tamilian Brahmin, he ate no meat or eggs, nor did he drink anything stronger than fruit juice. No tobacco and no girls for him either. Bhaskar's only vice was money. He loved the stuff with passion and he hoarded it like a miser. He couldn't spend a paisa on buying anything but the bare minimum to live, and never had more than three pairs of clothes in his life. Seeing his general run-down appearance you would think that the poor guy probably did not know where his next meal was coming from, whereas I knew for a fact that Bhaskar had more ready cash with him than many a businessman. His wife Padmavathy was a government CGHS doctor, a rather simple soul who could be seen in winter wearing thick-soled canvas shoes beneath her brightly coloured kanjeevaram saris. She wore a nose pin with four diamonds and ear studs of seven diamonds each and tied her long oiled hair in a single plait for all occasions. I had known the couple since the days he aspired to be part of Sanjay Gandhi's gang, and so I know that he had not changed his furniture since nineteen seventy-seven: his drawing room contained the same cane-bottomed sofa, the same chatais and the same bronze Nataraja on the same coffee table. There were no curtains in his windows and he had precisely four stainless steel plates and glasses in his house. It was lucky that he had no children. It would have killed him to spend money on them. What the man did with all the money he had was a mystery. How he acquired money was a story that needs to be told.

The story, which is a true one, goes like this. Bhaskar, an unimportant, uninspiring man, had political ambitions and he tagged along with Sunny Miyan, a member of parliament and an important member of the Congress party. As a reward for all the sewa Bhaskar did for Sunny Miyan, the latter introduced him to Sanjay Gandhi as a useful 'jobling'. And so Bhaskar became a jobling, who fetched and carried for Sunny Miyan and sometimes on his behalf, for Sanjay Gandhi. He made himself so useful that soon Sunny Miyan began using Bhaskar for fund collection, a job normally reserved for those who really had the confidence of the politician. Sunny Miyan had become member of parliament from Rampur, a difficult feat considering that he had quarrelled with the nawab of Rampur. Rampur was a rich place full of old-moneyed Muslim families living in the city area, and rich, hard-working Punjabi farmers in the rural areas of the district. These farmers had come to the wilds of the terai region bringing their farming skills with them and they took to sugar cane cultivation in a big way, transforming the district into a mini Punjab in no time. The farmers built themselves beautiful brick-and-cement homes with all modern amenities. In the middle of nowhere you could come across an absolutely modern home with air-conditioners and cooking ranges. One characteristic feature of the area was the fact that every man had a gun licence and carried his twelve-bore across his back. It was a common sight in the district to see big bearded farmers on their tractors and motor-bikes carrying guns. Sometimes their wives rode pillion on the motor-bikes, similarly armed. These rich farmers had endless property and money disputes and they paid the politician a good amount of protection money. Part of this money went to the party through Sunny Miyan.

It was the summer of 1980 and Sunny Miyan called Bhaskar to his house and gave him a briefcase of money, twenty-five lakh rupees in hard cash, and told him to go to Delhi and give it to Sanjay Gandhi.

Bhaskar took the briefcase and tied a thin nylon rope around it as a further safeguard. Then he went to the inter-state bus stop and took the next bus for Delhi. Clutching the briefcase this short, dark man went to the house of the prime minister and spent three hours at the gate trying to see her son, Sanjay Gandhi.

Finally when he was able to get a message across to him, Bhaskar was told to come back the next day at eleven o'clock. Sanjay Gandhi was too busy to see him that day. But the briefcase, Bhaskar protested. Tomorrow, he was told and there was nothing to be said after that. Bhaskar went to his brother's house in R.K. Puram, ate a dinner of sambhar and idlis and slept with his head on the briefcase, even taking it with him when he went to the bathroom. He told no one about the precious load that he carried. The next day he could not even reach Sanjay Gandhi's house. The young Turk, the hope of India, the light of Indira Gandhi's life, had crashed his plane near Teen Murti. He was flying his own plane and died along with the pilot. And C.V. Bhaskar became a lakhpati, twenty-five times over, in the flash of a second.

With his newfound wealth Bhaskar became a freelance journalist in name and a middleman in reality – that strange breed of men in Delhi whose job it is to look respectable and know all the politicians and officers who matter, then get people's work done for a fee. They don't call it a fee. It is known as a commission, usually a lucrative one, some of which is shared with the officer or politician who lends a helping hand. These middlemen are suave and well-informed. They throw parties where whisky flows. They never go anywhere empty-handed. They are generous at Diwali and New Year. They have their ear to the ground and pick up snippets of news like collectors' items and use them discreetly and efficiently. Bhaskar knew many politicians because of his connections and he set up shop in a two-room office in Shankar Market. He kept a battered typewriter there and often used it to write nasty articles in the press and thus find the right lever against a politician who was acting difficult. For this purpose he used the pseudonym,

Vidushak. But his main job was to use his unique talents as a middleman to get results for the moneybags and to make his own packet in the process. He was excellent at his work.

I met Bhaskar quite by chance at a party soon after I finished college. My athletic mind and body was not suited to long hours at the desk stooping over figures and files, and I was beginning to regret having studied Economics. Then Bhaskar came into my life. It was an instant meeting of souls and I found my vocation – being the perfect middleman. It took time and training, but I learned to cultivate the pretentious snobbery of the IAS man on the one hand, and the populist, often pedestrian, interests of the politicians on the other. Everyone has a price in this world. You only have to know it. Not everyone wants money. Some want a better posting, the allotment of a house, a holiday with the family in Scotland, liquor, women – anything really. All you have to do is to find out the man's weakness. For this, you have to cultivate the art of listening. Your face has to reflect the perfect blend of sympathy without sycophancy, and you have to be able to stomach a great deal of bullshit. I was good at it, but Bhaskar was better.

I went to office after my Lodhi Gardens rendezvous with Nagina. I greeted Bhaskar with a slap on the head that knocked off the ridiculous cap that he wore. For some reason this guy wore a white Gandhi topi all the time.

'Stop it.' He hit back at me but brushed air. I had already moved away. 'Where have you been, Anmol? I must have telephoned at least fifteen times. You weren't at home and you weren't in office. Where have you been?'

I sat down heavily behind my desk and blew on my hands. 'This place is really crummy. We have to do it up. Yellow paint on the walls, camel-coloured carpet on the floor.'

'Husains on the wall and bonsais on the desk! Why not? It's raining money here.'

'One reason why we are not getting the big clients is this office. Look at it!' I put my feet up on the desk and lit a cigarette. The wall in front of me had pictures of Lord Venkateshwara, Ganapathy, Murugan and Lakshmi. And they weren't just there to hide the damp patches on the wall; Bhaskar ardently wanted to be on the right side of the gods. 'At least we can buy an air-conditioner. There's no need to be a martyr in the heat.'

'Ten thousand rupees, five from you and five from me.' Bhaskar had his silly cap on again. The South had done nothing for the Independence movement and had no affinities with the Gandhi topi. And it was ridiculous for Bhaskar to be wearing the Gandhi topi in 1990 when even the Congress guys were no longer wearing it. But Bhaskar's real strength was that he was like a babu in the defence ministry. All the other Tamilian babus of the ministries loved him and he could ferret information from the most secret file that existed. 'You know that Maharashtrian fellow who wants to float new issues? Well, his case is through. Somehow he managed to get the letter from the finance ministry too. Now he is refusing to pay us.'

'Is that so? The bastard! You mean he's paid nothing?'

'No. He paid fifty per cent advance. He says that he gave the guys in the ministry the rest directly, so nothing is due to us.'

'I could twist his arm. Threaten to push him off the Qutub Minar.'

'No good. It's an occupational hazard. There's no contract binding him to pay. But we are not really losers. We never paid the ministry guys!' Bhaskar grinned.

'Then why are you weeping?' I stared at him.

'Look, Anmol, you talk properly to me, understand? I do all the dirty work and you get to go to the parties and drink the booze.'

'You are welcome to the parties,' I answered shortly, irritated by Bhaskar. He was whining a bit too much and I wanted to be left alone to think about Nagina. 'Do me a favour, Bhaskar, find Dost Mohammad. I'm dying for a cup of coffee.'

We shared a peon with the office next door where an impoverished, mournful lawyer sat all day. His name was Mahajan and he looked like a mouse. Time and again I had told him to give up and go home, he wasn't cut out to be lawyer, but he wouldn't listen. He came at ten in the morning in a crisp white lawyer's collar and sat at his desk till one o'clock. Then he went out and ate a lunch of chhola bhaturas and came back at two. Precisely at two-thirty the peon went out and got him a glass of tea. After drinking this he dozed on his chair, chin on his chest, snoring softly and rhythmically. At five he got up, collected his briefcase and, locking his office, went home. His peon was a cheerful fellow called Dost Mohammad who was quite frankly bored with his job. So he doubled for us and in return we gave him lunch and three cups of tea – one at eleven, one at two-thirty and one at four.

'Listen, Anmol, remember this Andhra party I spoke to you about who wants a licence for potable liquor and beer? The problem is Food Processing has put a ban on new licences. They are just not considering any applications.' Bhaskar stared at me over the rim of the cup. 'They are preparing a policy paper. The bastards! They want to lay down rules and priorities. Now, I ask you, where is the need to form a committee for this purpose? The whole world drinks and is better off for it. But in this land of hypocrites we set up committees to assess how much liquor a man can drink or needs to drink.'

'So?'

'So catch Mathur, the new joint secretary and find the loophole.'

'And what will you do?'

'I will expedite the file after you have found the loophole.' Bhaskar removed his cap in excitement. 'This is a good case, Anmol. Get past the ban and have the case processed. Ten lakhs each and five for expenses if the case goes through Industrial Development and the chap gets a licence. I know it's not easy. But the money is big. I've met the fellow.'

'What fellow?'

'The Andhraite.'

'Andhraite?'

'Concentrate, Anmol, please. The Andhra party is the one that wants the liquor licence. You must meet him once. He's in Delhi today. Shall I telephone and fix up an appointment?'

I nodded. Twenty lakh for a case was a lot of money.

Bhaskar picked up the phone and dialled a number. On his forehead he had made three horizontal chandan lines with a red bindu in the middle. Religion was important for Bhaskar. 'Hello? Hello, Mr Nagaraj Rao? Bhaskar here. Hain? From Goodwork Consultants, Sir. Yes, I'm fine, thank you. Yes. My partner, Mr Anmol Malhotra, would like to meet you to finalize the details. No, no, like my brother, all confidence. Okay? Four-thirty at Taj Mahal. Hain? Oh, he's tall, very tall and fair. Looks like movie-star, sure, sure. Okay, goodbye.' He put down the phone, picked up his coffee and drank it in two gulps.

'You are all set up now,' he said. 'Go meet Nagaraj Rao and get him the licence.'

I walked up to the window and watched the pouring rain. Rain shattered my peace of mind and made me morose and depressed. I wasn't my best on rainy days. Just the sight of the grey day, the huddled figures and the muggy, oppressive atmosphere made me miserable. Give me dry weather any day.

'I'll meet this Nagaraj Rao,' I said. 'But how do you think I'm going to catch Mathur? Liquor licences are the devil. The most difficult thing on the earth is to get a liquor licence.' I glared at Bhaskar who was looking smug and carefree. I knew why he had that expression on his face. Bhaskar had trained me well and now he thought he had done his bit as soon as he had passed on the problem to me. I was angry with him. What was he so happy about? 'Even if I'm able to persuade the joint secretary, what about the secretary and the minister? Do you think he's going to hand over the licence to me on a platter?'

'I know it's not going to be easy.'

'Easy? It's bloody impossible!'

'Talk to Nagaraj Rao first. We'll commit only if you think we can pull it off, otherwise goodbye, he can find someone else.'

'There can be no commitment. I'm not even sure it can be done.'

'You know Mathur.'

'Okay, I know Mathur. I knew him years ago. That doesn't make us buddies.'

'What's biting you, Anmol? This is the biggest case that we have got and it will really make us rich. Go and talk to this guy and feel your way around. What's the problem in doing that?'

'I've got too many problems,' I said. 'There's Guddu and Majhauli and Vidya.' I looked at Bhaskar. 'Do you know what Vidya's doing these days? She's joined the anti-Mandal agitators.

I don't know what's wrong with her. As if agitations and dharnas achieve anything.'

'They achieved independence.' For a second Bhaskar and I locked eyes.

'Maybe, but all this slogan shouting and breast beating is foolish. And that serpent of a prime minister that we have loves what he has done. Do you think he's going to give up his manifesto because of a student agitation? Forget it.'

'We should ask our neighbour Mahajan about the Constitutional position on reservation.'

'You ask him. I hear enough of it all the time from Vidya and Guddu. I tell you, partner, this Mandal business has given Guddu another reason to become a wastrel. Now he says that all the jobs are going to the scheduled castes and scheduled tribes so who's going to give him a job? Never done a day's work in his life, and talks of reservation. If all the jobs were to go to the high castes, he would even then not get a job, the nincompoop! I know him. Anyway, goodbye. I better go and see your guy. What Rao did you say he was?'

'Nagaraj Rao.'

Glumly, I went out into the muggy, wet day.

The bomb dropped by Prime Minister V.P. Singh about the implementation of the Mandal Commission Report on the backward classes had gained fire by his crowing about it from the ramparts of the Lal Quila on Independence Day and had started a tremendous stir in the country. From Punjab, Haryana, Uttar Pradesh, Bihar, Andhra Pradesh, Gujarat, Rajasthan, and of course, Delhi, anti-reservationists came out on the streets and protested against the implementation of the report. The bulk of the protestors were students because the reservation was affecting them directly – in admissions to colleges and in jobs. They took out rallies and processions, blocked roads, shouted slogans, pelted policemen with stones, gheraoed police stations, disrupted road and rail traffic, burned buses by the score and called for bandhs. They were greeted by tear gas, lathi-charges and firing by the police. The newspapers were full of reports of the Mandal stir. Every day the headlines screamed about death and destruction: *Sixty Students Hurt in Lathi-Charge, Normal Life Disrupted in Chandigarh and Jabalpur, Heavy Brickbatting in Udaipur, Fifty Agitators and Twelve Policemen Hurt in Shimla, Abortive Bid to Burn a Bus in Ahmedabad* and so on. But the strongest agitation was brewing in Delhi where every day hundreds of students took to the streets and faced lathi-charges. Gole Methi Chowk, near the prime minister's residence, became a popular demonstration spot. The police beat up the demonstrators left and right. Even the girls were not spared. As always happens in such situations, the harassed policemen on duty went berserk when the students staged an anti-Mandal and anti-V.P. Singh play on the street at Gole Methi Chowk. There was a pitched battle between the students and the police and the police even lathi-charged the students inside a bus from which they could not escape. An Anti-Mandal Commission Forum was formed and its spokesperson said, 'The attempt to strangle this democratic movement will not succeed and we will not rest till we achieve our objective.' And all along the BJP refused to give up their plan of the long Somnath-Ayodhya rath yatra, covering eight states. They kept giving the prime minister heart attacks by saying that the BJP support could not be taken for granted. The rath yatra was a calculated plan to mobilize Hindu support.

In this scenario Vidya became a crusader in shining armour fighting the forces of casteism and communalism. Pitaji supported her anti-Mandal stand, but was not with her in her anti-BJP stand. He was a knicker-wallah and totally opposed to the topi-wallahs. He discoursed endlessly on the wrong caste-based and religion-based policies of the Congress party that had left the Hindus disoriented from their faith. It is our country, he thundered, and we are treated in a step-brotherly fashion. How dare the Congress appease the Muslims and ignore the timid Hindus? Well, the timid Hindu was now going to take out his trishul and change his image from a thin, brown fellow with a concave stomach taking holy baths and eating spinach to that of a strong, Hanuman-like figure capable of taking on the strongest beef-eating Muslim and making mincemeat out of him. But he couldn't convince Vidya who was a die-hard secularist. He condemned her strongly on this point and called her a convent-educated, pseudo-secularist who thought it fashionable to laugh at her own gods, but it was no use. Vidya refused to listen to him.

However, when it came to Mandal, they joined hands and did their bit by writing letters to the editor and contributing to the anti-Mandal forum. Soon Vidya was involved in active agitation. The students were thrilled to find support among the adults and she was invited to the strategy meetings. She was getting so involved in all this anti-Mandal business that it was getting impossible to see her. Meanwhile the stir intensified. The All India Institute of Medical Sciences was renamed the Sangharsh Chowk by the students, INA crossing was named Shanti Chowk and the Gole Methi Chowk became Kranti Chowk.

*

The day I went to see Nagaraj Rao was a typical day of rallies, processions and slogans. To reach the Taj Mahal Hotel from Shankar Market meant that I had to cross Rajpath at some point, an impossible task. It took me an hour to reach the hotel. I didn't give my car to the attendants to park. They all steal petrol. It was raining and by the time I reached the lobby after parking the car my head was soaked. The sudden blast of air-conditioning made me shiver. I wiped my hair with a hanky as I looked around. Was that dark man with intense eyes Nagaraj Rao? The man got up, revealing a tough, muscular body. He was dressed in a white bush-shirt and white pants with a thick gold chain gleaming at his throat. He extended his right hand.

'Mr Malhotra?'

'Mr Nagaraj Rao?'

Credentials established, we went to the tea lounge and sat down. Rao was not the kind of man who wasted time on niceties. He came straight to the point. 'Mr Malhotra, I want a licence for Indian manufactured foreign liquor and for beer manufacture too. I'm told that you're the man to come to.'

'By whom?'

'By Himmat Singh.' Nagaraj Rao mentioned the name of one of the most powerful and influential guys in the Congress party. 'He said the best team in Delhi is Bhaskar and Malhotra, north and south.' He smiled suddenly and showed me two sharp canine teeth. 'Brains and brawn.'

'Am I the brains or the brawn?'

'Oh brains, of course. A north Indian with brains is a formidable opponent.' Again the Dracula smile flashed and his eyes grew rounder. 'Don't mind me, I like to joke. Fact is, Mr Malhotra, I also know you are a good friend of Mathur's.'

'And how do you know that?'

'I have spies. It's no use coming to Delhi and choosing the wrong man. It's a waste of time and money. So I did some research of my own and settled on Goodwork Consultants.'

'If you know so much why don't you get the licence yourself? Why come to me?'

'Because Mathur won't talk to me.'

'Mathur is not the last man in the hierarchy. There's also the secretary.'

'Your man.'

'And the Minister, Industries.'

'Your man.'

'You talk as though I am prime minister of the country.'

'I give regard where regard is due. I know you can do this. I have already given Bhaskar the terms of the agreement. He must have already told you. I'm prepared to give an advance, and further advances as and when you suggest, at different stages of the case.'

I looked at him carefully. He was good looking if you like Dravidian looks : thick lips, thick eyebrows, and plump cheeks. In fact I thought he looked somewhat sinister, like the liquor baron with an army of goons whom he aspired to become. 'What about the various people who may not be so anxious to do the work of Nagaraj Rao out of natural love and affection?'

'Additional five for the minister. Officers you handle.'

'What about the formal applications? Have you made them?'

'Yes. And I'm already approaching financial institutions.'

That was that. I couldn't think of any more questions. It was the chance of a lifetime. I could get at least a clean eight lakh as my share after paying off the babus, maybe more. And there were ten more already in the pipeline. The thought of all that money made me dizzy just thinking of all the things I could do with it. I looked at Nagaraj Rao. 'Okay. I'll have a go at it.' We shook hands and Nagaraj Rao gently pushed a briefcase towards me. I picked it up and strode out.

It was getting dark but I knew Bhaskar would be waiting. We closed the door of the office and opened the briefcase. There were two lakh rupees in crisp notes and two diaries with pictures of various Nataraj Hotels. We stared at the money and grinned happily. There is something about new notes that sets the adrenaline pumping and the nerves tingling. We decided to keep fifty thousand as expenses and take seventy-five thousand each to begin with.

I drove home thinking about how to approach Mathur. In a situation like this it was a disadvantage to know the man too well.

I reached home to find the family in the middle of a serious debate about the Mandal Commission. The army had been called out in a number of states because of the district administration's failure to stop the rampaging mobs of the pro and anti-reservationists from clashing. The prime minister had declared in a rally that he was prepared to sacrifice his government but would not go back on the reservation decision. Delhi University had suspended teaching. In fact, Delhi was being held in an almost siege-like state by agitators of various kinds.

'V.P. Singh wants to Mandalize the country,' said Pitaji.

'And you are bent upon vandalizing it,' I said wearily. Nobody had thought about dinner, it seemed.

'Nobody can control the students now. They have started on the road to self-destruction. It's a do-or-die situation,' said Vidya. 'Why can't this PM understand that the students are genuinely affected.'

'But why paralyse life, damage public property and harass people?' I was tired, wet and hungry. 'This is not the way to seek solutions. Every bus in Delhi has broken window panes.'

Pitaji stood up and pointed a finger at me, 'People like you scare me more than V.P. Singh. He is a cynical politician who only wants a vote bank. But you are an irresponsible hypocrite! How dare you pretend to be so unconcerned!'

'I'm not unconcerned,' I shouted. 'I'm only sick of being pushed around and I hate violence.'

'Sometimes violence is the only answer,' said Vidya. 'Nobody listens when we talk quietly. What is going to happen to our children? For some years now people had stopped worrying about castes of friends and colleagues. Now it has begun again. Whenever I see a person getting unfair advantage over me because of his caste, my blood boils.'

'Papa, see this,' the children waved two stickers for the car. One read, 'Don't Blame me, I didn't vote V.P.' and the other, 'I'm sorry I voted V.P.' They proceeded to paste them on the glass front of the crockery cabinet. Every car in Delhi was carrying the first slogan. If they didn't vote V.P., then who did? At least the second slogan was more honest.

'Don't worry, folks, the Mandal Report will never get implemented. It will lie forgotten in some cupboard,' I said.

Vidya faced me in anger. 'You talk like god from Mount Sinai. The government has decided to implement it.'

'He looks like a crook.' This from Mataji, her homely face bristling in unaccustomed anger. 'Shifty-eyed serpent! Rajiv Gandhi was worth ten of him.'

'This is what V.P. Singh has done to the country, he's brought us to a situation where we think a guy like Rajiv Gandhi is better than him,' said Pitaji sadly.

Vidya lifted her heavy plait and twisted it into a bun at the nape of her neck. Her smooth face was innocent of all make-up, not even the tiniest hint of lipstick. Her unplucked brows were heavy and dark, a bit shaggy too. But they suited her and went well with her broad brow and plump generous lips. Vidya had a serene, womanly look about her which didn't really go with her mission in life. Her figure was warm and plump, she invited confidences. She soothed the children simply by gathering them to her bosom. She was almost like a mother to me too. What I felt for her was not the love I felt for Nagina. There was no grand passion, only the comfort of habit and dependability. She sat on the sofa with her legs tucked under her, the black-and-white printed fabric of her shirt stretched tight across her hips and thighs. With her crumpled dupatta she wiped her neck and upper bosom, then flung the dupatta over her shoulder. The gesture disgusted me a little.

'When you have finished your discussion I would be grateful for some dinner.'

Guddu whirled to face me. 'How can you think of food? The students are ready to die and you are so unconcerned.'

'A few dead hardly matter,' I said and went up the stairs to my room. I didn't mean to sound so cynical, but Guddu really irritated me. A grown man like him, old enough to marry and have children, went around berating the world like a spoilt child. I poured myself a drink in the bedroom and removed my wet shoes and socks. Vidya came into the room.

'I think you better go slow on all these rallies and meetings which you have been going to, Vidya. It's having a bad influence on Guddu.'

'I'm not going to stop! Sometimes I think Guddu's right, you are the most selfish and self-centred man that I have seen.'

I removed my clothes and pulled on a pajama-kurta. 'I don't want to quarrel, Vidya. Fact is, I also don't want reservation but I don't want a dharna in my house either. And nor do I want my wife taking to the streets. Leave it to the politicians whose job it is to run the country.'

'It's our job too. We have to point out the mistakes. We voted for them, we can throw them out. Mandal will destroy us.'

'Nothing will happen. In this god-forsaken country there is always a loophole. 'Show me the man and I will show you the rule.'

'If we keep quiet future generations will never forgive us. History will call us cowards!'

'Why are you so emotional? You either hate or love, nothing in between. When Rajiv came the whole country couldn't stop mothering him. Then you hated the sight of him, calling him a shopkeeper, a thief, everything. Then V.P. was the answer, and now he is a combination of Hitler, Mussolini and Nadir Shah!'

'He's worse!'

I finished my drink and made another before lying in bed with my head against the pillows. 'Do me a favour, Vidya, get me my dinner here. I can't face the family downstairs.'

I lay in bed in the semi-darkness and brooded. There was a strange restlessness in me. Vidya, Guddu and the Mandal issue, Bhaskar, Mathur and the middleman deals, visions of a comfortable life and lots of money – all seemed to move in and out of my life. I didn't want these worries. They restricted me and took away my freedom. Was there ever an escape from them? If only all these worries would fade away, I would be free to think of Nagina. There, I had said it. I had said Nagina's name. It was Nagina's name that tore at my heart like an unhealed wound.

*

The next morning Delhi woke up to the news that a student by the name of Rajiv Goswami had set himself on fire at the Safdarjung Hospital crossing. Rajiv Goswami, a student of Deshbandhu Gupta College, made a self-immolation bid and by that act also set aflame the tempers of the students who came out in hordes. On 19 September, 1990, there was a crowd, about three-thousand strong, of boys and girls at Sangharsh Chowk. The time was about eleven-thirty in the morning. Rajiv Goswami, who had been sitting on hunger strike for the past several days to protest the decision of the prime minister to implement the recommendations of the Mandal Commission Report, doused himself with kerosene and lit himself before jumping into the middle of the crowd. The slogan-shouting crowd would not let anyone near him and it was with great difficulty that one policeman managed to reach Rajiv and put out the fire. The crowd then broke out in a fury and began stoning and brickbatting in a frenzy, and prevented the police from removing Rajiv Goswami to hospital. A number of policemen were hurt in the process. Almost at the same time, outside police headquarters, two thousand students gathered and shouted slogans against the prime minister – V.P. Singh *hai hai*, Delhi Police *hai hai*. They beat drums and blew trumpets and shouted slogans while they squatted on the road and demanded the immediate dismissal of the four police officers of New Delhi who had led the attack against the students at Gole Methi Chowk.

As if that was not enough, there was a lathi-charge at one-thirty by the police in an attempt to disperse the crowd. The lathi-charge only provoked the students further. They immediately retaliated by hurling stones and brickbats at the police. Total bedlam prevailed in the area for the next two hours and the heavy exchange of stones on both sides injured at least two girls, fourteen boys and nine cops. Water cannons were used in an abortive bid to disperse the agitationists, nineteen tear gas shells and twelve hand grenades fired at them all failed to bring the situation under control as the students rushed into several government buildings located in the area and hid themselves inside the offices. In some offices the police were prevented from entering by the staff members themselves, but in others they entered and removed the students forcibly. The indiscriminate lathi-charge did not spare the press or the people in the offices that the police entered. At least five buses were burned and thirty others damaged. Three police vehicles and vans belonging to the Delhi Milk Scheme were also damaged. Traffic was held up at a dozen points all over Delhi. Processions were taken out by students of Vivekanand Mahila College, Jesus and Mary College and Maitreyi College. Several students of the Delhi University sat on a twenty-four hour hunger strike in the campus to protest against police brutalities on students.

But all news about the anti-reservation stir paled into insignificance against the self-immolation bid by Rajiv Goswami. Photographs of the boy engulfed in flames were on the front page of every newspaper and many were the eyes that wept for him. Rajiv Goswami, a thin ordinary-looking boy with a week's growth of scanty beard, became a real-life tragic hero. Some newspapers even reported that he had not set himself on fire but that others had made a scapegoat out of him, and further, that the boy would never have done it if the crowd had not goaded him into doing so. Whatever be the truth, I do think it requires the courage of a dozen lions to set oneself on fire. The message sent by this self-immolation bid was unmistakable and the emotional appeal was such that after Rajiv Goswami there were such news items every day from all parts of the country. The entire nation was in a state of shock. But the prime minister refused to relent. There was no let-up in the state of affairs, and the entire northern part of the country, from Jammu to Madhya Pradesh, and from Maharashtra to Bihar, was, literally, burning.

'Come in, come in,' sang out Bhaskar the moment I stepped into office. 'Where have you been? I thought you had joined the anti-Mandalites like Vidya.' He threw something at me. I caught it in my left hand. It was a wad of hundred-rupee notes. I didn't have to count it to know that there were ten thousand rupees there. 'For sending a file underground for one month in environment. Good money for the job, hain?'

'I suppose so. Why are you giving all of it to me? Finally had your fill of money, have you?'

'This is for the fridge and the curtains and whatever you want. I agree with you, we need to do up this office.' This was so unlike Bhaskar that I could only stare at him. He touched the lobes of his ears. 'I have another job in the environment ministry for you. There is this fellow who has a liquor factory and he's been dumping chemicals in the Ganga near Allahabad for years. Now a smart new collector has closed his factory. Environment wants a report. You have to ensure that the right report goes to the ministry. Good money.'

'Why don't you handle this yourself with all your wonderful contacts in the ministry? You have a stranglehold on the Tamil babus of the environment ministry.'

'The fellows who are going to inspect are not from the ministry, they are from the state government. Isn't your brother-in-law the excise guy in Allahabad?'

'So?'

'The case is about dumping chemicals from a liquor factory into the river. Who do you think is going to do the inspection but the local excise people?'

'Are you going to share the loot with him?'

'What do you mean? He's your brother-in-law.'

'He's also the excise fellow. These guys won't even go to the toilet unless they are paid.'

'You mean he will ask you for money?'

'He won't ask me, he'll ask the fellow whose factory it is.'

Dost Mohammad entered with my lunch. I was so hungry that I ate the first puri without even breaking it. Bhaskar watched every mouthful I ate with impatience. I knew what he wanted, he wanted me to get the work done through my brother-in-law and then he would split the money in half between him and me. But I was not in the mood for that. I had had enough of doing the dirty work and getting only half the money. All Bhaskar did was sit on his backside and order me around. I did all the work, all the contacts were mine, all the goodwill we had was what I had built up, yet when it came to sharing I didn't get what I deserved. Bhaskar could whistle for the excise report or do it himself. If my brother-in-law was going to do it, I wanted two-thirds of the money.

'You are really very hungry,' said Bhaskar watching me polish off my delicious lunch. Finally everything was finished. I sighed, at peace with the world. Then I turned to Bhaskar. 'If we do not involve my brother-in-law he will strike a deal directly with the factory chap and that will be the end of our deal. How much is the chap willing to give?'

'Thirty.'

'Not enough.'

'What do you mean?'

'Tell him that his licence is in imminent danger of being suspended and ask for fifty. Then we can give something to my brother-in-law too. Oh, by the way, I have to take Mathur to dinner today. I need some of that contingency money. At least two thousand.' That stumped Bhaskar but he couldn't say anything to me for I was only doing my job. He had to fork out the money.

I waited till Bhaskar had gone to the other room to fetch the money and then I called Nagina – I was going crazy thinking about her. I couldn't call her from home. I dialled her Sunder Nagar number. I got the answering machine and Nagina's husky voice asking me to leave my name and phone number. It was the first time I had spoken to an answering machine.

'Who's Nagina Aggarwal? Whom were you talking to?' Bhaskar's beady eyes were on me.

'A woman.'

'A woman? Anmol, what are you up to? Do I have to remind you that you have a wife and children?'

'So?' I tried to stare him down.

'So you tell me. Who's this woman, Anmol?'

'Just someone. No one,' I repeated.

'Anmol, be careful – especially with women.'

'I think you have done your duty, C.V. Bhaskar, loyal friend and concerned well-wisher.' I said sarcastically. 'Just don't say anything more, okay?' I gave him a two-finger salute and sauntered out of the office followed by his appalled gaze.

I knew why Bhaskar, the virtuous Tam Bram, was giving me so much unsolicited advice – he was jealous. He was this squeaky clean guy with oiled hair who had never screwed anyone but his wife and he couldn't stand it that I might have been in for some excitement. He just could not stomach my good luck. Well, he could lump it.

I walked in the gracious corridors of the inner circle of Connaught Place to while away the time. At the paanwala's I lit a cigarette and was told that V.P. Singh's days were numbered. If the stupid Mandal decision did not finish him, LK Advani, the BJP president, would, because Advani had threatened to withdraw support to V.P. Singh on the Ayodhya issue. There were also strong rumours that the Janata Dal had a rebel in its own ranks – Chandra Shekhar. So there wasn't a hope in hell for the prime minister. The paanwala, a diehard Hindu, said that all this was bunkum, the only important issue was Advani's rath yatra and the Ayodhya Babri Masjid issue. At the mention of the rath yatra a new light shone in the eyes of my smoke-mates and immediately the whole discussion took off on a tangent. You would have thought that the Hindus were in the minority in India and Hinduism in grave danger of being wiped off from the face of the earth. I shook my head and moved on. Why could people not take things normally?

'Sahab, totewali – try your luck!' called out a voice and I stopped. The totewali was a scrawny, cunning looking nomadic woman who wore the trademark maroon and black skirt and chunky silver jewellery of her tribe. Kilos of silver encircled her neck, wrists and ankles and her face was dotted with scores of tattooed black spots. Thick lines of kohl outlined her sharp eyes. She pointed to the two parrots in the cage and the stack of cards lying face down on the ground.

'I don't believe in this rubbish,' I said.

'Oh come on, Sahab,' she caught my hand and pulled me down. 'You will surely get the divine lady your heart desires.'

'What lady?' I asked, in spite of myself.

'The lady with immense life force – with prana – the lady with the snake eyes that can kill!'

'Snake eyes?'

'Tu-tu-tu!' She opened the cage and a parrot walked out, pushed a few cards and delicately pulled out one from the middle of the pile. The parrot laid the card near the woman and calmly walked back into the cage. The woman dropped my hand and peeked at the card. 'She's a beautiful devil,' the woman cackled. 'She will devour you with love.'

I arrived in the lobby of the Maurya Sheraton Hotel at precisely eight-thirty. I had already reserved a table at Dum Pukht, the restaurant that served authentic Awadhi cuisine. I hoped Mathur would have the delicacy to appreciate the food. Mathur was a full fifteen minutes late, but I didn't mind waiting. After all, the poor fellow was a joint secretary. Mathur had taught me in college for two years before joining the Indian Administrative Service. He was a dry sort of chap who wore thick glasses and had a face like a file. For some reason he had taken to me. I think this was because balding Mathur was crazy about girls, all girls, and these girls flocked to me and not to him. I didn't blame the girls. Even at that time, when Mathur was only about twenty-seven or twenty-eight, he looked like a sucked mango.

'Anmol,' said a plaintive voice near my right elbow. 'Where have you been? I've been waiting for you for so long.'

'I'm sorry, I thought I had told you to meet me in the lobby,' I said, steering Mathur down a flight of stairs towards the restaurant. 'I hope you had something to drink while you waited, Sir,' I said, though I knew he never would do that until he was sure that I was there. After all, he would have to pick up the tab in the event of my failure to appear.

The subdued atmosphere of the restaurant was a relief and I got down to concentrating on Mathur. 'What would you like to drink, Sir? May I suggest Scotch?'

'That sounds good. You have done well for yourself,' he repeated, almost in envy, I thought.

'Nothing to complain about. But tell me about yourself and about your postings,' I said. 'You are UP cadre, aren't you?'

That took care of the next one hour. All I had to do was to occasionally nod and say, Is that so? to keep the conversation going. I learnt how hard working and brilliant he was and how the government didn't appreciate him. Just because he consistently did a good job and refused to suck up to his bureaucratic and political bosses he had to suffer for eight years in the North-East while everyone else spent their time in Delhi or Goa. When they did take him out of the North-East he was shunted to the Andaman and Nicobar Islands. Oh! The injustice of it all! Well, he was a firm believer in god and he always told his wife not to lose faith, some day they were bound to get their due. But she was very unhappy, especially after a fourth daughter was born to them. Three were born in the North-East and the fourth in Port Blair. Having children in such remote places had ruined his wife's health and her mental health was not good either. But he never lost faith and good days came in the shape of Das, the present cabinet secretary who was distantly related to his wife. It was his wife who had gone to see Das and plead with him to give her husband a posting in Delhi. That's how he landed Food Processing with a house in Ravindra Nagar.

'Are you happy here?' I asked when I finally got a word in edgeways.

'Delhi is a strange place, when you are not here you crave to be here but once you do come here you are disappointed. Everything is so difficult and so expensive. If you ask me honestly, we were happier in the smaller places. The big houses, peons, drivers, fresh garden vegetables, these things are not to be sneered at.'

'I suppose not.' The food had been served and I had my first heavenly bite of Biryani Noorjahan, almost fainting with pleasure. 'Tell me something; is it really very difficult to make ends meet?'

'It is.'

'Then what do you do?'

'Struggle like the rest of the officers to keep up appearances.'

'Not everyone is struggling.'

'Maybe,' said Mathur and concentrated on his food.

I pondered a little over Mathur's behaviour. After talking all along about the money crunch he didn't seem to take the hint. Maybe he required more time. I ordered a liqueur with the dessert. He finished two helpings of the dessert and I was gratified to see that Mathur needed to open the top button of his trousers. We both made a trip each to the toilet and emptied our bladders which certainly eased the situation a little. While Mathur was in the toilet I thought that I should once again broach the subject by asking for help for Nagaraj Rao and gauge his reaction. If he was willing to help, I could suggest the gratification.

'Two more,' I told the waiter when Mathur came back.

'I really think I have had enough,' he protested.

'One more, and a slow one this time. We have to allow the bloated feeling to go away and brandy is the only thing for it.'

'Is that so?'

'Absolutely.' I waited for the brandies to come, and then spoke again. 'You know, Sir, I have a friend who is very keen to get a licence for liquor and beer manufacture, but I'm told that the government is not giving any new licences these days. Is that true?'

'One hundred per cent true. No new licences for this financial year.'

'Why?'

'The higher-ups feel that we are becoming a nation of drunkards. There is serious thought being given to totally stopping the manufacture of liquor.'

'But that's ridiculous! It can never happen. And even if you did pass a law, the only thing that will happen is that the manufacture of spurious liquor will go up. Prohibition has worked nowhere in the world.'

'I agree with you. People are never going to stop drinking. But right now there isn't a hope in the world of anyone getting a licence.'

'But I know of a case where a guy did get a licence just a month ago.'

'I know the case you are talking about. The party's from Punjab. That's a different story altogether, he was related to the chief minister of Punjab.'

'So one can get a licence.'

'If you know the prime minister or the president, yes.'

'But giving the licence in one case creates a precedent, doesn't it?'

'What are you getting at, Anmol?'

'What I'm trying to say is that my friend desperately needs a licence and he is willing to do anything for it,' I said, taking the plunge.

'He better go to the minister in that case. I can do nothing for him.'

'But you have to initiate the file,' I urged.

'Anmol, don't ask me to do something I cannot do. I cannot and will not do anything against the policy.'

'The policy is not finally decided yet. If an exception can be made in one case it can be made in another too.'

'I'm not doing it.'

'Why not? Listen to me, Sir,' I dropped my voice to a confidential whisper and leaned across the table to look him in the eye with a bare four inches of space between us. 'Everyone is doing it, everyone. You have four daughters to marry, and despite your best efforts you cannot be sure that you will find boys who won't ask for dowry. Help this friend a little bit he'll be grateful, I assure you.'

'Anmol,' Mathur's voice was suddenly weary. 'I need money as much as the next man but I'm not doing anything for money. My children are used to genteel poverty. The marriages of my girls are fated. Whatever has to happen will happen, nothing can stop that.'

I sighed a deep, disgusted sigh. After showing so much promise, Shriman Mathur was fizzling out like a damp squib. And what a waste of an evening, an evening spent listening to his woes and holding his hot, sweaty hand. I had no choice but to play the card I was hoping I wouldn't have to. I pulled out the pictures I had of Mathur having lunch with a female friend. So what's the big deal in breaking bread together? But it had Mathur in cold sweat. 'Where did you get these?' he gasped.

The rest was a cinch.

*

I was dreaming about the money I was going to make through Nagaraj Rao when Nagina called late in the evening and put out everything from my mind. Vidya was in the other room putting the kids to sleep. 'I'm going to my farm house in Mehrauli tomorrow. Why don't you come with me?'

I thought of the money I had to collect from Nagaraj. 'Farm house? You want me to come to Mehrauli?'

'Yes.'

'Why? Is everything all right? Has your husband found out about us?' I whispered anxiously into the phone.

'Meeting you after all these years, Anmol, I've realized what we have been denying ourselves. I want to make up for lost time…' Nagina's husky voice made me weak with wanting.

'What time?'

'Is seven thirty too early?'

'No, I'll be there,' I said unsteadily and disconnected the phone just as Vidya walked in.

nagina

I was named Nagina by my grandmother who said I was as rare, precious and beautiful as a gem. My mother did not agree. When I was born she wept for days and refused to breastfeed me. For a Punjabi woman to have a girl as her first-born is considered something of a failure. In the years to come, she could only muster a strange mix of love and resentment towards me and certainly none of that pure unconditional love she felt for my younger brother, Kulbhushan. All through my childhood, I resented the attention my mother showered on him and I did everything to gain her love. But I could do nothing, absolutely nothing, right in her eyes. To give her credit, I was a difficult, opinionated child to whom obedience did not come easy. After years of being unable to deal with her indifference I came to the conclusion that the reason why my mother didn't love me was that she didn't really love herself. She believed that the entire female race was not worth much else than bearing children.

Mummy had a strict moral code about the way girls were to be brought up. She got it from her mother who had six daughters and yet managed to marry them all into wealthy families. My maternal grandmother– whom I had met only about three times in my life– considered herself personally responsible for the sin of giving birth to six girls. The only way to atone was to keep them in their place and treat them all like dirt. I don't know how Mummy felt about being treated like dirt by her mother, but she sure as hell treated me no different.

Mummy thought all women were naturally licentious and devious, incapable of any intellectual depth and full of what Christians call original sin. In her thinking, women were naturally promiscuous and mothers had to take every precaution to ensure that their girls remained pure and untarnished for their husbands. Papa did not entirely believe that all girls were bad and had to be kept safe – like hot-house flowers – for their husbands, but he never expressed an opinion contrary to what Mummy said. I am eternally grateful to him, though, for not telling Mummy what happened between Anmol and me in Majhauli that night because if my mother had had the slightest inkling that I wasn't a vestal virgin at the time of my marriage, she would probably have slit my throat.

Why are girls disliked so much? Simple. Girls are resented because they don't fit into the two long-term objectives of the family i.e. the continuity of the male line and the intact preservation of inherited property. Daughters are disruptive of these goals. To give them dowries fathers have to portion off chunks of their own land which then – like the girl herself – become the property of another family. This I understood after I got married.

I was eighteen, back from finishing school in Switzerland and wondering what to do with my time. Though I kept telling Mummy that I hated marriage and the idea of being a subservient slave to a man, I simultaneously felt the need to be courted and loved by someone. Then my friend Ratna got married and told me such lusty tales about the marriage bed that having a husband was suddenly a very attractive proposition to me.

Mummy was thrilled when Satya Pal Aggarwal sent me a marriage proposal because he was moneyed aristocracy. Satya Pal had had money even in his great grandfather's time (his great grandfather had been the diwan of the Raja of Belgaum). While Papa had pots of money there was nothing remotely aristocratic about his lineage. We were refugees and too newly rich to matter in the social set up. Mummy was delighted because never in her wildest dreams had she imagined that a family like the Aggarwals would want to marry into a family like ours.

'Satya Pal Aggarwal!' exclaimed Papa. 'The guy's so old and a widower too. He has two children.'

'He's only thirty-three and he has more money than he can count. What's more, he likes Nagina,' said Mummy, relieved that someone could.

'Where has he seen Nagina?'

'I don't know. But he says he likes her style and that she's just the kind of wife he needs – educated, cultured and able to handle social life and children.'

'Children!' I screamed. 'I can't handle any children!'

'Well, you need not. Satya Pal already has two, a boy and a girl. He won't want more,' Mummy pointed out quickly.

Papa got up and began pacing the room. 'Nagina, go to the study. I want to talk to your mother.'

Kulbhushan, full of importance now that he had sprouted a fungus-like growth on his upper lip, looked thoughtfully at the picture of Satya Pal that was enclosed in the letter. 'He's like the Prince of Wales, dressed up in a suit and diamond cuff links. He rides too, like the Jaipur Maharaja.'

'Like the Prince of Wales? Show me the photograph.' I was suddenly interested.

The photograph showed a slim man standing in the middle of a green with a golf club in his hand, poised to take a shot. He wore white trousers and a red T-shirt, with a white golf cap on his head. His skin was a creamy chocolate brown and he had a square cut, distinguished face. I couldn't see his eyes because he was looking at the golf ball at his feet, but I noticed the aquiline nose and the pinched nostrils. A very French nose, I thought. He looked like every girl's image of a romantic hero and I decided there and then that I wanted to marry him. I must have shown some excitement on my face for Papa pulled the photograph from my hand.

'He's thirty-three and has two children.'

But my mind was made up. 'Older men are much better than callow boys,' I declared and married SP with much fanfare before my nineteenth birthday.

If Ratna had not told me tales of the absolute romp she and Ravi seemed to have twice a day, I would have gone on assuming everyone's sexual life was as boring as mine. And then I understood why SP lived so chastely with me. It was because of Radhika, his mistress.

Ratna tried comforting me but I was totally shattered when I learned that my husband had a permanent mistress. Things began to fall apart – or should I say that things began to fall in to place? – soon after. We are all, after all, only fulfilling our destinies. Of course I knew about SP's flings with his air-hostesses. Everyone knew about those. But they flitted in and out of his life like butterflies, fluttering bright-coloured wings one day and fading out the next. I didn't mind the air-hostesses but Radhika was another story altogether. Inevitably I was the last one to learn about her and even then I did not believe the stories until Ratna told me that she lived in our Golf Links house and was introduced at parties as SP's wife! I don't know what hurt more, the knowledge that my husband had a mistress or the humiliation that everyone besides myself knew about it. The day I found out I went home full of anger, my self-esteem shot to pieces. Then, afraid that I would burst with the horror of the situation, I took four valiums with a strong shot of brandy. The combination almost killed me. But later I felt better and quite able to deal with the anger and hurt.

I got over it, of course. Everyone does. The most immense of tragedies become memories or are simply replaced with larger troubles. But with the fading of the grief and bitterness there came an emptiness that would not fill. I plunged into a spanking social life. Dinner parties, ladies' clubs, lunches, poetry-reading sessions, book launches, wine-and-cheese sessions, art exhibitions – I was everywhere. I drank champagne and wine at parties and came home to a nightly dose of brandy and sleeping pills. Ratna told me I would kill myself with this lethal combination but I laughed it off. Brandy and a couple of pills were not going to kill me. They only made me sleep better so that I was ready for the next day. I lived this life for six years until one day, much to my surprise, I discovered that I was pregnant.

It was a difficult pregnancy. I was sick all the time and suffered from a nagging pain in my lower back that nothing seemed to cure. In every posture, sitting or standing, even lying down, it bothered me. As the pregnancy advanced the baby seemed to get heavier and heavier. It lay like a leaden lump in my lower abdomen, pulling downwards. 'Doctor, what's wrong?' I asked my gynaecologist. 'It's as though the baby itself doesn't want to be inside me. It wants to be released from me, from life.'

'My dear Nagina, how melodramatic!' Doctor Hirawala, the male Parsi gynaecologist who was my obstetrician, had little patience with the imagined ills of super rich women. He had a round pink face and a totally bald head with a few tufts of white hair growing above his ears. I always felt a little sick looking at him and I hated his thick, hairy hands examining me.

I won't believe anyone who tells me that children don't smile before four months; Nishant smiled just hours after he was born. He looked healthy enough and had a voracious appetite– he was even eating cereal at four months. But he never learnt to hold up his head. Or crawl, or sit up, or stand or talk.

What went wrong, or more specifically, what did I do wrong? Over and over again, with myself and with my doctors I have debated this question. I'm told that Nishant has cerebral palsy. He is a spastic. What could I have done about that? I don't know. In my worst nightmares I had never thought this was in store for me. And if someone had predicted such a fate I wouldn't have believed it. Things like this happened to other people, not to me, not to Nagina, the beautiful, pampered daughter of Rai Sahab of Majhauli. But it did happen.

With every passing day, month and year it was clear that Nishant, my beautiful son, would not improve. He grew in size with a long, gangly frame and stick-like arms and legs. His skin was fair and free of blemishes and he had thick wavy hair that grew at an astonishing speed, but his eyes were dull and lifeless. His neck could not support his head and his entire body was inert, lifeless as a vegetable. He responded to nothing, no one. He had no control over his bodily functions and he could do nothing for himself. I had two male nurses taking care of him who fed him and cleaned him and massaged him. Initially I spent endless hours with him, talking to him, reading to him, telling him jokes, begging him to respond, even shouting at him, desperate to hear his voice. But he remained lifeless. He did not even know I was his mother.

Every day was a painful revelation, and years were lost in trips to doctors, trips to temples and gurudwaras; years were lost in weeping before astrologers and godmen. Nishant remained a vegetable. I somehow felt responsible. As though there was something I had overlooked, something that I had neglected to do, that I could have done for him. I was plagued with guilt for the drugs and the drinks I had taken before he was born.

The whole world has children and in India they drop them while cutting wheat in the fields, but when I set about doing a simple thing like having a baby, what did I produce? A hypotonic spastic with severe retardation. I know now from my extensive reading that retardation is not always hereditary, that India has two to three per cent mentally retarded children, and that the problem is insoluble. Even Sweden, with all its medical advancement, has not been able to eradicate it fully, only limit it to point six per cent. And, as with most serious diseases, it doesn't distinguish between the rich and the poor, between the high and the low castes. But does that deaden the pain and the guilt?

Sometimes I think that Nishant loves me and responds to me, but in reality he doesn't. Oh, he knows me all right and maybe some instinct tells him that I'm his mother. But I think he would respond in the same way to anyone who fed him and kept him warm and dry. But he's so happy – an idiot who doesn't understand unhappiness, he loves music and colour. Maybe there is something in those dead grey cells of his. A tiny spark that sometimes gleams through that lopsided grin of his, and pulls at my heartstrings. It's too difficult to talk about Nishant but that's all I can do. Talk and endlessly wonder – what went wrong?

So I spent the next ten years rushing Nishant to specialists in the day and partying hard through the nights, often drinking myself to oblivion. When the doctors all gave me the same answer, I tried to shop away my stress. The more I cracked internally the more externally I shone. The more my self-esteem fell, the more I dazzled on the social scene. The empty space inside my heart just would not fill.

Nine years had passed since the birth of Nishant and I was still running to every mystic, mendicant and medicine man in the vicinity, and running away from myself.

I first heard about Siddh Baba from a rich socialite at a party in Maharani Bagh and the very next day I headed for Dehradun with Nishant in my Mercedes. Siddh Baba, as everyone called him, spent his time on a high wooden platform, almost five feet above the ground. He was so thin and emaciated that each bone of his body was visible through his skin. A good case study for a student of medicine, I thought. But for all his undernourished appearance, the Baba was alert and his quick darting eyes were everywhere. Anyone who could survive on three glasses of liquid a day for thirty years had to have something going for him, I thought as I stood in line with the rest of the devotees. We were made to stop ten feet away from the Baba. Most stood and stared for a while, then made their obeisance and moved on.

I stood glued to the barrier of wooden poles and willed the Baba to look at me. In my white and black printed salwar-kameez and my sunglasses and white shoes I looked and felt like an exotic stranger. What could a rich woman want from the Baba? The bunch of devotees around the Baba looked at me with a mixture of resentment and pity as I stood there, hour after hour. When I could no longer stand, I looked for a convenient stone and, spreading my handkerchief upon it sat down to wait. He had to call me. I would wait here till he did. After a long time I felt a tap on my shoulder and I turned around to face a young man dressed in saffron clothes. 'Baba is calling you,' he said. 'Follow me.'

Up close, Baba looked so ordinary that I was disappointed. Like any unwashed sadhu with tangled hair and an unkempt beard, but without the staring hypnotic eyes. I wasn't sure how to greet someone who sat so much higher and wondered whether I should touch his feet or say namaste. In the end I settled for namaste because groping for his feet would have been too embarrassing. I stood there looking up at him, waiting for him to give me my cue. His eyes were fixed at a point above my head. After an eternity he spoke. 'Beti, you have come to Baba. Your problems are over forever.'

Even I, with my blind faith in sadhus, couldn't buy that. Something of my scepticism must have shown on my face because he looked me straight in the eye and said, 'Some problems are insoluble. As long as you have this body,' he indicated his own body, 'to care for, you have to save it from pain and discomfort. This is an insoluble problem. All insoluble problems are the result of your karma, your deeds, bad or indifferent. Those you cannot escape, you can only hope to have the strength to bear them. God does not have the power to preserve you from the consequences of your own doing. You will reap what you have sown. The tragedy is some of the sowing you did in your previous birth which you don't know about. So you wonder, why me? What have I done to deserve so many trials and tribulations? It is your shortsightedness, your impatience, your lack of faith that is responsible for your pain. There is a pattern in everything, a cycle. Come to terms with the insoluble problems that have been served to you, like you come to terms with the family you are born in. Accept them and control your soul, don't let it wonder around covered by a layer of discontent. I see a red aura around you. Red means anger, lust, desire, dissatisfaction. Calm down, beti, and accept things as they are.'

'That means there is no solution! Nishant will remain like this, the body growing and the brain not growing, mentally retarded, a vegetable!' I was beginning to sob, huge, dry racking sobs that tore at my throat painfully.

'Is this your son?'

'Yes,' I sobbed, thrusting Nishant's wheelchair forward, anger and pain a rising storm within me. I wanted to scream and kick with grief. I wanted to roll in the dust and pull my hair out, to howl till the pain in my heart lessened. I forgot that I was in public, that the driver and a crowd of Baba's followers were watching me. I forgot even the Siddh Baba and I sank to the ground, put my head on my knees and cried, 'Do something Baba, do something! I have gone abroad to all kinds of doctors... allopaths, homeopaths, ayurvedas, naturopaths, quacks, everyone. And I have gone to temples and dargahs, to Hindu and Muslim saints, to astrologers and palmists. There must be someone who can perform a miracle for my son! There must be someone who can put his hand on his shoulder and cure him. There must be a sanjeevani booti somewhere. Baba, please, I'll give you gold, silver, money, whatever you want. You are Siddh Baba, you can do anything, *anything*. You have amazing powers. If you have ever done anything to help anyone, Baba, I beg of you, help me. I appeal to you. I embrace your feet. Help me! Please help me, Baba! Please!'

There, in the foothills of the Himalayas where the sun sets early, where grief is a lonely cry in the jungle that no one hears, where the howl of the jackal reassures you on long lonely paths up the mountain, there I screamed my anguish and cleansed my soul of bitterness and grief.

Baba said nothing during my outburst and nor did anyone else. In fact, the few sadhus and chelas who were hanging around quietly disappeared. Siddh Baba made no attempt to stop me or console me with inane words of sympathy. The taste of dust was in my mouth when I finally quietened and wiped my tears. I wasn't the kind of woman who felt incomplete without children. Not for me the agony of constant child-bearing to prove my fertility or whatever. But the fact that I had produced Nishant, the paraplegic, who had to be strapped in a pram before he could be taken for a walk, was more than I could bear. He couldn't even hold up his head, for god's sake. Yet his hold on life was so tenacious I believed a will existed inside him. Once, when he was about four, Nishant had vomited. I still remember the strain on his face and the horror in his eyes as he induced spasm after spasm, desperate to regurgitate everything, to stop himself from choking on his own vomit.

'Daughter, you may or may not believe this, but sometimes if you want something very badly, you have to give up something else that is equally valuable. A sacrifice, you understand?'

I bent to touch his feet and climbed back into my Mercedes.

An hour out of Dehradun I told the driver to stop. Time for my coffee and pills. I swallowed a vitamin tablet, my antioxidants, a painkiller and an antihistamine with a glass of water, then washed them all down with two cups of coffee. Then, because I wanted to have a third cup, I took two Gelusils to prevent acidity. The coffee tasted sickly sweet, but I liked it. The caffeine sent my blood soaring and the sugar gave me energy. I felt wonderful and decided to walk a little and search for a discreet bush for the essential business of life. The driver could have a smoke in my absence.

I found not a discreet bush but a field of sugar cane. Well, I thought, nothing like a cane field to hide your indiscretions and chose to squat there. Unless you crash around and announce your presence, no one can spot you in a cane field. In Punjab, the sugar cane fields in the border areas were the safest hiding places for terrorists. All along the border areas sugar mills were made to stop crushing so that farmers would stop planting cane and the terrorists could be exposed. I pulled a few leaves off the top of the cane and almost cut my hand. The long, narrow leaves had razor-sharp edges. The cane was ripe and ready for cutting. The farmer must have been told when to start. Maybe he was not allied to any factory and was looking for a kolhu to sell his cane for jaggery making. I wandered around, inhaling the heady scent of the sugar cane and thinking of the cane fields of my youth.

That night I lay in bed with the scent of sugar cane juice in my nostrils and thought about my life. From what Baba had said I understood that Nishant would not get better. And neither could I wish away the life I had with SP. Meeting Baba was an important turn in my life. It made me think and I now knew what I had to do. I had to leave Nishant and go back to Majhauli and I had to work in the mill. I wasn't meant to while away my time at parties. I remembered the heady scent of the sugar field and smiled to myself. It had to be the sugar mill. Sugar was in my blood.

In the middle of the night I sat up and hugged my knees in excitement. Such a simple solution, why hadn't I thought of it earlier? I would go back to Majhauli and work there. Then I would be happy, truly happy and the mess around SP and Nishant would fade away and everything would begin to make sense. I got out of bed and began to pack. I would leave early in the morning, I decided. I was full of energy and excitement and could hardly wait to begin.

As usual, I rushed into things without thinking and without even giving my long-suffering family a warning. The only place that would give me solace was Majhauli. My heart ached for it. The tall fields of sugar cane with their sharp-edged long leaves, the dusty fragrance of new mango leaves, the smell of roasted corn and the chilly winds that blew from the foothills of the Himalayas...

It was August when I reached Hariyali. The factory had to begin crushing in a couple of months. Early crushing was better than late crushing in the months of May and June because the cane began drying in the heat. The farmers' cane was doing well in the fields and they would be ready to supply the factory sugar cane by the first of October, except for a minor hitch – we hadn't paid the farmers for last year's cane, and the cane arrears were huge, more than five crores of rupees.

Once there I was greeted with the news that Som Dutt Bihari and Imtiaz Khan, the MLA of the region, had decided that they were going in for an agitation, and a dharna in front of the factory gates would begin soon. Papa was depressed, Mummy angry and Kulbhushan in a towering rage. The only way now was to woo Bihari and Imtiaz Khan so that they could persuade the farmers to supply cane without insisting on payment of arrears.

The farmers led by Bihari were insisting on the arrears being paid before the boilers were fired and that was the trouble. They wanted payment of arrears first, only then would they supply cane and allow the factory to run. And if we did not start the factory we would lose the season and the farmers would beat up the factory people for not crushing. It was a Catch-22 situation. Either way, the factory lost, unless Papa and Kulbhushan could make arrangements for five crores of rupees in hard cash, which was owed to the farmers. The problem was compounded by the expansion. If he hadn't decided to go ahead with the expansion of the mill Kulbhushan might have had some cash to spare.

I sat around the dining table with Papa, Kulbhushan and Kulbhushan's oily new engineer, Harshvardhan Gupta. Gupta was dressed slickly in coffee brown slacks and a green polo-neck shirt. He had a brown sweater knotted around his neck. His dark fleshy face had more than a seven o'clock shadow and his right arm rested casually on the back of Kulbhushan's chair. Both Papa and Kulbhushan had had meetings with Bihari; disastrous meetings as it happened. Kulbhushan was in a towering rage and he'd called Bihari a bastard and an untouchable who did not know his place and had ended up in a fist fight with him – a most surprising situation for I couldn't imagine my finicky brother bringing himself to touch the riffraff. But apparently Bihari had incensed him enough and they had both rolled around in the dust till Harshvardhan had stepped into the fray and told Kulbhushan to stop. As if that was not enough, Kulbhushan then tried to bribe Bihari and a ruffled Bihari threw a fit and said that he would die rather than touch a paisa of the Rai Bahadurs' filthy money. I sniffed when I was told the story by Harshvardhan and let Kulbhushan know that if this was the style of the managing director of Hukam Singh Mills, then god help the factory. After all, bastard or not, Bihari was the secretary of the Cane Union and the factory couldn't run one day without his active co-operation. But the most surprising thing was that my normally calm and collected father had entered into a battle of words with Bihari! He'd tried the Lord of the Manor act with him saying that he was responsible for the upbringing of Som Dutt Bihari and therefore Bihari, the ungrateful wretch, should not dare to go against his benefactor. This was the last straw for Bihari who said that he had enough of being treated like a servant and that this was independent India and not the feudal heritage of Rai Sahab. He ended by saying that nothing was going to stop the agitation except the immediate payment of five crores of rupees, otherwise not a single farmer was going to give cane to the factory. We will set fire to our fields, he said, but we will not give you cane.

'But why did you go and speak to this Bihari character?' I asked Kulbhushan in exasperation.

Harshvardhan's swarthy face was impassive but he was watching me under hooded eyelids. 'Do you have any suggestions?' he asked me.

'Yeah, do you have any suggestions?' echoed Kulbhushan belligerently.

'As a matter of fact I do,' I said icily. 'First, I think you should speak to Anmol. He is an old friend of Som Dutt Bihari's. And second, I suggest we talk to the MLA, what's his name?'

'Imtiaz Khan?' said Kulbhushan.

'Yes,' I said.

'It's a good idea,' said Papa to my surprise. 'Imtiaz is an educated man and it would be easier to make him understand the compulsions of economics. The banks are refusing to lend us any more money. There's nothing I can do short of setting up a printing press and printing hundred-rupee notes.' He said nothing about my suggestion that we involve Anmol.

'I think you should invite him for breakfast, Papa,' I said.

'Gupta will go. He will invite Imtiaz Khan on my behalf.' Then Papa turned to me, 'I don't think you should talk to Anmol, beta.'

'Where's the choice? ' I snapped and then flicked a finger at Harshvardhan. 'You'd better go immediately and invite Imtiaz Khan. Didn't you hear what Papa said?'

I could see Kulbhushan's brow darkening with anger at the dismissive way I had spoken to his friend but he said nothing. Harshvardhan was as suave and cool as ever. He stood up to go and gave me a mocking salute before strolling out casually. Kulbhushan made to go with him but Mummy signalled him not to. The relationship between my brother and Harshvardhan was becoming somewhat clearer to me now. I wondered if Mummy and Papa realized that what they shared was deeper than friendship.

Imtiaz Khan did not arrive till eleven o'clock, but Papa was not ruffled. He had expected him to be late and he'd had toast and lukewarm tea to stave off the hunger pangs. Kulbhushan starved and fumed while Harshvardhan drank three cups of coffee. I sat in the window niche of the breakfast room and admired the Hariyali gardens. From where I sat, the lawns stretched for at least half an acre, undulating and lushly green with not one weed to be seen anywhere. The continuous green was soothing and helped me consolidate my thoughts. 'MLA Sahab has come,' a servant finally announced.

I gathered my trailing dupatta and walked to the front hall. I was dressed in a green and white crepe suit with sequins on the yoke and I wore my hair loose. I had got it permed recently, against everone's advice, a month ago, and it flounced and bounced about my shoulders. I was pleased with the result. That was the look I was cultivating those days – a wild, elfin look, a little frail, a little helpless. I could see the impact I made on poor Imtiaz Khan and I smiled at him maliciously. Let him drool, the poor sod!

'Adaab.' Imtiaz Khaṇ had a very handsome beard, jet-black and trimmed to perfection. He wore the traditional Congress uniform of white kurta-pajama, only his wasn't cotton.

'Welcome, Khan Sahab,' I said and pretended to look over his shoulder. 'You haven't brought your wife? Oh, you should have. I would have had an opportunity to chat with her.'

'Namaskar, Khan Sahab.' Kulbhushan and Harshvardhan came out together and led him to the main drawing room, a room that was almost forty feet long and entirely wood panelled. It was really a party room and had five different arrangements of sofas around it. It was an overwhelming room, but Imtiaz Khan didn't seem particularly fazed.

'Imtiaz Bhai.'

'Rai Sahab!'

Papa and Imtiaz Khan embraced each other and grinned. They sat down opposite each other and the rest of us arranged ourselves around them like trusted aides. Imtiaz Khan was confident and relaxed. Papa made some small talk, even kidded him about the second wife he was rumoured to have taken.

'Why do you joke with your poor servant?' said Imitaz Khan in typical Lucknowi fashion. 'I tell you this MLA's job is very difficult. It has ruined my life! Or would I have just one wife? God forgive me, I would never be guilty of such a sin!' All of us laughed.

'And you should see the haji's daughter, she's like a piece of glitter, a jugnu, lighting this and burning that with the glow of her eyes!'

'May you get your haji's daughter if you covet her,' laughed Papa.

'I'm a connoisseur of beauty, Sahab. I look at and admire every beautiful thing.'

After chatting a while about this and that we moved to the dining room. I had laid out our finest crockery. Snow-white napkins glowed in silver napkin holders. The spread was worthy of a king. To drink there was a choice of three fruit juices, buttermilk (sweet and salty), tea, coffee and milk. And to eat the MLA could choose between a traditional Punjabi breakfast of stuffed parathas and halva, a South Indian breakfast of idli-dosa and sambar, and, if he felt like going English, there were muffins, sausages and eggs. Not to mention a number of side dishes and a variety of sweetmeats, trays of roasted nuts, and every fruit that grew anywhere in the country.

Imtiaz Khan did not go gaga over the spread, but he ate well enough and kept everyone amused with his jokes. Finally breakfast was over and we all retired with cups of coffee to a smaller drawing room.

'Well, Rai Sahab, how is business?' asked Imtiaz Khan, finally giving Papa an opening.

'Khan Sahab, nothing is hidden from you. The factory must begin crushing on the fifteenth of November. My repairs are almost over and I have made all arrangements for the firing of the boilers. The calendar has been given to the cane secretary, Som Dutt Bihari. Purchase centres have been opened, weigh bridges checked and rechecked. We are all anxiously waiting for D-day. All that remains is for the farmers and Bihari to co-operate.'

'I see. And what does Somu Bhai say?'

'He says no farmer will give us cane until last year's arrears are paid.'

'Sounds reasonable to me,' drawled Imtiaz Khan.

'How can the closure of Hukam Singh Mills sound reasonable?' growled Kulbhushan.

'Quiet, Kulbhushan,' Papa admonished him and turned back to Imtiaz Khan. 'You might think it sounds reasonable but I have no money. Not only myself, no mill owner in Uttar Pradesh has the money. You know, Khan Sahab, how unnaturally high the cane prices have become. Every mill owner has arrears!'

'Not to this extent they don't.'

'That's because of the expansion of Hukam Singh Mills. Our cash flow is a little tight. But we'll break even this year and by next year we'll be making a profit, I promise you.'

'I'm sure you will. But I still don't see what is wrong with Bihari's request for payment of arrears. After all, the poor farmers have to eat.'

'Khan Sahab, I'm not running away with anyone's money. I only need two months' time. Payment for the fresh cane will be made within a week as required by the law and payments of arrears will begin after two months, as soon as the sugar starts moving in the market. I am neck deep in debt, the banks are refusing to advance me any more money. Once we start crushing, these problems will be behind me.'

'Rai Sahab, I know enough economics to understand the words "cash crunch" but do the farmers? Cane, as you well know, is a one-year crop. The poor farmer has waited one whole year to get his house repaired, to get his daughter married, to buy his wife a new sari. The hardships they have suffered are tremendous!

And now you won't pay them. What do they eat? How do they buy seed and fertilizer? I know every argument that you can give – there is a cash crunch, the state-advised prices have gone up, seventy per cent of sugar goes to levy, the sugar market has been in the doldrums the whole of last year, you are still using the carbonation process, and so on. There could be a hundred and one reasons for not paying the farmers but not one of them will fill their children's empty bellies. Hundreds of farmers and their children are eating only one meal a day. What do you have to say to them, Rai Sahab?'

'I have to say thank you for being so patient with us. And I have to say that the worst is over. A little more patience and all their difficulties will be over.'

'And I have advised Som Dutt to lie down on the road in front of the factory and not allow any cart, any truck of cane to go inside! The poor farmer sweats blood and tears to raise a year-long crop of cane and all he gets at the end of it are empty excuses and false promises!'

'But...'

'But what? What does he get at the end of the year? An empty parchi that he carries around with him till it is torn and tattered? This parchi is a cheque, said the chief minister, a cheque to encash whenever he needs money. But has he been able to encash it?' Imtiaz Khan put a hand inside his pocket and pulled out a torn pink slip. 'Even I carry my parchi with me all the time. I know that I can get my money any time I want. But I'm not going to ask for my money. I will come for my money only when every farmer in my area has been paid. Rai Sahab, I too am a farmer. I know the pain of the farmers who give you everything in return for a torn piece of pink paper. I have no faith in the mill now. When I don't want to give you cane, how can I ask the farmers to do so?'

'Will the closing of the factory give them their money?'

'No, it won't.'

'Then?'

'Then what?'

'Then there has to be compromise.'

'I agree. But where is the compromise that you are offering? As I see it, it's we who are going to forgo our money for another two months, maybe more, while you continue to rake it in!'

'I think you are being unfair, Khan Sahab. I am in genuine difficulty and a compromise...'

'Okay, compromise. You want to talk compromise, I'll talk compromise. What are going to give us?'

'I told you payments will begin in two months. Give me two months, that's all.'

'That's no compromise, that's what you want!'

'I can offer nothing more.'

'The farmers are ungrateful bastards!' Kulbhushan jumped up. 'They live on our charity.'

'Kulbhushan! Papa's voice was like a whiplash. 'Leave the room. And you too, Harshvardhan.'

I sat down besides Papa and looked at the unperturbed MLA. He was too seasoned a man to let Kulbhushan's outburst trouble him.

'Why don't you borrow from the market?' Imtiaz Khan said finally putting down his cup of coffee.

'I have no collateral to offer for such a vast sum of money.'

'Has the stock of Hukam Singh Mills gone down so much that you cannot borrow a few rupees from the market?'

'Unfortunately, it's not a few rupees.'

'This is my offer to you, Rai Sahab, pay the farmers at least fifty per cent of the money owed to them before the fifteenth of November and I guarantee you that the factory will begin crushing on time. Otherwise...'

'Otherwise what?'

'Agitation. And it will have my support.' There was silence. Nobody knew what to say after that. 'Well, I should be moving now. Thank you for the delicious meal. Let me know what you have decided.' He raised his hand in an adaab.

'Fifty per cent is still a crore and a half of rupees,' said Papa after Imtiaz Khan had left. 'Do you think Satya Pal could help?'

I shook my head. SP could help but wouldn't and I didn't want Papa to risk humiliating himself. 'We will have to get Anmol.'

'You are right, you will have to convince him to come. He is your childhood friend, after all.' Papa whispered the last words to himself.

'I shall go back to Delhi and meet him. He will come,' I said and left it at that.

That evening the Rai Sahabs sat down together for a family dinner. Papa sat at the head of the table, Kulbhushan and Mummy to his right and I on his left.

'I hate it when people don't sit in their allotted places,' said Mummy smoothening the pleats of her impeccably tied sari.

'What?'

'You are sitting in Kulbhushan's place and he is sitting in mine. If, there is no order in the things around you there is no order in your life.'

'What order, what places? I don't understand all this nonsense,' I said reaching for the grilled fish.

'Be patient, Nagina, the bearer will serve you.' Mummy tapped my hand with the handle of a serving spoon.

I jerked it back in anger. 'Stop treating me like a delinquent child, Mummy! I can serve myself. By the time your bearer serves the food, it is all cold!'

'Your behaviour is obnoxious!'

I ignored my mother and continued to serve myself. Sometimes I saw so much of myself in her that I was truly frightened. I wanted to be totally different person from Mummy and I was shocked to see that the older I got the more like her I was becoming.

'Nagina,' Papa intervened before I could react, still troubled about the morning's run-in with Imtiaz Khan. 'Will Anmol listen to you and come?'

'Yes, Papa, he will.'

'What makes you so confident?' Kulbhushan asked petulantly.

I looked at his smooth pink face with the thin nose and bow-shaped mouth and watched him cut his food into small square pieces before piercing one with a fork and placing it delicately in his mouth. Then I looked at his bony wrists protruding from his shirt's cuffs and imagined pink and silver bangles on them. I laughed aloud at the thought. 'Why are you laughing?' Kulbhushan sounded suspicious.

'Never mind. But you don't worry. I guarantee you, Anmol will come.'

'What I don't understand, Rai Sahab, is why Nagina is taking so much interest in the mill's affairs?' said Mummy archly. 'Surely Kulbhushan and you can handle it. Satya Pal will not like Nagina spending so much time in Majhauli.'

'I agree,' piped up Kulbhushan. 'Why trouble sister dear.'

'I don't agree,' said Papa firmly. 'We are in the middle of a crisis and we can use all the help we get.'

'But what can Nagina do? She knows nothing about the problems here.'

'I know enough!' I thumped the table with the flat of my hand. 'I've grown up here. I belong here.'

'Softly, Nagina, softly. If I may be permitted to say it, you don't really belong here, do you? You now officially belong to wherever SP's village or hometown is.' Kulbhushan was snide.

'I agree,' said Mummy. 'SP and Nishant need her in Delhi. You shouldn't keep her here, Rai Sahab, what will the world say?' She passed me a plate of beautifully cut fruit. 'Have some fruit, dear.'

'Hang your fruit!' I pushed back my chair and stood up. 'Papa, let me make my position clear. I came here for two reasons; one, because it's my father's house and two, because you, dear brother, are unable to solve the crisis the sugar mill is facing. You misbehaved with Imtiaz, you treated Bihari like a bloody slave and you tried to talk to Anmol and failed there too! If you think you can handle the problem yourself, go ahead and do so. Not one of these people is likely to co-operate with you!' I slumped back into my chair and picked up my fork and began to eat. 'This food is tasteless.' I threw down my fork with violence. 'I want some black coffee.'

'Look what you have done, Nagina!' Mummy shouted pointing to the gouge mark that the fork had made on the polished table top.

'What's this obsession with things, huh?' I spun around. 'Try to think of people, real people and their feelings for once.

The days of feudal lords are over. You cannot run the factory if you treat people like slaves.'

'Who are you to advise us? It's you who treats everyone like a slave. Look at the way you are behaving with us.' Mummy was furiously rubbing the mark on the table with a napkin. Her carefully cultivated poise was slipping.

'Go home, Nagina, we don't need you here. You only spread unhappiness.' Kulbhushan stared at me with venom.

'Stop it all of you,' Papa's voice cracked across the room like a whip. 'And understand me, Kulbhushan. Ours is a family business, we have to stick together. Tomorrow I might need to borrow money from SP.'

'Rai Sahab,' began Mummy, rearranging her features and changing her tactics. 'Nagina is our daughter but she belongs to another family now. Her interests and her loyalties are there and so they should be. The mill and its problems are Kulbhushan's. He should take care of them.'

'Kulbhushan should take care of the problems provided he can do so. And what is all this about everything belonging to Kulbhushan? Get this clear…'

'No, Nagina, you get this clear. The mill, the distillery, Hariyali, all belong to Kulbhushan and will always belong to him. Rai Sahab, I don't think you are doing the right thing.'

'I think what you are saying is totally unnecessary, Vimla. Kulbhushan is the son of the house. Agreed. But we need help at the moment and Nagina is the daughter of the house. Not only can she help, she is willing to help. That's all. There is no need to read anything more in this. So stop all this nonsense right now.' Papa turned to me. 'Nagina beta, I want you to get Anmol here quickly. I fear that after today Imtiaz and Bihari will be in a hurry to start their dharna. We have to prevent it.'

'Yes, Papa. I will leave early in the morning.' I smiled sweetly at Mummy. 'Don't worry about SP or Nishant. Neither of them is likely to miss me.'

I went up to my room in triumph. Kulbhushan was the son of the house but Papa needed my help and wanted me in Majhauli. That was enough for me. Majhauli was my home. I belonged here. Nothing moved me more than the sight of carts piled high with cut cane lined up outside the gates of Hukam Singh Mills. I had tried to make a space for myself in SP's life but he didn't want me. Like an uprooted tree I could not grow there. My roots were still in Majhauli and it was in Majhauli that I would grow and flower and prosper.

But I understood Mummy's fear. Mummy feared that if I came back I would begin to take control of the mill and she knew I was more capable then her precious son, the light of the family. Well too bad for her. She would have to live with me for a while. Right now, the first thing I needed to do was to talk to Anmol and get him to come to Majhauli.

I went back to Delhi and had Kulbhushan call on Anmol. I knew that one meeting with him was all I needed. If I got him to agree to help then Papa would finally understand which of his children was more capable.

Meeting an old lover after fourteen years is quite an experience. I sensed the old electricity between Anmol and myself the moment we were together. I had forgotten what a strapping man he was and the feelings I once had for him. Kulbhushan had invited Anmol and his wife to dinner at my house in Sunder Nagar. I sized up his wife Vidya in one glance and I just knew she wasn't the sort who could make Anmol happy. Just as I knew from one look at him, that Anmol was still deeply in love with me. Accustomed to years of SP's indifference, it was a relief to fall into the arms of a real man again. After a meeting at the Lodhi Gardens I wanted to meet Anmol on my own turf and I wanted to meet him alone. I decided to call him to SP's farm house in Mehrauli.

Anmol arrived at the farm at seven thirty in the evening after I had called him up three times and driven myself up the wall in mounting panic. Anmol was central to my game plan. Without him I was sunk.

'Hello, Anmol.' I was all soft smiles and soothing pastel colours when he finally arrived at the farm.

'Hello, Nagina.' He stood in the doorway and stared at me, 'You look wonderful.'

'Come in.' I led him to the patio we had in the back of the house, a lovely bower-like place with plants and creepers and white wrought iron furniture and loads of toys and things to amuse Nishant. The farm was one place where I didn't hide Nishant. He was allowed to sit everywhere and anywhere.

When Anmol entered the patio the first person he saw was Nishant strapped to his chair, watching a robot that moved forward, turned around and somersaulted, all the while emitting robot-like sounds and flashing lights like crazy. Nishant's head was tilted at an unbelievable angle as he tried to keep an eye on the toy that constantly moved out of his line of vision. Drool dripped from his slack lips.

The first sight of Nishant is shocking. People avert their faces and gulp down the bile that they feel rising within them. They want never to have to look upon such an apology of a human being again. Anmol reacted in horror too. Then the horror was replaced by tears, not for Nishant, but for me. At least he had the sensitivity to say nothing to Nishant. The ones who tried to talk to Nishant were really the worst. Nishant could respond to nothing. Anmol sat at a safe distance from Nishant and tried to hide the tears in his eyes.

'Take Nishant for a walk,' I told the nurse after some time and made sure Anmol was watching as I made a great show of adjusting the straps on Nishant's wheelchair, even though that was something his nurse had done for years and for which she needed no assistance. 'Let's walk outside too,' I said finally taking pity on Anmol who looked as though he was about to burst into tears again.

It was a relief to get away from Nishant. I hated myself for displaying Nishant as I had done, but I had done it deliberately. Altruism has never been the most motivating influence in my life and I have no qualms in saying that I am rarely moved by feelings of love and brotherhood. I don't even want to be a martyr on the altar of maternal duty. Why should I be? Nishant does not even recognize me as a mother. I hate sickness and disease and I cannot keep pouring out love for a stone that does not respond. I had displayed Nishant for a purpose.

Outside it was cool. My dress was thin and wasn't really meant to be worn in mid-October. I hugged myself closely and hoped the walk would warm me up. I meant to give Anmol a tour of the rose garden but we walked further and further away from the house, beyond the boundary, till we reached a thick mango grove that fell in the neighbour's territory. There among the trees we were hidden from prying eyes and there, finally, Anmol spoke. 'I'm sorry about Nishant, Nagina.'

To my horror I felt myself beginning to weep. There was no reason to cry but suddenly I was swamped with a terrible sense of longing and despair and I wept with abandon. Nishant, my mentally retarded son and the biggest tragedy of my life. I think it was the sense of loss I felt when I saw Anmol and Nishant together – a vision of what could have been – that triggered my grief. I wept for myself and for all the tragedies in my life and for the terrible fact that no one loved me or wanted me. Anmol, the clumsy stupid oaf, stood there helplessly making weird soothing noises till I was forced to do what he should have done. I walked into his arms and holding his elbows, put his arms around me. Then I abandoned myself to clutching hot hands and frenzied lips, trying to rid myself of all the pain. Passion threatened to crescendo when sanity returned as a result of the overgrown baby's inability to deal with the buttons on my kurta. I thrust his thick fingers away and looked around in terror. There could be a hundred lurking eyes in the grove. I was horrified with myself and immediately began walking back home. I must be crazy walking into the woods alone with Anmol. Every servant and every child on the farm would know exactly where I had gone and what I had done. I almost ran home, dragging him behind me, stopping to breathe only when I reached the house.

I led Anmol straight into the drawing room and rang the bell imperiously. 'Tell ayah to get my shawl,' I told the attendant. 'And ask the gardener to cut two dozen of the best roses for Sahab,' I indicated Anmol. 'Ah, and please get us something to drink. Would you like some wine, Anmol?' I knew the servants would not think it odd that I ordered wine. It was my standard drink when in company, though I'm sure Anmol wanted a whisky and I could have actually done with a brandy.

Having set the scenario for the servants and ensured that one or the other of them would keep coming and going in the room,

I heaved a sigh of relief and sank into the sofa. Anmol looked at me with deep longing and I found myself shrinking a little in horror. My wayward steps were taking me into an adulterous relationship that the heat in my loins told me I wanted. Anmol downed his wine in one gulp and stood clutching the fragile glass in his enormous hands. He smiled at me and told me I was the most beautiful woman in the whole world and that he loved me more than anything else, even more, he added without hesitation, than his children. I was silent. For the first time since I couldn't even remember I was loved for who I was and I was filled with gratitude.

'I love you too, Anmol,' I said and we sat like that devouring each other with our eyes, quite lost in a lush romantic haze till the servants disturbed us. I knew that I need have no doubts about his loyalty. 'When can you come to Majhauli?' I asked.

'Whenever you say.'

'Tomorrow?'

'Yes.' Then he shook his head. 'Make that the day after tomorrow. I have to wrap up some work here.'

'Okay,' I said briskly. 'Things are hotting up in Majhauli and Papa and Kulbhushan are in a complete panic. We have to reach there quickly so that you can begin talking to that Bihari guy.'

'When is the factory supposed to begin crushing?'

'Fifteenth of November. And it's already nearing the end of October.'

'Don't worry, I'll be ready to go the day after tomorrow.'

'Good. You better pack for at least a week.'

'Okay. And I'd better talk to Bhaskar too. Let him know that I will be gone for a while.' Anmol grinned his boyish grin.

'Who's Bhaskar?'

'My partner,' said Anmol. 'The Madrasi Babu! He'll cut his throat when he knows I've gone.'

'That's settled then,' I said smiling at him. 'I'll pick you up day after tomorrow.'

'Okay,' he whispered. I felt a bit smothered by his overpowering maleness. I bared my teeth in a smile at him. What fools men were. Their brains were between their legs. I don't think there is a man alive who cannot be manipulated by a clever woman to do exactly what she wants.

After Anmol left, I wrapped my shawl around me and went out again. Our farm house was huge and sprawling with the best rose garden in the whole of Delhi. SP spent a fortune on the roses. I walked on the narrow path between the rose beds staring at the ghostly white blooms and the red blooms that looked black in the dark. The red desi roses were SP's pride. He tended them for their perfume and even had a small lab that distilled pure rose essence that was used by perfume and rose water manufacturers. The night sky was clear and twinkling. I began to wonder why I had invited Anmol to the farm house, and made him promise to come to Majhauli to solve the crisis in Rai Bahadur Sugar Mills. Of course I wanted to help Papa but there was a hidden personal agenda here that I could no longer deny.

The next morning I woke fresh from dreams of Anmol. He was a handsome bastard. I remembered his crushing embrace and the wet excitement I felt. It would be much easier to seduce him in Majhauli. There was nothing wrong with what I was doing. If SP could sleep around and keep a permanent mistress why could I not have a lover? And the best part was that the configuration of events was such that Papa and Kulbhushan needed

Anmol, and Anmol needed me. It was a heaven-sent opportunity to go to Majhauli and get involved with Hukam Singh Mills.

Two days later I left Nishant in Sunder Nagar, told my mother-in-law I was off to Majhauli, ignored her comment that I was spending an inordinate amount of time in Majhauli these days and asked about SP. She looked at me strangely, didn't I know that he had gone to Bali? He had, had he? I seethed in anger at SP's behaviour but it only strengthened my resolve. I was going to Majhauli and I was going to work with Papa. I knew SP would be very angry when he came back. He wanted me to be the ideal housewife and take all his indiscretions without protest. I had had enough of being the long suffering wife, thank you very much. I would now do things for myself. Without waiting to answer any more questions, I packed my bag and left for Dehradun. I had to see Baba and seek his blessings before I began my new venture.

The moment he saw me, Baba climbed down from his perch to sit under the shade of a tree. 'Baba, I am going to start a new venture,' I said. 'I want your blessing.'

'I see raj yoga for you,' said Baba. 'Nothing that you do from now on can go wrong. Everything that you touch is going to turn into gold. But there is no happiness, no family life. Do you remember what I said to you about sacrifice? Sacrifice is the touchstone of life. To get something we have got to give up something else. So don't be surprised if you too are asked to sacrifice something valuable, something that means a lot to you.'

'You mean Nishant?' I asked.

'That I don't know. But you will not get everything. You have made a choice in your life, there is no way you can avoid the consequences. You might think that you have been asked to make more sacrifices than other people, but that's not true. There's balance in nature. You might think some people have not faced as many trials in life as you have but it's possible that they may not have wanted all that you have wanted from life.'

'I don't understand you, Baba, and I am scared. I don't want to give up anything in life. I want everything. What have I got in life? Tell me, what have I got? I don't have the love of a husband, or the love of a child. I don't even have the support of my mother and brother.'

'You are an intelligent and ambitious woman. I don't know whether it is for the good or the bad, but you are yourself seeking change and you will get it. As for success, there is a great deal of success in the material sense of the word. You will be on top of the world.'

'I came for your blessings.' I stood up looking at him.

'Nothing positive comes without a negative reaction, child. I told you that you will get what you seek, but you will have to sacrifice for it. If what you seek is very important to you than the sacrifice is worth it, isn't it? That's all I can say. Now go.'

anmol

Life had turned full circle.

I was going back to Hariyali and Majhauli. Going back because the Singhs of Majhauli needed me. I was filled with a self-righteous feeling of triumph. I had left in disgrace but I was returning in an air-conditioned Mercedes, seated next to Nagina. I was Nagina's first lover and obviously first was best. I had spent fourteen years of my life under a shadow. I had been thrown out of Majhauli and I was the reason Pitaji lost his job and had to leave the place he loved. If only Pitaji could see me now. At the thought of my father I felt my smile slip. I knew he would not regard my return to Majhauli as a triumph. He was a rigid, passionless man who would never forgive me for getting back with Nagina.

As I sped in the car towards Majhauli my heart beat painfully at the thought of seeing Hariyali again. I had often imagined myself descending the staircase of Hariyali in my dreams, one hand lightly resting on the polished balustrade of Burma teak, my glance casual and calm like that of owners of old wealth who don't have to talk about their inheritance. And always Nagina stood at the end of the staircase and waited for me. After fourteen years I was finally able to forgive Hukam Singh. I understood why he had thrown me out. It was not Nagina he had been protecting, it was his home.

'Is there something on my nose?'

'What?'

'I mean you are looking at me so strangely.'

'Am I? I'm sorry. But I wasn't really staring at you, I was thinking of something.' I opened the window a crack. The air-conditioning was making the car uncomfortably cold. 'I suppose the guest house at the mill is complete?'

'Oh, yes.' She turned to me, impulsively leaning closer so that her perfume enveloped me. 'But you are not going to stay there. You're going to live in Hariyali.'

'Certainly not,' I was shocked. 'Besides, it would not do to live at the kothi. Somu and company will immediately conclude that I am your man.'

We were nearing the factory now. I looked around with excitement as the car turned into the gates of Hukam Singh Mills. It was so painfully familiar, yet so different. There were large groups of farmers standing around the gate smoking beedis. All eyes followed the white Mercedes as it turned into the gates. I pressed back behind the curtains, grateful for the dark tinted windows that prevented them from peering inside the car. Nagina noticed my sudden shrinking and smiled; as the 'sahab log' she was used to being stared at.

'You have not started the trial run of the factory,' I said, staring at the silent factory.

'Must be trouble with the machinery. I told Kulbhushan that the new engineer he had hired was no good. But he went ahead and hired Harshvardhan just because he played a good game of golf!'

We reached the guest house and the driver opened the door and took my bag. 'I'll send the car in an hour's time,' Nagina said as I turned to say goodbye.

In exactly one hour I strolled out of the guest house and stood in the garden with my face lifted to the blinding blue sky. The sky, the purple foothills, the chilly wind, the scent of the flowers and the trees, all were so beautiful and life-affirming that I felt tears come into my eyes. This was where I belonged. I stopped to admire everything on my way to Hariyali including the new school building, the crèche, the concrete-lined drains and the co-operative store. I was disappointed to meet nobody familiar. I was standing and staring in wonder at a tree filled with brilliant mauve flowers when a passer-by greeted me.

'Adaab huzoor.'

'Uh, adaab. What is the name of this tree, do you know?'

'Sahab, ask me anything about the factory and I can tell you. What do I know of trees? But it's a beautiful tree nonetheless.' The man smiled at me and his short orange beard moved like a live thing. 'You are new here. Have you come to work in the factory?'

'No, I'm just a visitor. But I grew up here among the mountains and the cane fields.' I sat down beneath the flowering tree. 'If you have grown up here and seen the glow-worms wink in your fist and tasted new honey from the bee hives beneath the roof of your home, your heart is forever here.'

'You are a poet, Sir,' he laughed. 'But if you feel so strongly about the place, why did you leave?'

'I was a young fool, enamoured by the lure of the cities and the glitter of neon lights. I wanted quick money, cars, clothes.'

'You can do without all that here,' the man said lighting a beedi and giving it to me. 'I'm from Bihar and we have the mountains there too but you are right about this place. It does have an intoxication about it.' For a while we smoked companionably. I enjoyed the strong beedi. Then the man spoke again: 'Forgive me for saying so but this place is not perfect, it has all the complexities of a town. We even have the Mandal agitation here.' He laughed heartily. 'I'm a backward Muslim, imagine that!'

I nodded, not really interested, and squinted up at the sky as my companion hauled a rock beside me and sat down on my left. Lotus-eaters, that's what we all are in rural India – lazy, slow, impractical, more interested in the twists and turns of arguments, shades of meaning, turns of phrase. We were not really disturbed by the silent factory and the still chimneys. Progress didn't depend on them. In any case, what is progress but maya, illusion? We were content to smoke.

'When's the factory going to start?'

'Who knows,' he said following my glance and looking at the smoke-free chimneys.

'You seem like a man of the world,' I said. 'I'm sure you have ideas and solutions.'

'I have ideas.'

'What's the solution to the factory's problem?'

'Who's asking me?'

'I am.'

'Who are you?'

'A friend.'

'Fire the engineer.'

'What?'

'You asked me for a solution and I say, fire the engineer. Get rid of him.'

'The engineer?' I asked, not quite understanding what he was saying. 'Who's the engineer?'

'Harshvardhan Gupta.'

'Harshvardhan Gupta?' There swam before my eyes a vision of a huge man who had been at Nagina's party. He'd looked more like a hoodlum than an engineer. 'He's the engineer?'

'Yes, he's the new engineer. But he has no time for the factory. He spends the entire time buttering the Chhota Rai Sahab. In our time the servants and the owners did not sit or eat together. There was a reason for that. The owner can't drink with the servant at night and haul him up in the morning.'

'You are talking about your time as though you are an ancient.' I got up and dusted the seat of my pants. 'So tell me, what is the new engineer like?'

'Guptaji? He is very smooth. He says only what Kulbhushan wants to hear and Kulbhushan believes only him. Today Guptaji has the power of the life and death over everyone, including him.'

'Kulbhushan?'

'Yes. They are like man and wife.'

'Who?' I said bewildered.

'Kulbhushan and the engineer, Harshvardhan Gupta.'

I was shocked. 'What about Rai Sahab, didn't he object? He is such a shrewd judge of character.'

'True, but he's getting old and he is afflicted by son-stroke.' He laughed merrily at his joke. 'Kulbhushan is the son and heir, he can do no wrong.' I started to interrupt but he waved me down. 'Oh, he knows *why* Kulbhushan doesn't want to marry, but what can he do?' My friend flicked away his beedi. 'Blood has a terrible hold on the emotions. The love of sons is the blindest of all loves because its only basis is blood.'

The ravages of time are heartbreaking. The Rai Sahab who stood before me when I was ushered into Hariyali was the same Rai Sahab who had ordered me to get out and stay out, but what a difference! That Rai Sahab had been a colossus who was known to make men weep and tremble. He had a strong jutting chin and frightening eyes. This Rai Sahab's eyes were weary and shifting, his shoulders drooped, his hands opened and clenched. I stood there stupidly wondering how to greet him. Should I shake hands, fold them in a namaste or touch his feet? He put me out of my misery by extending his hand. I gripped it strongly and was startled to see him wince. 'You are strong,' he said. 'And tall, taller than before.'

Life is not a fairytale and the differences between right and wrong are not as defined as they are in stories. Also, perceptions change with time. As I sat in the drawing room of Hariyali and saw the loose folds of skin, the thinning grey hair, the shrunken frame and, most of all, the uncertainty in Rai Sahab's eyes, I found my fears fading. In the old relationship I had been the underdog, in the new one I was the messiah called to solve their problems.

I sat down to lunch with Rai Sahab and Nagina and heard more about the situation in Majhauli. Actually I knew what the problem was; what I really heard was Rai Sahab's bewilderment and hurt at finding himself confronted by a situation that was not responding to his attempts at resolution. Som Dutt Bihari, the secretary of the Cane Union, had the farmers solidly behind him and he also had the active support of Imtiaz Khan, the MLA. He said that no farmer in the area would give Hukam Singh Mills cane until all the arrears of the previous year were paid to the farmers.

Som Dutt Bihari was a UP man, not a Bihari, and he was the son of Yagya Dutt Bihari, who had been an out-and-out opportunist. During the freedom struggle Yagya Dutt had turned nationalist, worn the Gandhi topi, acquired the certificate of freedom fighter, and thus benefited from the monthly freedom-fighter's pension scheme while ensuring admission to schools and colleges for his progeny.

When land reforms began, Yagya Dutt was at the forefront in all the processions. And why not? He had nothing to lose. By the time the land reforms were complete and the boundaries squared, Yagya Dutt had forty acres of land in his name. Nobody dared ask how because by that time Yagya Dutt had graduated from local dada to local leader with his own army of goons. In his forty acres of irrigated land he grew sugar cane and he sold his cane to Hukam Singh Mills but also went and joined the jaggery and khandsari units when they protested against the mill. When it became clear that the mill was here to stay, he became a champion of the mill workers' cause. When the old man finally succumbed to his various ailments, his son, Som Dutt Bihari, was ready to take on the mantle.

Thus was born the leader of the Cane Growers' Union, Som Dutt Bihari. But I remembered the boy, Somu. He was older than me and was totally responsible for the toughening up of Anmol Malhotra.

Rai Sahab's wife, Vimla, was proud of her socialist ideology so in her school she had children from all backgrounds. Shishu Mandir was basically a school for the factory workers' children, but Yagya Dutt's son was allowed admission to the school. Of course his admission was more a tribute to Yagya Dutt's nuisance value than his own intrinsic merit. In those days the school's classroom hierarchy was quite flexible and children two-three years older and younger sat together and learned the alphabet. Som Dutt was being trained by his father to be a local dada so he was adept at using his fists and had no qualms about using them either.

'See, Som Dutt, how beautifully this small boy writes,' said the schoolmaster one day, showing my copy book to Som Dutt. I wasn't really small, I was eight years old, but parents didn't spend sleepless nights over their children's education back then. On the other hand, Som Dutt was much too old to be struggling with the alphabet. 'If you spend more time on your studies and less being the star ruffian of the class, you too can write as well,' he chided Som Dutt.

Som Dutt's face burned with shame and anger. He was a thin, dark boy, much older than the average boy in the class and the insult was unbearable. He clenched his hands into fists and stuck out his lower lip in a pugnacious scowl. But the teacher didn't take heed. 'Not only is Anmol small, but he is the newest boy in the school. Today I want you to sit with him and practise the alphabet.'

Som Dutt moved towards me like a wounded tiger. The first clue I had of what was coming my way was when he caught a generous chunk of my thigh between his filthy thumb and forefinger and twisted the flesh till I screamed.

'What happened?' asked Masterji.

'He pinched me,' I said between sobs and showed him the welt on my thigh.

Masterji was livid and threw Som Dutt out of the class, telling him to send his father to see Vimla Singh. Som Dutt looked at me with hatred and stalked out of the room. And boy! did he give it to me later. He thrashed me so hard I almost cracked a rib. I tried valiantly to fight back but he was just too good for me. However, the strangest thing was that it didn't make me an enemy of Som Dutt's. He respected me for trying to fight back and as for me, I learned how to fight. I noted the way Somu kneed boys in the groin, the way he twisted fingers till they almost broke and the way he went for the ribs. After that I made him my guru and followed him around like a faithful dog.

But Rai Sahab didn't even say anything against Som Dutt – that was not his style. 'Som Dutt is a true champion of the farmers,' he began. 'I don't blame him or the farmers for their anger. Payments are late by a year. We wouldn't have been so short of money if it hadn't been for the expansion. Still, cane prices are inordinately high this year. I'm thinking of going to Lucknow tomorrow to speak to the chief minister. If the state government could give us an advance to pay the farmers, it would save the situation. In the meantime, it would help if you could speak to Som Dutt Bihari and request him to give us some time, about three months.' Rai Sahab's voice had begun to peter out awkwardly; he was embarrassed to ask a favour of me.

'I'll see what I can do, Rai Sahab,' I said and stood up as he raised his hand in a half salute and went out of the room.

Happiness is an emotion that is usually felt in retrospect. I mean, when we are actually happy we never seem to realize it. As I strolled with Nagina that evening in the Hariyali lawns, I was such a bundle of excitement that I didn't realize that what I felt was real happiness. Nagina had used her dupatta to tie her hair in a high ponytail and walked barefoot in the grass. It was early evening and the crows were making the most unearthly racket. I could see every blade of grass that poked between Nagina's bare toes and I could distinguish every shade of colour in the flowers. I lifted my head and sniffed the scented air and gazed upon the purple mountains with a sigh of contentment. If only I could capture the day and the atmosphere forever.

'Sahab,' called a respectful bearer. 'Phone from Delhi.'

'For me?' I asked.

'Yes, Sir.'

I hurried in and picked up the ornate white-and-gold handset. 'Hello, Anmol Malhotra here.'

'Anmol? Thank god I got you. Partner, there's trouble here. Vidya's in jail!' It was Bhaskar.

'What do you mean? Are you drunk?'

'No, I am serious! Vidya is in jail.'

That was the most comical thing that I had ever heard and also the most annoying. I didn't know how to react. 'If this is your way of getting me back to Delhi, Bhaskar, try again,' I said.

'I'm serious, Anmol. Vidya came back to Delhi a few days ago and took part in an anti-reservation dharna along with other parents. I don't know exactly what happened but the police lathi-charged the parents and some arrests were made. Vidya apparently was the leader of the mob.She charged at a policeman with a steel curtain rod.'

'Good god!' I was flabbergasted. It was all very well to protest and take part in rallies, but to go armed with a steel curtain rod was unthinkable! It showed premeditation and intent to harm. 'Curtain rod?'

'I'm afraid so,' said Bhaskar. 'Of course, a lot of the other parents also had rods, rolling pins and wooden clothes-washing bats, but I suppose Vidya got carried away.' I made no reply, I didn't know what to say. 'Are you there? Anmol?'

'Yeah, I'm here.'

'You better come home. Vidya's frantic and so are your parents. Only Guddu is elated. He thinks Vidya is a heroine.'

'He would,' I said bitterly. 'All right, Bhaskar, I'll leave as soon as I can. Can you and Mahajan come to my house by midnight? I should be home by then.'

'We'll be there,' promised Bhaskar.

I put down the receiver and turned around. 'I have to go back to Delhi. Tell Rai Sahab that I'll be back as soon as I can.' I took out a hanky and wiped my face. 'I suppose I can get a bus from here.'

'Sit down, Anmol. The driver has gone to Meerut for petrol.' She looked at her watch. 'Let me see, it's almost six o'clock. You should be able to leave by seven. Is it serious? Is someone sick? Your wife?'

'It is my wife and she isn't sick, she's in jail!'

'In jail?'

'Yes in jail, for having knocked a policeman on the head with a steel curtain rod.' I still didn't believe it. 'She thinks she's the world's greatest social reformer, a human rights activist or something! I'm sick and tired of her causes. The way she carries on you would think that the world was coming to an end just because there is reservation for the wretched OBCs. I better go to the guest house,' I said at last. 'Will you tell Rai Sahab that I will be back as soon as I can?'

'Of course. Listen, Anmol, can I ask my lawyer to help? He's very good.'

'Give me his phone number. If I need him I'll call him.'

I left Majhauli at about seven-thirty, and it wasn't the Mercedes that I travelled in this time but the lowly Fiat. I would be lucky to reach my house by one o'clock in the morning. Everytime I thought of Vidya in jail my heart sank. I remembered every horrendous story that I had ever heard about police brutality and the conditions of jails in the country. By this time my anger had been replaced by fear. Vidya must be devastated. Why couldn't she be a normal mother and cook and look after the house and the kids? Before this Mandal business she had restricted her activities to giving talks on the radio and speeches in civilized fora and joining various committees and societies. Though even that irked me, because I'm not the type of person who takes up causes, I was able to ignore them most of the time. But this!

I reached home at exactly twenty past one to find a long foreign car parked outside along with a uniformed chauffeur. I ran into the house fearing the worst only to be greeted by Pitaji, Mataji, Bhaskar, Mahajan and two very distinguished looking gentlemen having a midnight feast. Vidya was serving them. It was a tea-party! For almost twenty seconds I stood there unnoticed as Vidya pressed the distinguished looking gentlemen to have some halva and insisted on squeezing lemon juice on their green peas herself.

'Anmol!' – Bliss! Finally my dear wife had seen me – 'You have come!' cried Vidya.

This was too much like a scene from a movie. 'What do you mean, I've come? What else could I have done after the frantic phone call I received from Bhaskar? He told me that you were in jail! Will someone tell me what on earth is going on? I have come running all the way from Majhauli, worried sick, only to find my dear wife in the middle of a midnight tea-party. What the hell is going on?' I shouted.

A sullen silence descended upon the party. Pitaji gave me a filthy look and left the room. 'You spoil everything!' shouted

Guddu. 'Why didn't you stay on in Majhauli?' It was his turn to stalk out.

'Why don't you sit down, Anmol,' said Vidya, a flush mounting in her face.

'Ah Mr Malhotra, I'm Desai,' said one of the smoothies, smiling at me and returning to the peas as though that explained everything.

'I don't know you, Mr Desai,' I said as rudely as I could. 'I came as soon as I could because I had been told that my wife had knocked a policeman on the head, and here I find a... a...'

'A celebration! Ha ha,' laughed Desai. 'Understandable. Well as you know, Mrs Aggarwal telephoned me and I was able to use my influence to get Mrs Malhotra out of the lock-up. Hence the celebration.' He smiled at me and asked Vidya for some more halva.

'Mrs Aggarwal? Oh, you mean Nagina.'

'Yes, I mean Nagina. I'm her lawyer. When she called me and told me about the problem I immediately called the police commissioner and asked him where was the evidence that it was Mrs Malhotra who had hit the constable on the head? It could have been anyone in that melee. I'm glad to say that he was inclined to agree with me. Of course, she was still booked for rioting and disturbing the peace, but I was able to bail her out.'

'Nagina did this?' I whispered.

'What?' said Desai. 'Yes, Mrs Aggarwal phoned. She was very upset to see you so upset. Well, we must be going now. Mrs Malhotra, if you decide to whack another policeman on the head, just remember to let me know in advance. Goodbye.'

*

Finally Vidya and I were alone in our bedroom. I lit a cigarette and inhaled deeply. 'Vidya, let me make one thing very clear: This is the last time you go for any rally or anything. You are going to sit at home. I've had enough. I want a wife who looks after her home and children, I don't want a leader. This time, thanks to Nagina, you're home safe and sound. Next time I'm not going to ask Nagina to bail you out, understand?'

'I didn't ask you to bring in Nagina,' Vidya retorted. 'In fact, I didn't even ask you to come. It was Bhaskar who telephoned.'

'Oh yeah! And what would you have done for yourself? It would have served you right to spend the night in jail with rats and mosquitoes. You do a person a good deed, and what do you get in return?'

'Whom are you calling a "person"? Am I a "person" for whom you have to do a good deed? Answer me! Am I?'

'That's not the point...'

'It is the point, if you do something for me, your legally wedded wife, and then crush me under a sense of obligation. Whereas for this Nagina, you give up everything and go off to the ends of the earth!'

'How you exaggerate,' I shrugged in disgust. 'One can never have a reasonable conversation with a woman.'

'What do you mean "never" and what do you mean "woman"?' demanded Vidya.

'Just be thankful that Nagina bailed you out and put a stop to this nonsense once and for all!'

'Nagina, Nagina, Nagina!' Vidya almost hissed in anger, and turned away wiping her face and neck with her crumpled and dirty dupatta. Nagina was two years older than me and Vidya was four years younger. That made her six years younger than Nagina but nobody would believe that. Vidya's clothes were unironed and there was a stale smell of sweat and something else around her that I could not identify. Her thick oiled hair was plaited as usual and her nose shone brightly. I willed myself not to compare the two women and looked away from Vidya.

'What do you mean "Nagina, Nagina"? Surely you understand that you would be nowhere without her?'

'And me? What about my trauma? I... I...' she hid her eyes.

I don't know what reaction she expected from me but I was irritable, angry and tired. I could not sympathize with Vidya. Vidya made no movement, no sound, and I said nothing. After an age she turned her back to me and I heard the sound of low sobbing. I knew Vidya was feeling ugly, unloved and rejected, but I had Nagina on my mind and in my heart. I lay down on the bed fully clothed and lit a cigarette. 'Switch off the light, Vidya,' I said. 'My eyes hurt.'

Vidya turned off the light and went into the bathroom. For a while I heard the normal sounds of water and teeth-brushing and I closed my eyes. I was exhausted. Vidya came out and lay on the bed beside me. She had washed and the smell of sweat had been replaced by that of talcum powder.

'Anmol?' There was a question in her voice.

'Haan?'

'Since when have you known Nagina?'

'Since birth.'

'But before that dinner at her house, I had never heard you talk about her.'

'Since when have you started to listen when I speak?'

'Anmol!'

'Besides, what is this inquisition about?'

'It's not an inquisition. I am trying to understand why you went to Majhauli with her and why her lawyer interfered.'

'I didn't see you making any such inquiries with the Desai fellow, in fact you were feeding him halva.'

'Be reasonable, Anmol. I couldn't ask him...'

'Ask what? What is it that you want to know?'

'How well do you know Nagina? And why did you go to Majhauli?'

'I know Nagina as well as you would know any person whom you grew up with. And I went to Majhauli because she asked me to help out in some mill affairs. Satisfied? Or is there anything else you want to know?'

'Anmol, why are you so angry?' There were tears in her voice. 'I have had a horrible day and...' She turned towards me and put her arm across my chest.

I don't know what happened to me. I went a little bit crazy. I didn't want Vidya, the talcum-smelling lump. I wanted the perfumed and silky Nagina. So I pushed her away. I pushed Vidya away and turned my back on her.

I returned to Majhauli the next day and went straight to see Som Dutt Bihari. He was a friend from childhood and it was natural that I should go and look him up on my first visit back. I had been told that his house was on the corner of the main road going to Meerut. I reached the road with ease and I spotted the house too, I think, but just as I got off the motorbike I had borrowed from Nagina, the power went out. Nothing is as unrelentingly dark as the countryside in the night. I cursed as I felt my way to the front door of the house and knocked.

'Who's it? Who comes?' called a voice.

'I'm looking for the house of Som Dutt Bihari,' I said, almost stepping into the door.

'Who seeks him?' asked the voice.

'A friend.'

'Does the friend have a name?'

'Yes, but does Somu live here?'

'First tell me your name.'

'How does my name matter?' As I spoke the power came back on and I blinked as I found myself in a small room with virulent blue walls.

'Who is it at this time of night?' asked the voice again. 'Have you lost your way?' I squinted at the five men in the room.

'No,' I said. 'I'm looking for Somu.'

'Anmol Bhaiyyaji!' shouted the voice that had been questioning me and I found myself facing a grinning Somu who grasped both my hands and pumped them. Then he flung himself into my embrace. 'My God! I can't believe it. Is it you or Shivji descended from Mount Kailash?'

'Somu, you son of a gun,' I said, taking a playful swipe at his stomach. He let out a tiny scream and I looked at my fist in amazement. I'd forgotten that I was finally stronger than he was. 'How are you, yaar? And what was all this threatening? Why didn't you say who you were when I asked?'

He looked a bit sheepish. 'This area is not safe after dark. Look,' he showed me a tamancha, a country-made pistol. 'Everybody keeps these by their side. Lucky the lights came on when they did.'

'I'll say! Otherwise you might have shot me!' I said. 'Let me have a good look at you. You look a bit thin but seem to be enjoying yourself,' I winked at the open bottle of liquor and the glasses on the table.

Somu grinned in delight. We were old buddies and had shared many a bottle of country liquor in the old days. He introduced his drinking companions: 'This is Imtiaz Khan, the MLA of the area, and Ras Bihari, my cousin. You will remember him, Bhaiyyaji, for he was a permanent tail behind me, just in the way I was yours,' – a blatant lie! – 'and this is Hashmat Bhai, Nathu Pradhan, and my younger brother, Bhanu.' I nodded at the fresh-faced boy. 'Stand up, boy, and touch Bhaiyyaji's feet. He's only a boy but he is studying for his B.A in Meerut. I wanted him to be a doctor but he won't agree. Too much to study, he says. Silly boy.' He cuffed his brother lovingly.

'No, no,' I protested. 'Don't touch my feet. I'm not a great man.'

'Welcome to Majhauli, Malhotra Sahab,' said Imtiaz Khan, the MLA. He stood there running his fingers through his beard. I couldn't help staring at it. It was a beautiful beard, well-oiled and obviously dyed. So this was the influential MLA Sahab. I had already learned that Imtiaz Khan was liked by every caste and religious group in the region, including the sizeable Sikh population. Some people said that the Sikhs had come during Partition while others, especially the nasty, jealous ones, said that they were actually criminals and they had been settled here by the government in an attempt to rehabilitate them. For some reason the Sikhs of this area took to Imtiaz Khan. The Punjab problem had something to do with this. It turned traditional friends, the Hindus and the Sikhs, into enemies, and it turned traditional enemies, the Sikhs and the Muslims, into friends – a most unusual situation. The result was that the Muslims and the Sikhs thought Imtiaz Khan was wonderful. All this I had already learned from the maalis and the bearers in the guest house. But Imtiaz Khan was somewhat unusual, I thought, looking at him carefully. Compared to the average Congress politician of UP, he was suave, somewhat educated, and most surprising of all, more than a little concerned with the problems of his electorate. Of course, Nagina thought most of it was a pose, as with all politicians, but he did have a remarkable credibility in the area and even Rai Sahab admired him, though reluctantly. I had been told by Rai Sahab to keep an especially close eye on him and gauge his mood. Rai Sahab felt there was a great deal smouldering underneath Imtiaz Khan's smooth exterior.

'Thank you,' I bowed my head at Imtiaz Khan. 'But I'm not new to Majhauli, you know. I was born and brought up here. I'm only reliving old memories and meeting old friends.'

'Is that so?' he looked at me speculatively. 'But Majhauli today is not what it used to be. The development work started by me has changed the face of the town. I have built roads, the middle school as well as the fountain in the town square. It is the only fountain of its kind in the whole of Uttar Pradesh and, listen to this, it has never run out of water! Summer or winter, the fountain flows with water!' He looked at me expectantly. Evidently this was my cue for applause.

'You are absolutely right, Imtiaz Bhai,' said Somu soothingly. 'What is Majhauli without Imtiaz Khan but a body without a heart!'

'Who can deny the role of the politician in building a nation,' I said. 'And for building up their own area, a politician of the ruling party is always the best bet. You sanction the funds yourself, you release them and you utilize them! Perfect formula for success!' I was being sarcastic, but Imtiaz Khan lapped it up.

'Why don't you sit down, Bhaiyyaji,' said Somu, 'and share a drink with us. It's not the best drink but it's English whisky. Read the label for us, Bhanu.'

'Old Tavern,' said Bhanu. Somu looked at him as proudly as if he were reading Persian.

Somu was only a couple of years older than me but he looked older. He was thin and dark with big black eyes and a shock of grey hair that looked as though it had never been combed. At first glance he looked unremarkable. But Somu was too intense to be ordinary. I remembered that even as a child he was very persevering. He stuck to a thing and hammered at it till he mastered it. He was determined and single-minded in his approach. Like Arjuna he saw only the target to be achieved, nothing else. If Som Dutt Bihari had decided to be sticky about the agitation, it would be difficult to make him shift his stance. I sat down on a tin chair vacated for me and tried to make my bulk inconspicuous.

'Bhanu, find a clean glass for Bhaiyyaji,' said Somu. 'And run down to the bus stop for some boiled eggs. Take the cycle and come back quickly.' He turned back to me, 'Bhaiyyaji, sit on this chair, please.' Somu offered me the better chair and it took me a full minute to convince him that I was comfortable.

'So, Somu,' I said as I took the glass of whisky he offered me – it was important to be accepted by Somu – 'How are things? Do you have a job?'

'Don't you know? He's the secretary of the Cane Union, the most important man in the area,' said Imtiaz Khan.

'Surely not more important than you? Even I know, living far away in Delhi, that you are the most important man around here,' I raised my glass to Imtiaz Khan. Imtiaz Khan smiled at me but only with his lips. Flattery was not the right way to this man's heart, I realized, so I turned back to Somu. 'How's the factory doing? How are Rai Sahab and the family?'

At the mention of Rai Sahab the atmosphere of the place changed. There was a surreptitious exchange of glances among the others. Then Ras Bihari got up and went to the door and spat in the darkness. Somehow that said much more than words ever could. I looked at Somu expectantly while he avoided looking at me. It struck me suddenly that he probably knew the circumstances in which I had left Majhauli. For a second I felt myself flush with shame at the memory of the incident, shame and fear that Somu may think badly of me. Then it passed. Men looked at the deflowering of beautiful virgins in a different way.

'The factory's okay.' It was Imtiaz who finally found his voice. 'They have expanded the capacity of the mill to two thousand five hundred tonnes crushed per day. There is even talk of a paper plant to be set up shortly. Oh, all's well with the factory for sure. It is only the people who are suffering.'

'Why, what's the matter?' I again looked at Somu, but Imtiaz didn't give him a chance. He was a politician after all, and he could never give up centrestage to anyone else.

'What's the *matter?*' Imtiaz echoed in astonishment. '*Everything's* the matter! The factory is earning in crores and swallowing up all the money while the poor farmers haven't been given their dues for more than *one whole year.* Is this just? Is this fair? Should the rich lick butter and cream while the poor starve? Eighty per cent of our farmers are poor and they cannot be expected to wait for payment. The hardships they suffer are tremendous. Legally, the mill owners are supposed to pay the cane price in a fortnight's time but here one year has gone by and there is no sight of the money!'

'You mean the factory has paid the farmers nothing?' I asked.

'Oh, it has paid something, but a lot remains to be paid.'

'How much?'

'About five crores,' Imtiaz answered quickly.

'Five crores? Are you sure of the amount?'

'Oh, it might be a few lakhs here and there, but the amount is near enough.'

'I don't understand,' I said, while Somu looked at the door longingly. He wasn't happy with the conversation, I could see that. 'Tell me, how much cane does a factory purchase? I mean in cash terms, how much does a factory pay towards cane in one season?'

'Tell Bhaiyyaji what he is asking, Somu.' Imtiaz passed this one.

'The factory requires about four lakh tonnes of cane for its expanded capacity and the cane price last year was three hundred and sixty rupees per tonne. That comes to fifteen crores of rupees. Out of this, at least five crore or a little less is still outstanding. My position as secretary of the union is very difficult. On one hand I have to listen to the curses of the farmers, and on the other I have to listen to the owners who make threatening noises if there is talk of not giving them cane. Ah, here comes Bhanu,' he turned thankfully to the door. 'What took you so long, boy? Walking like a pregnant woman instead of running?' Quickly Somu began shelling the eggs and I ate three of them in quick succession before I remembered Vidya's lectures on my cholesterol. God, they were tasty!

'Bhaiyya,' whispered Bhanu to Somu. 'Bhaiyyaji seems hungry, shall I get some bread too?'

'Yes.'

'No,' I protested. 'It's only that I haven't eaten eggs for a very long time.' I reached for a fourth.

'Why?' asked Bhanu.

'You won't understand. But we were talking about the factory's arrears.' I turned to Imtiaz Khan. 'Forgive my obtuseness, but if the factory ran for the whole season last year, where has the money gone?'

'It's gone nowhere,' said Imtiaz. 'It's right there in their backyard!'

'It's in the personal coffers of Kulbhushan,' said Ras Bihari.

'It's in Rai Sahab's safe.'

'It's everywhere, but not paid to the farmers.'

'It's in the Mercedes cars and holidays abroad,' said Ras Bihari more aggressively.

'No, no,' said Somu loudly. 'That's not entirely true. There's a cash crunch in the company right now, the mill has no ready cash. I understand that. I understand about levy and low market prices of free sale sugar and the higher cost of extraction by the carbonation process...' he trailed off.

'Whose side are you on?' demanded Ras Bihari belligerently. His face and eyes were red with anger. 'This is a battle, Somu, and the battle lines are already drawn. We have decided to protest and so have you. This is not the time to find excuses for the owners!' He gulped down his drink and wiped his mouth with his sleeve. He wasn't eating, I noticed, only drinking.

I looked with interest at Somu, waiting for him to respond. Somu looked troubled, but kept quiet. Here was a man beset with self-doubt.

'He is not with the owners,' said Bhanu, sitting up straighter and looking at Ras Bihari in anger. 'He understands the pain of the farmers more than anyone else and he is not backing out of leading the agitation!'

Somu smiled weakly and patted Bhanu on the back. 'Softly, beta.'

'I know Somu is no coward,' said Ras Bihari. 'But in a situation like this you cannot talk in favour of the owners. There could be three hundred reasons for them not paying the farmers, but will the excuses fill the bellies of the children? Will you explain the sulphutation-carbonation process to farmers who have gone to sleep hungry tonight? What does the process mean to them?'

'I'm not saying I sympathize with Rai Sahab...' began Somu.

'Look, Somu, you are the secretary of the union. Your job is to look after the interests of the farmers, that's all. You alone carry so much authority that your Rai Sahab is afraid of you. Do you think he can even dream of running the factory without your active cooperation? Stand up to him and say that you will not let the factory run until every paisa is paid to the farmers. Inspire the farmers with your conviction. Be a leader and lead the people. They look up to you, you are their only hope. You can't have doubts, Somu. The time for dilly-dallying is over!'

'He's right, Somu,' said Imtiaz Khan. 'I'm with you. Why are you worried?'

'I'm one hundred per cent with you,' said Somu. 'I swear by Ram Lalla that I will not rest till every farmer in the area is paid. But where is the need to say all this in front of Bhaiyyaji? He has come to our house after so many years, he doesn't need to hear only about our troubles.'

'I cannot sweet talk anyone, Somu. If he doesn't have the guts to listen to the truth, then you sweet talk him,' said Ras

Bihari angrily. This was interesting. Obviously Somu was not entirely convinced that he was doing the right thing.

Imtiaz Khan broke in harshly: 'I think that this is not the time for a debate. We have decided our course of action and we are going to stick to it. Tomorrow we have a meeting in the pradhan's village at which we shall officially launch our agitation. Are all the arrangements made, Pradhanji?' He turned to the quietest and least obtrusive member of the party.

The pradhan, a man of about fifty with a dark, weatherbeaten face, looked more like a dacoit than the head of a village. Somu later told me that he had been a gangster and could wield a lathi with more dexterity than a butcher wields a knife. Apparently he had once killed a man with a single blow of his lathi. Talking of lathis, Somu also told me of the time when he, Somu, had broken a man's skull with a lathi during a gang war. Luckily for him the man did not die and the head injury left him so unfocused that, because of his confused testimony in court, the prosecution was unable to prove its case.

'Netaji,' began the pradhan, addressing Imtiaz Khan with deference. He hadn't spoken till then and I was taken aback at the sound of his voice, which was deep and hoarse, like a chain-smoker's. 'I am a Congresswala and I will support the party with whatever I have. Individuals are not important. Don't worry, Netaji, all arrangements will be made for the meeting. The only thing needed is patience. Patience is the key to an agitation. Wear down the other party by sheer tenacity. Nothing is achieved by breaking the egg, certainly not the chick.' He delivered what sounded like a rehearsed speech and what he meant by the egg and the chick I couldn't for the life of me understand.

'Well, well,' said Imtiaz sardonically. 'Words of wisdom from a history-sheeter!'

'I agree with you entirely, Pradhanji,' said Somu. 'I'm confident that tomorrow's arrangements are going to be absolutely wonderful.'

Somu was obviously the middle-path guy who himself had doubts, but who kept everyone together. This was not the Somu I knew. The Somu I knew had been a tough-talking guy who used his fists more than he used words.

'What is the agitation going to be called?' asked Hashmat, Imtiaz's principal side-kick.

'*Majhauli Ganna Kisano ka Sangharsh Morcha.*'

'Sounds impressive,' I said. 'And where is this morcha going to be?'

'It will begin at the pradhan's village and then move to the gates of Hukam Singh Mills, where else,' said Imtiaz Khan. 'I, of course, will be behind the scenes. Somu and the haji, who's the chairman of the union, will be in the forefront.'

'The haji can do nothing but dodder on shaking legs. It's Bhaiyya who will be the soul of the agitation,' Bhanu stared with admiration at his brother.

'Don't speak like that of the old, Bhanu,' admonished Somu though he smiled at him.

'Can I attend tomorrow's meeting?' I asked.

'Of course,' said Imtiaz Khan. 'As long as you are on our side and not Rai Sahab's.'

'Well, that's settled,' I said getting up. 'I'll be making a move now, Somu. How do I reach the pradhan's village?'

'Bhanu will pick you up, Bhaiyyaji. But I haven't even asked you where you are staying. My humble doors are always open for you.'

'Thank you, Somu, but I'm staying in the mill's guest house.'

'The mill's guest house?' I could see the shock on every face around. It couldn't have been worse if I had said I was in jail.

'Mill's guest house? Do you know Rai Sahab?' asked Imtiaz.

'Yes,' I replied easily. 'I told you, didn't I, that I was born here? My father worked for Rai Sahab.'

I shook hands with everyone and moved out, followed by Somu. I waited till the others went back inside before I spoke. 'Somu, you are serious about the agitation?'

'Yes, Bhaiyyaji, I am.'

'Why?'

'We just told you...'

'Yes, I know about the suffering etcetera. But Somu...' I looked at him in exasperation. 'How did you manage to involve Imtiaz Khan in this affair? What does he have to do with the mill's affairs?'

'He's the local MLA, no agitation can succeed without his blessing.'

'What is in it for him?'

'He thinks we are going to have elections soon. He thinks with the mess V.P. Singh has made of the Mandal business the elections are round the corner so he's cashing in. The whole agitation will give him a cause, a forum. He will get publicity.'

'And you? What will you get?'

'I think the farmers have suffered too much and I think that we have rights too and should not be pushed around! We are treated terribly by the upper castes. For too long have we suffered in our own country at the hands of our own people!'

'So you are a Mandalite?'

'What's wrong in being a Mandalite? For once someone is thinking of us as human beings and the rest of the country can't stand it.'

'Whoa! I have nothing against the Mandal Commission, Somu. Relax, will you? What time will Bhanu pick me up?'

'Eleven o'clock.'

'I'm your friend, Somu.'

'You are also a friend of the owner's daughter.'

I ignored his jibe and kicking the motorbike to life roared off into the darkness.

On reaching the guest house, the first thing I did was strip and take a long hot bath. Just as I finished I heard what I thought was a surreptitious knock on the back door, the one that led to the garden. I turned down the volume of the TV to listen better. A second later there was another knock, soft but persistent. Someone was there. Tightening the towel around my middle, I walked across and opened the door. 'Nagina!' I was shocked.

'Quick, get out of the way,' she said and I stepped back hurriedly. She entered and immediately shut and locked the door behind her. I stood staring at her in surprise as she did a quick round of the room, bolting the doors and settling the curtains so that nothing was visible. Still afraid, she switched off the ceiling lights so that the room was now lit only by a table lamp and the flickering light of the TV. Only then did she relax. And she burst out laughing.

'What's so funny?' I asked in astonishment. I was still standing near the door with my mouth open, only now it was hanging open because of her luminous beauty. Nagina wore a black sweater and skin-tight black jeans. The only colour on her was the bright orange lipstick on her lips. She looked like a *Vogue* model.

'You are,' she said, still laughing and pointing at me.

'Me?' I looked down at myself and realized that I was still wrapped in a towel. 'I... I'll get dressed.' Turning my back to her I pulled on a pair of trousers and quickly shrugged on a shirt. I turned back to face her and, much to my consternation, she burst out laughing again.

'Now what's the matter?' I asked in exasperation one hand going instinctively to my fly to check whether I was safely zipped up. I was.

'Your hair is standing on end. You look as though you've received an electric shock.'

'I have received a shock. Why have you come? And why not through the front door?'

'Because I shouldn't be meeting handsome guys alone at this time of the night in their bedrooms.' She arched an eyebrow at me.

'Then why are you?'

'Because, you nut, I want to.'

'Hmm?' We were standing facing each other now and she stopped laughing.

'Anmol?' Her voice was husky and intimate and feeling nervous I began to talk rapidly. 'You want to know what happened at Somu's house? Well, I met everyone there including your MLA. He's dead against you guys, I tell you. And he has a tremendous influence on Somu. My feeling is that he is financing the agitation too. He's worried about elections, you know. He thinks elections are approaching.' I babbled on without looking at her, afraid to stop.

'Anmol,' she interrupted me softly.

'Huh?'

'I came to see you, Anmol. Is this all you have to say to me?'

I stared at her helplessly. Again I was in Majhauli and again I was with Nagina. I knew I should have pushed her out of the room and taken the first bus back to Delhi, to safety and to sanity. But I couldn't do it. The sexual chemistry between us was so strong I could not control it. Nagina flung herself into my arms. Lost, totally lost, for a long time we just clung to one another in desperation. It had been such a long wait. We stared at each other with burning eyes and heaving chests as we gasped for breath. I fought for control, telling myself that I was no longer eighteen. But Nagina wouldn't let me go. She gripped me with arms of steel and whispered my name over and over again.

'Nagina,' I said, lifting my head and trying to prise open her arms.

'Anmol, please don't send me away. Please.'

What could I do or say after that? We stood for a long time, cleaved together, thigh to thigh, lip to lip, working off some of the heat. I was losing control of the situation when rescue came in the shape of a knock on the door. We sprang apart guiltily.

'Sahab,' called a voice. 'Shall I lay the dinner?'

'Yes,' I called back. 'I'll be there soon.'

Nagina raised her hands self-consciously to her hair and smoothed it down. 'I had better go,' she said looking at me.

She was just inches away from me and I wanted to fold her in my arms again, but I backed away a little. 'Go home, Nagina. I will come and see you tomorrow after I have attended the meeting in the pradhan's village.' She didn't move. 'Nagina, my darling, please go. Someone will see you and the consequences will be terrible.' She still didn't move.

'Nagina?'

'Anmol,' she whispered. 'I don't know what has happened to me. I'm not normally like this. I've never kissed another man except my husband before.'

'I know, Nagina.'

'No, listen. Something has happened to me. I can't sleep, I can't work. I think of you all the time.'

'Me too.'

'Is this love, Anmol?'

'Nagina leave, please.'

'Tell me, is this love?'

'I've always loved you. You know that, don't you? But we are no longer children, Nagina. Let us leave things as they are and try not to analyse them.'

'Anmol.'

'Yes.'

'I love you.'

'Nagina,' I whispered in despair.

'Have you heard what I said? I love you, Anmol.' She held out her arms to me and again we were cleaved together, kissing with desperate urgency.

'Sahab?' Another knock on the door.

'Next time we will definitely make love,' she whispered and breaking free Nagina slipped out of the room towards the garden, banging the door behind her. I stood there with the taste of her lips on my mouth. What a woman! I wanted her more desperately than ever.

The next day I overslept. It was natural because I didn't sleep till dawn, dreaming all the while about a life that could never happen.

When Bhanu came to pick me up I was on my third cup of coffee, still trying to shake off my languor, but I got dressed in a jiffy, giving my shave a miss. I was going for the launch of an agitation, not for a beauty contest. As it turned out it was the right thing to do for the amount of dust raised by Bhanu as he drove through the untarred village roads ensured that I would have to bathe again before I faced Rai Sahab and his daughter in the evening. He was one crazy driver.

We roared into the village, a tiny one with the usual huddle of katcha houses and dusty, unpaved alleys and open wells. In the centre of the village was a middle-sized dusty opening with a chabutra around an old shady tree and the primary school through whose glassless windows I could see the village elders sitting inside with patient, glazed eyes, totally undisturbed by questions of time. But I was taken aback by the size of the crowd that milled outside. There were at least three to four thousand people. The meeting had not yet begun because Imtiaz Khan had not arrived. I left Bhanu to do whatever he had to and wandered amid the crowd of farmers who, after their initial curiosity, ignored me.

It was already past noon and the October sun was high in the sky. The farmers sat in groups of fours and fives on their haunches and gossiped and smoked beedis. Everyone was discussing the cane price arrears, especially what each was personally owed by the mill. They were restless, keyed up and unhappy. Sugar cane is a year-long crop and to get nothing at the end of it was more than disappointing, it was devastating. The small farmers were suffering from prolonged malnutrition; though they were getting some food it was not enough. With winter upon them they worried about repairs to their houses and winter clothing. The new crop was ready and they were desperate to cut and sell it so that they could get some money. At least the mill would pay them immediately for the new cane. They resented the call for sangharsh because they felt it would only prolong their agony and deprive them further of the essentials of life. If the factory started crushing, then there were chances that they would be paid. Rai Sahab had promised payment for the new crop within a week and payment of arrears after two months. There was greater hope in this scenario than in sangharsh. In fact, some of them said, Rai Sahab had threatened that if there was talk of sangharsh, he would not run the factory at all this season. He would lose a great deal of money but he could take the loss whereas the poor farmers might as well commit suicide. The jaggery and the khandsari units couldn't take all the cane. Besides, they too paid better prices only in competition. Once word was out that the factory wasn't going to run, cane prices would crash in the region. And, unlike the sugar factories, the government had no way of ensuring that the jaggery or the khandsari units paid the farmers the minimum cane price. They would pay the bare minimum, not the government decided minimum cane price.

'Bhanu, my boy,' I said sitting down next to him and lighting a cigarette. 'The farmers are not very happy with this agitation of yours.'

Bhanu refused the cigarette I offered him. 'Bhaiyyaji, they are uneducated yokels! They have to be told what is good for them.' The boy was not more than nineteen or twenty and still had a smooth, unshaven skin and clear whites of eyes.

'And agitation is good for them?' I tried to sound sarcastic.

'When you fight for a principle, some sacrifices have to be made. Some of them are bound to suffer.'

'I am still not very clear. Who on earth gains from this agitation? The farmers don't gain, the factory workers don't gain, the owners don't gain. I mean, what is the purpose of the agitation? As I see it, everyone suffers.'

'Bhaiyyaji, we gain in principle! After this agitation succeeds no factory owner will dare to take the farmers' cane and not pay them for a year. Nobody will dare to commit such an injustice! And we have a host of other demands too, like correct weighing, no deductions for driage, interest-free loans from the factory for seed and fertilizer, employment for the sons of farmers as factory workers, more collection centres, free transportation of the cane from the fields to the factory, and so on.'

'I see. And what about those who will starve, should this agitation reach an impasse and the factory not run this season?'

'It's easier said than done. If the factory does not run how will Rai Sahab pay off the instalments of the huge loans that he has taken for expansion?'

I looked at Bhanu's smooth brown face. Here was an idealist, a newly initiated priest who was bound to quote the scriptures and interpret them more strictly than his teacher. He really was a lovable boy and I could bet that he would end up as a munshi in some office keeping exact account, tallying the left column with the right and laying down his life for a ten-paisa difference. These intense types really did waste too much of their energy. It was no use talking to him. I thought of looking for Somu, but all of a sudden the passive crowd was galvanized into action. To their eternal gratification the MLA Sahab, Imtiaz Khan, son of Wali Mohammad Khan, had made an entry.

And what an entry! He came riding into the square in an open jeep as though it was election time. He wore a black achkan and snow-white pajamas with a white Nehru cap and a red rose in his buttonhole as if he was Jawaharlal Lal Nehru himself.

For some minutes there was utter confusion as the jeep braked to a stop and the crowd milled around. Slogans filled the air again and again. Everyone was thrilled. Imtiaz Bhai was every inch the neta. He allowed himself to be garlanded and then threw the garlands into the crowd; keepsakes for the crowd to cherish. Whatever doubts I might have had about his possible influence were dispelled once he started to speak. Without waiting to be introduced, Imtiaz Khan, while still in the jeep, snatched a portable mike and started speaking spontaneously into it.

'Brothers and sisters, I have not yet been asked to speak, but I wish to ask you a few questions. Will you answer me?' He got only a lukewarm response to this. He raised his voice and shouted into the microphone, 'Have the British gone?'

'Yes.'

'Louder. Have the British gone?'

'Yes.'

'Is this the white man's regime?'

'No'

'Are we slaves still?'

'No.'

'Then why are you behaving like slaves?'

No answer.

'If you behave like slaves you will be treated like slaves! When India was slave to the English, who came to help us? Nobody. Today when we are treated like dirt and made to fill our bellies with water, does the cane commissioner or the collector come to our rescue? No. Is this not self-rule? Is this not a parliamentary democracy where every bastard who sits on the chair must give the sum total of his achievements and failures to the people? If what I say is correct, why are you behaving like slaves and taking all that is being dished out to you? Stand up and say, "No!"'

'*No!*' screamed the crowd.

'Will you allow the atrocities of the rich seths to continue?'

'No!'

'Will you fight?'

'Yes!'

Somu, who had been standing with Imtiaz Khan, suddenly snatched the mike from him and bellowed into it:

'Brothers, I will tell you a story. There was once a farmer, a poor farmer, who watered his fields with blood, sweat and tears to make it fruitful. Mother Earth was so moved by his labour of love that she gave forth in abundance. She burst forth and offered all her treasures to him. The farmer, his heart overflowing with love and gratitude, cut his crop and loaded it on his cart. As he left home, he told his wife and children to wait for him, he would come back with food, clothes and gifts for them. In the marketplace the trader who bought wheat, the rice miller who bought paddy and the sugar mill owner who bought sugar cane, lay in wait for him. The poor farmer made his rounds. He went from one to the other and do you know what they did? They lied to him! They lied to him about quality, they under-weighed the crop, they cheated him, and as if that was not enough, they said, "We don't have money, come tomorrow and collect your money!" They took his goods and didn't pay him. The wealthy trader, the rich rice miller and the rich sugar mill owner, all of whom wore silk next to their skins, said that they didn't have money! They drove in air-conditioned cars followed by an army of flunkies to wipe their asses, and they said they had no money! Is this not dacoity? Is this not daylight robbery? I ask all of you who have assembled here, is this just?'

'No,' screamed the crowd. 'We want our money!'

'My friends, I too am a poor farmer. My heart bleeds for you. I promise you today, in front of all of you as witness, that so long as Rai Sahab Hukam Singh owes any one of you one single paisa, I will not eat my fill. I will get up hungry from my plate and I will not rest till every paisa is paid to you. This is my mission! Too long have we listened to petty excuses and false promises. No more I say, no more. Repeat after me:

Nahin chalegi, nahin chalegi,
Yeh factory nahin chalegi!
Jab tak paisa nahin degi,
Tab tak factory nahin chalegi!'

The mood of the crowd was jubilant, optimistic, upbeat! It was unbelievable! The crowd that a few minutes ago was uncertain and despondent, unsure whether agitation was the right way out of the crisis, was now ready to set fire to its own fields if Somu or Imtiaz asked them to do so. They forgot their ripening cane, they forgot all the time and money they had spent in their fields, they forgot driage, they forgot that they would not get any money unless they cut their cane and sold it. They forgot everything except the mood of the moment. I was sure this mood of euphoria would not last once they reached home and saw the unlit hearths and the despairing faces of their families, but right here and now it was different. They felt part of a cause. Suddenly, life had meaning.

'Bhaiyyaji!' Somu stood before me. He was in ecstasy. 'We are going to do it! We are going to bring the factory to its knees! Not one man in the area is going to give Rai Sahab cane even if he begs! Nothing can go wrong now. It's only a question of time, and we are patient. We farmers know patience. For a thousand years we have eaten half a belly full in the hope that things will change and the dacoit will change his ways. We have an infinite capacity to suffer! We will suffer but we will not give in to the oppressor!'

I stared at Somu in admiration and despair. In this mood it was no use talking to him. He was displaying none of the anxieties and doubts of yesterday. I'd thought that I could play on his fear of taking on the responsibility of so many people – their hopes, their fears and most important of all, their hunger. I wanted to ask him what would happen if his threats didn't work. What if Rai Sahab wrote the year off and decided not to run the mill at all? How long could they carry on the agitation? What if the farmers who were screaming in euphoria today, started screaming for Somu's blood tomorrow? The moment they began to scream for Imtiaz Khan's blood he would simply wash his hands off the whole affair and run off for the Assembly to Lucknow, leaving Somu to handle the monster.

But this was not the time to say all this to Somu. Imtiaz Khan had begun his formal speech, rambling, repetitive and full of self-praise and we moved off together towards the pradhan's house. It was quieter inside the house and at least we could hear one another speak. It was deserted too, for everyone was outside. I was tired so I flopped down on a rather dirty diwan and leaned my head against a greasy round pillow. Somu sat on a stool opposite me and lit a beedi, offering one to me. He looked tired. Bhanu had said that Somu had come to the village the previous night and since then had been supervising arrangements.

'I'm hungry,' I said. 'Do you think we can get something to eat here?'

'The pradhan has made arrangements for feeding the entire crowd, puri-sabji is being prepared.'

'For the whole crowd?' I asked in disbelief.

'Yes.'

'There must be at least three thousand people outside.'

'Four thousand, more likely,' said Somu. 'Pradhan has an army of women cooking for them. It is a matter of pride for him that everyone who has come to his village eats before he goes away. That's izzat.'

'It's going to cost him a fortune!'

'Not a fortune. It won't be a feast, just simple food to fill the belly. Still, he is a generous man. It's not many who would feed so many people. Actually it is also good strategy. Every man who eats his salt today will be beholden to him.'

'Come on, there are not many who subscribe to this "beholden" theory. This is not satyug.'

'No, Bhaiyyaji, it still matters, especially in some castes.'

'So?'

'So the pradhan is killing many birds by feeding the people today. The people are beholden, Imtiaz Khan is impressed, and I'll have to keep his interest in mind.'

'I suppose so. Well, I don't mind being beholden to him. I haven't even had breakfast.' On cue, as though someone were listening, the door opened and a lady, her face covered with a veil, came in carrying two brass plates of food. She was followed by a boy who carried a stack of chapattis and two glasses of water. I looked at the plates in surprise. The pradhan couldn't be feeding the crowd this food. There were at least four different varieties of vegetables there, dal, a bowl of ghee and red chillies, rice, and for dessert, two besan laddoos, each the size of a tennis ball! It didn't take us long to devour the lot. 'Food inside the belly gives you a totally different view of life,' said Somu belching in satisfaction.

I grunted in reply, adding, 'Good food, good smoke and the company of a friend in a remote village with no telephone and no television, this is the formula for instant bliss.' I lay back on the greasy pillow and lit a cigarette.

'I can't understand what you city-dwellers find so wonderful about rural life. All we have are flies, dust, mosquitoes and filthy water. I don't think that's a formula for instant bliss.'

'No?'

'Women carrying pots of water on their heads for miles, children studying in schools with no roofs, roads that turn into rivers of mud in the monsoon...'

'Okay, okay. I get the idea,' I interrupted. 'Let's talk now about the one thing that can improve life in the rural areas: money.'

'Money.'

'Money that will come only if the factory runs. Somu, I think you are making a big mistake in this agitation. Call it off and let the factory start on time,' I urged him. 'Listen, I know the Rai Sahabs and I know Kulbhushan. He is a self-opinionated, stubborn, arrogant bastard! Rai Sahab no longer calls the shots, it's Kulbhushan who is important and he is crazy; abnormal. He is quite capable of shutting down the factory permanently and declaring himself insolvent.' I got up from the diwan and pulled up a stool close to Somu's. 'Somu, listen to me, please, I have an idea. I suggest that you make a counter offer to Rai Sahab and say that if the payment of arrears does not begin on the fifteenth of January, exactly two months after the factory starts, *then* you will stop supplying further cane. That gives you a chance to test what Rai Sahab is saying, and the farmers also get some money.'

'Bhaiyyaji, you say that one man, one Kulbhushan is uncontrollable. How do you think I will be able to control lakhs of farmers? Once the factory starts and the farmers begin supplying cane, there is no way I can stop them. Don't you see that in such a situation some will be paid and some won't? How can I discriminate between one farmer and another? And if I now ask them to believe Rai Sahab on the strength of my beliefs and he lets them down, what credibility do you think I'm going to have?'

'But – '

'It's too late, Bhaiyyaji. The decision has already been made and I am not going to reconsider.'

'Why don't you talk once to Rai Sahab?'

'I have talked to Rai Sahab and I have talked to Kulbhushan. But my meeting with Rai Sahab was like one between the king and the lowly serf. All I wanted to know was when he was going to pay us. He didn't even reply to me. On the contrary he treated the question like an encroachment... how dare this serf, this slave, question me, the king? Is this independent India or what? I mean have we no rights? All I wanted to know was when he was going to pay us. That's all. For that he called me a namak haram.' Somu glared at me in anger. Then he shrugged and had the grace to look a little chastened. 'So what if Rai Sahab educated me. Does it mean that I am to remain grateful to him the rest of my life? Should I offer my backside to be kicked by him? Generation after generation?'

There was silence for a while till I prompted him again, 'And Kulbhushan? What happened with him?'

'Kulbhushan? He prefers men!' For Somu that sentence contained all the contempt in the world. 'Kulbhushan is a totally self-centred man, even the factory comes second to his pleasure. How else do you explain the hiring of a person like Harshvardhan

Gupta? Gupta is a fraud and a cheat. The whole world knows that. He was thrown out of his earlier job on charges of embezzlement which could never be proved, but the amount of money involved was a staggering fifty lakhs. Perhaps Rai Sahab should borrow money from him,' Somu laughed hollowly.

'Yes. But what happened?'

'Kulbhushan sent me a message asking me to come and see him in Dhai Din Ka Dera, Beeji's house. Beeji was a wonderful lady, wonderful. Things began to deteriorate after her death. Rai Sahab lost all control of the mill though he continued to retain the title of chairman. Kulbhushan officially installed Harshvardhan as his partner in crime and Rai Sahab effectively stopped dealing with factory affairs. As you said yourself, Bhaiyyaji, Rai Sahab is merely a figurehead now.' Somu sat silent, lost in thought. I didn't prompt him for I was shocked too. Though I knew by that time about the kind of relationship Kulbhushan and Harshvardhan shared I was shocked that everyone seemed to know about it.

'Anyway, to continue the story, I arrived at Dhai Din Ka Dera at exactly eleven o'clock in the morning as I had been asked to, and the servant told me that Chhote Sahab would be with me shortly. I sat down on the sofa in the veranda and waited for half an hour. Finally, Kulbhushan sauntered in dressed in a pink shirt, looking like Dev Anand – he really is a handsome bastard, isn't he? He looked more than handsome that day. Like a polished diamond! He lounged against the door frame with straight and narrow shoulders and stared at me with his typical insolent look. I stood up to greet him and was mystified by a sudden, strange phenomenon. Behind Kulbhushan's head there appeared, as though by magic, another head. This huge, shaggy head was dark and evil and appeared to hang there watching all the while. It was as though Kulbhushan had two heads. It took me a moment to realize that it was none other than Harshvardhan, but the way his profile appeared slowly, with its predator-like hooked nose, shook me to the depths. Harshvardhan looked at me as though I were a low-caste rag-picker. And then without provocation, while I was sitting there and telling them about the problems of the farmers, Harshvardhan called me a namak haram. I told him to stay in his limit and then suddenly Kulbhushan went crazy. He called me a motherfucker and attacked me. I let him have it then, Bhaiyyaji, and punched and slapped him in turn till Harshvardhan stepped in and broke us up. Then, Bhaiyyaji, Kulbhushan offered me money. He said take money and end the agitation. Harshvardhan tried to calm him down and kept making soothing noises but Kulbhushan would not stop. He called me names and said money was my god. Money is everyone's god, Bhaiyyaji, but every man has his self-respect and the way that rich bastard spoke, the contempt he put into the words, made me say instantly from the bottom of my heart, "I'll die before I betray my farmer brothers. Nothing will make me touch your filthy money. I'll starve before that!"'

I had listened to Somu's account without comment and now I truly didn't know what to say. What kind of influence did Harshvardhan wield on Kulbhushan? Was Rai Sahab aware of the extent of this influence? Surely he was not blind to the fact that Kulbhushan had already lost all the goodwill created by him in the region. I didn't think that Rai Sahab suffered too much from a blind, all-consuming love for his son. Then why was he letting the reins of the factory slip from Kulbhushan's hands to Harshvardhan's?

'Look, Somu, I have a suggestion. Meet Rai Sahab once more. I'll be present at the meeting and we will try to have a reasonable conversation.'

'No.'

'Why not?'

'Nothing will be achieved.'

'Listen to me. I'm not the owner and I am certainly not either a farmer or a worker. I am a well-wisher. I have nothing to gain or lose personally. I ask again, do you trust me?'

'I trust you, Bhaiyyaji,' he said after a longish pause. 'I trust the friend of my childhood.'

'Will you come for a last meeting?'

'Okay,' he sighed after a while. 'I will come, but tell me Bhaiyyaji, how did you get embroiled in the mill's affairs?'

'Kulbhushan asked me to help.'

'And you felt you had to help out of the natural love and affection that you felt for him?'

'No, and you know that. I decided to help because of two reasons: one, because Rai Sahab had decided to forgive me and forget everything; and the second reason you know.'

'Yes. Nagina.'

I could sense the disapproval in his voice and not wanting another harangue I made as if to get up. Somu caught my hand and pulled me down. 'Bhaiyyaji, don't misunderstand me please, but I want to say something to you.'

'Nothing about Nagina,' I warned.

'Listen to me,' he pleaded. 'You know, Bhaiyyaji, that I am a bhopa.'

'What's a bhopa?'

'A bhopa is a devotee of the devi and one to whom the devi has granted special powers. I'm not truly a bhopa, my father was. But I do have some psychic powers. My father died before he could train me fully, so whatever I know I have learned with my own devotion and hard work.' He fell silent and I was quiet too. When he spoke again Somu's voice sounded different, hoarse and raspy. 'Bhaiyyaji, some women are not good. They are inauspicious. Do you understand what I am trying to say, Bhaiyyaji? Such women are witches, churails! They are beautiful nagins but they...'

'Somu, I will not listen to your nonsense.' I didn't know whether to laugh it off or to get angry.

'No, no listen to me. It is true, such women exist. They suck out your life blood and leave you to die!'

'That's enough, Somu!'

'Bhaiyyaji, Nagina is a beautiful churail. She is a blood-sucking leech. You won't even know it but she will use her beauty to entice you until you are totally in her control. Go home, Bhaiyyaji. Go home to your wife and children. Leave the Rai Bahadurs to solve their own problems. They will destroy you, she will destroy you. Listen to the words of a bhopa – Leave the churail alone!'

Somu spoke the last sentence in a strong, husky whisper that seemed to reverberate in the room. It frightened me and I flung off Somu's arm in sudden terror and stalked out.

I went back to the guest house and shaved and bathed with a vengeance, cleaning and scrubbing every inch of my body. When I came out of the steaming bathroom I was as red as a ripe tomato from the hot water and the vigorous scrub. It was only eight o'clock and too early for dinner, but I was hungry and decided to eat before sitting down to do some serious drinking. Once in a while I get into these moods; I need to get a whole bottle of whisky inside me. I am a whisky man and I like it almost neat, with just a splash of water and no ice.

'Dinner is served,' said the bearer and I fell upon my food with a savage hunger. I was thankful to see saag meat and red chicken legs. Vegetarianism is fine for party talk and Vidya, but that's it. I get constipated with too much of the green stuff. I ate four tandoori rotis and abstained from eating the onion rings soaked in vinegar even though I loved them.

It was only when I sat in the veranda outside my room after dinner and poured out my third drink that I allowed myself to think of Vidya, not for the first time in all these days, and wondered if she had cooled down. She had packed her bags and left for Ambala the night I'd left for Majhauli. Vidya was a good wife, if somewhat self-righteous about a number of things and she had political ambitions. I had married her not because I loved her but because she was chosen for me. She wasn't Nagina. No, she definitely wasn't Nagina.

When I'd spoken to my father-in-law before I left Delhi he had told me, man to man, not to worry about Vidya. Women are like that, he said, they all have leaky faucets in their heads. Ignore them, never pamper them and if necessary, the judicious use of an occasional slap often solves the problem. And then he delivered the best piece of advice: leave her alone for at least a week before you call her. How did my father-in-law, a rip-roaring, thigh-slapping crude Punjabi manage to produce a girl so prudish and principled? I drank steadily, staring into the dark night, totally oblivious of the cool night air. And taking her father's advice I pushed Vidya's self-righteous image out of my mind.

It was pitch dark and silent in a way that only the countryside can be. No constant drone of traffic, horns, vendors and general chaos. I looked up at the black dome that was the sky. I could see some stars and a vague outline of the mountains, but not much more. The veranda where I sat faced no house, so there were no lights anywhere. Nothing disturbed the complete silence and darkness. I was replete with good food and pleasantly tired; the whisky was settling nicely through my veins. There was no point in ruining the peace of the night by worrying about my wife. Anyway, I was being a dutiful husband and leaving Vidya alone when she needed the space.

Then, as always my thoughts turned to Nagina. What was it about her that fascinated me so much? Granted she was beautiful but so was Hema Malini, and I didn't drool over Hema Malini like that. Nagina made up her eyes boldly. She wore eyeliner that she drew out to the corners, like dancers did. I had never really liked that over-made-up look, but on Nagina it looked divine – theatrical, but divine. Her nose was like her father's, thin and curved but not so curved that it detracted from her beauty, just enough to give her a haughty look. It was the arrogance that attracted me. That, and perhaps the fact that she was pursuing me. Even if it was because of her own agenda, the fact that she was pursuing me was immensely exciting.

Nagina had a typical Indian figure: broad-shoulders, heavy breasts, slim waist with a deep navel and solid buttocks. She was a tough, self-opinionated, arrogant woman who thought there was no one like her and that everyone should bow to her. She was a woman like no other and I wanted to possess her and make love to every inch of her flesh. She was rich and she was ambitious, she had wealth and social connections, she was feted and she was courted, she was ruthless and clever and she had captured my entire being in such a way that I couldn't stop thinking about her. I had left my home, my wife and my kids and I had followed her into the wilderness. Something about Nagina brought a heightened awareness to every nerve-ending of my body. Her touch singed me. I wanted to undress her and study every limb, every crevice; smell every odour, explore all her contours. God, I wanted her so bad I was afraid of being in the same room as her.

By the time I had poured my fifth drink I had come to the conclusion that even if I wasn't really in love with Nagina, I was completely obsessed with her body. Once I'd had my fill of her I would get over her as naturally as I would get over the hang-over I was bound to have next morning. At that moment a black shadow flitted across the lawns and stepped lightly on to the veranda where I sat. And in a minute we were inside the room. Nagina and me.

With my fingers I traced her lips and kissed them. Then my fingers found her smooth jaw line and I buried my face in the fragrant mass of her hair. Slowly I pushed her shirt off her shoulders and kissed her neck where the skin was satin smooth and soft. Very slowly I removed her shirt and let my hands run over her long arms, her arched back, and her waist. Only then did I allow myself to run my fingers lightly over her heavy, round breasts. I traced the dark aureoles and tugged her nipples until she arched her back and moaned for more. But I was in no hurry and took my time touching every inch, kissing, exploring. I pulled her pants down over her hips and let my hands run over her smooth thighs. Nagina shivered with pleasure. I felt I would burst and closed my eyes as I hooked my fingers around the waistband of her panties and very slowly pulled them off. I wanted to touch before I saw. But the feel of Nagina's smooth, hairless pubis, with its wet muskiness, absolutely destroyed my patience and I went down on my knees to see and taste this wonder. And then Nagina was tugging at my clothes whispering, Hurry, hurry, hurry, and gripping me strongly, she simply opened her legs and impaled herself, rotating her hips and moaning with desperate urgency. I came quickly but she would not let me go. She tightened her inner muscles and held on to me even as she gripped my buttocks with her legs and thrust her breasts into my mouth. I was ready again and thrusting with frenzied strength. Nagina's wild response was incredible. She loved it.

We were still trying to get our breath back when there was a loud noise outside, followed by a cry and a curse.

Crash!

We pulled apart in fear.

'What was that?'

'I had better go.' Nagina was in panic and so was I. Quickly we made ourselves presentable, pulling on our clothes and running our fingers through our hair. I ran to open the side door that opened into the garden and Nagina slipped out like a silent wraith, melting into the night.

'Sahab?' Servants and bearers alerted by the noise had gathered. Had Nagina escaped undetected?

'Someone was on top of the roof,' said one of the servants. 'And he jumped down or fell off. See how this bush has flattened? There is even a broken piece of concrete. Look,' he pointed to the roof with his torch. 'Someone was on the skylight's ledge, which broke with his weight.'

Oh god, I thought. The news would be all over town by morning and this time surely Rai Sahab would shoot me through the heart. And what about her husband? Old Satya Pal Aggarwal, the phoney diplomat who screwed around? I had forgotten all about him. He would probably have me assassinated! He looked like the sort who had mafia connections. I must have been mad to get involved with a married woman.

'We could find no one, Sahab.'

My mind was in turmoil. Why did this happen to me every time I came close to Nagina? It seemed Majhauli had nothing to do except worry about the two of us. I wanted to catch the bastard who was up on the roof and beat the shit out him. But there was nothing to do except hope he had not seen anything, or pray he cracked his head and developed amnesia. There was nothing to be gained by staying up and freezing. One might as well sleep and face the situation when and if it came.

The next morning I arrived at Hariyali at precisely ten to eleven since Somu had promised to be there on the hour. I rang the doorbell a little apprehensively and waited for someone to open the door, gun in hand. Nothing so dramatic happened. I was received most courteously and shown into the main drawing room where Rai Sahab, Nagina, Kulbhushan and Harshvardhan already sat.

Nagina looked stunning. She wore white and blue, white tights with a blue and white striped sailor sweater that was small enough to show me some of the goods I had seen last night. Her hair was tied in a high ponytail with a white chiffon scarf and she wore some kind of white hearts as earrings. The sleeves of her sweater were pushed up to her elbows. I forced myself to look away from her and concentrate on Rai Sahab, who sat ramrod straight with an unapproachable expression. The Rai Sahabs would never change. I sat beside Rai Sahab. I wanted to remind him that this was not going to be a master-serf meeting, it was not even an employer-employee meeting, Somu was a free bird. I suggested that Rai Sahab should meet Somu alone. I would, of course, be present to mediate. Kulbhushan gave me a dirty look and flounced off with his mate, but Nagina refused to go, saying her father needed her by his side. I didn't think it was a good idea because Nagina can be very arrogant and disdainful, but it was too late to argue as Somu was already at the door.

'Namaste, Rai Sahab,' said Somu limping into the room.

'What's the matter with you, Mr Som Dutt? Why are you limping?' asked Rai Sahab with courteous formality.

'Nothing. Just met with a slight accident yesterday.'

'Slight?' I asked as Somu winced when he sat down. 'What's the damage?'

'A couple of broken ribs. That's all.'

'That's all?' echoed Rai Sahab. 'Sounds serious to me. Let me send my doctor to examine you.'

'Broken ribs!' exclaimed Nagina, as I stared at Somu with narrowed eyes. He had been fine when I left him yesterday.

'No, no.' protested Somu immediately sitting up straighter and smiling. 'I'm not one to be frightened by a small thing like this.'

'You must see a doctor,' insisted Nagina.

'No, no, no doctor,' said Somu vehemently.

'Well, okay then,' said Rai Sahab. 'I do hope that apart from the cracked ribs you are all right, Somu Sahab?'

'Don't embarrass me by calling me Sahab,' Somu replied. 'What is my status in front of you?'

'Don't say that! You are the Cane Union's secretary! Our existence is nothing without you.'

'It's your greatness that makes you speak thus, otherwise what am I capable of?'

This nauseatingly sweet exchange went on. I felt like getting up and shaking Rai Sahab. If he was waiting for Somu to make the first move he would have to wait forever. Somu was here at Rai Sahab's insistence, he wasn't going to reveal his hand first.

'Well, Somu,' said Rai Sahab, finally losing patience with the small talk. 'I hear you people have decided to hold us to ransom.' He tried smiling at Somu as though the whole matter was just a joke but Somu held his ground and waited. He was smart, for the next thing that Rai Sahab said showed that he was losing his cool. 'I don't understand what it is that you people want? Will you be benefited if the factory does not run?'

'No.'

'Then?'

'But we were not paid even when the factory *did* run.'

'Don't you believe me?'

'Believe you?' It was Somu's turn to raise his eyebrows.

'Believe me when I say you will be paid in two months' time?'

'It is not a question of whether I believe you or not, it is a question of whether the farmers believe you or not. And they were not paid even when the factory did run. They don't have faith anymore. Cane was crushed, sugar was made and sold for one whole year but what did the farmers get? Empty promises and false hopes.'

'I don't want to go into the reasons for our heavy arrears again, Somu, you know them as well as I do. All I want to say is that I came as a refugee and brought prosperity to Majhauli. I made Majhauli my home and the people of Majhauli are now my people. The economy of the place has changed because of me. I appeal to my people to give me two months' time. Can you give it to me?'

It was a good appeal. It sounded sincere and had the right touch of pathos in it. I thought Somu would be moved.

'If you are asking me personally, then the answer is yes. But if you are asking the farmers of Majhauli, then the answer is no.' So Somu had not been moved.

'Only two months,' whispered Rai Sahab. I could feel Nagina squirm as Rai Sahab spoke. She didn't like to hear Rai Sahab plead before Somu.

'No.' Somu folded his arms and looked straight at Rai Sahab who looked at the floor.

Immediately Nagina got up and stood between her father and Somu: 'You never listen to me, do you, Papa? What he wants is money. Give him the four to five lakhs that you can spare and see how he laps it up.' Nagina's words dripped venom. Her eyes were full of contempt.

Somu sprang up and shouted: 'Keep your money. I thought we were going to discuss this in a civilized manner.'

'Money is the only language *you* people understand!'

'*Nagina*!' There was a momentary glimpse of the old Rai Sahab who, people said, could wither souls with the power of his hawk eyes. 'Get out of the room!' Rai Sahab waited till Nagina left and then continued: 'Sit down, Somu, and please don't misunderstand what I say. If you can help me gain time I'm willing to reward you in any way that you like. A mutually advantageous agreement is what I have in mind.'

'Like four lakhs of rupees?'

'If you like,' Rai Sahab's voice was soft.

Somu looked at me in sorrow. 'That makes all the Rai Sahabs. All of them have now offered me money.' He turned and stared at Rai Sahab. 'Let us suppose, Rai Sahab, that you do succeed in bribing me. What then? Will I be able stop the agitation? It's not me who wants money. I'm sure you will pay me money, a lot of money, if I wanted it. But you need to understand that if I back out of the agitation there will be others to take my place. How many people will you bribe, Rai Sahab?'

'It's not a bribe.' Rai Sahab tried to salvage the situation. 'We give you money every year.'

'True. But this year is different. Try to understand if you can that it is not Somu who is opposing you, it is the entire farmer community. They – we – are tired of starving while the owners get fat and rich. We are willing to discuss a compromise in which half of the money is paid before the factory starts crushing. That is the best offer that I can make. Let me know if you find that acceptable.' Somu stood up. 'I am thankful to you for giving me so much of your time.' He folded his hands in a formal namaste and limped out of the room. I hurried after him, leaving Rai Sahab to contemplate his non-existent goodwill.

I caught up with Somu outside the house and walked down the driveway with him to where Bhanu waited on his motorcycle.

'I told you that it was no use meeting the Rai Sahabs, didn't I?' Somu looked at me with eyes that were filled with anger and pain.

'Somu, we had to try, didn't we?' I could hardly look at him.

'Why? So that they could humiliate me once more? Look, Bhaiyyaji, it's no use talking any more. The agitation is on. We go on dharna from tomorrow and there's nothing you or your Nagina can do about it.'

'Somu,' I tried to sound threatening, but failed.

'I don't know what there is between you and Rai Sahab's daughter, but I can see that you have decided not to take my advice. So be it. Don't tell me I didn't warn you.'

'It was you, wasn't it?'

'What do you mean?'

'It was you on the rooftop yesterday,' I pointed a finger at him in anger. Somu didn't deny it, only chewed his lip and tried to stare me down. 'Listen, Somu, what I do with my life is my affair. And if anyone hears of yesterday's incident I'm going to kill you. Do you understand?' I was standing almost on top of him, he was so much shorter than me now. 'For the last time, Nagina is my business. Lay off!'

Somu didn't blink an eye, he only continued to chew his lip. 'This love-shove is only good for the movies, you know ...'

'Somu!' I glowered threateningly at him.

He turned and started to walk away. 'I don't have time for a man who spends his time buried in a woman's pallu. Do what you like. Jump into the well or bang your head against the wall, or make friends with a churail – it's all the same to me.'

'I'm going to ask you once more, Somu, give up the sangharsh business.'

'It's too late. Everything is ready for the agitation.'

'I can only presume that you have thought about all the consequences. Don't blame me for anything that happens now, Somu.'

Bhanu, who had been waiting outside for Somu spoke up: 'What will you do now, Bhaiyyaji?' He looked at me with a challenge in his bright black eyes

I looked from him to Somu before I spoke. 'That's for you to find out. All I wanted to say was that if this is war then there is nothing fair or unfair in the methods that might be used.'

I returned to the house. Rai Sahab had not moved an inch in the interim. He sat quiet and immobile while Nagina, Kulbhushan and Harshvardhan hovered around him. They looked strange together – Nagina, a fashionable socialite who was actually quite hard-boiled and determined, as I was beginning to discover; Kulbhushan, the fairy, concerned about the mill, but more concerned with Harshvardhan; and Mr Gupta himself, a satyr looming over the family, wielding his evil influence over Kulbhushan who behaved like a lovelorn maid.

'Anmol! Our very own hatchet man!' Harshvardhan said snidely. 'I thought you were going to break the strike, pull down the barriers and get us all going. What happened?'

'You know what happened. They are not listening.' I said shortly.

'And we thought you were going to work miracles.' Harshvardhan spread his arms deprecatingly and looked at Rai Sahab from the corners of his eyes.

'I'll tell you what happened,' I said hotly. 'What's happened is that you and Kulbhushan together have successfully ruined whatever goodwill Rai Sahab had created in the region. You are arrogant, obnoxious and partisan. That's no way to run a company.' I looked at Kulbhushan and pointed a finger at him, 'You are seen to be favouring an undeserving employee for personal reasons. Not only is this guy not a good engineer, but you chucked out an excellent engineer and a perfectly good man to bring *him* in.'

'I don't have to listen to Anmol giving me a lecture. Harshvardhan is here because I say so and the first person who disagrees with that can leave!' Kulbhushan broke in hotly.

'Harshvardhan Gupta should be here because he is good at his job and not because you want him here, Kulbhushan,' said

Rai Sahab. 'I don't want to quarrel with you because of him but if his presence is creating such a furore in the factory then perhaps you should do something about it. Too many sudden changes are not always welcomed by the people.'

'All Harshvardhan's done is make a few changes and all for the best,' said Kulbhushan defensively.

'That's not the way people see it.' I said. Then I continued, 'Do you realize that Harshvardhan's been here for only three months and three of your top people have resigned and gone? And you have not done anything to replace these men.'

'I was going to but this agitation came along,' Kulbhushan muttered.

'I wish you had the sense to hire good people, Kulbhushan, so that no more people leave and you can make up some of the ground that you have lost.'

'A change in the old order was needed. These old fogies didn't even know how to spell computer.'

'Maybe, but they were good men and people respected them. If computers are so important, maybe you should let the computers handle the agitation.' I passed a hand over my eyes. I was getting tired.

'You are going too far, Anmol,' warned Kulbhushan.

'You think so? The truth is that your pal here is morally and financially corrupt along with being a no-good engineer!'

I had barely finished speaking when Kulbhushan launched himself bodily at me. I was prepared and easily fended him off. But it was Harshvardhan who was able to calm him. He put a heavy hand on Kulbhushan's slim, hairless arm and shook his head. Immediately, Kulbhushan's temper subsided and shaking himself free, he went and sat on the sofa with his back to me.

'Look, let's forget everything else and concentrate on how to resolve this issue. Any ideas on where to go from here?' Nagina looked from me to Harshvardhan to the back of Kulbhushan's head.

'Yes,' said Harshvardhan. He ticked them off on his fingers. 'One, Rai Sahab should go to Lucknow and meet everyone: the chief minister, the cane and sugar industry minister, the chief secretary, the cane secretary, the cane commissioner and whoever else there is. Kulbhushan and I will go talk to the bankers again, and Anmol should continue talking to Somu and Imtiaz Khan.'

'What about my suggestion to you, Nagina? What about the cash you were supposed to raise?' Kulbhushan spoke from the depths of the sofa, still with his back to us.

'I'm working on that now,' said Nagina shortly. 'I should have something soon.'

'It had better be quick if it has to work.'

'I must say I agree with Mr Gupta's ideas,' I said. 'He has covered all angles.'

'Well now, look at that!' Harshvardhan pretended to be shocked. 'I am pleased that you approve, Mr Anmol Malhotra.' He raised two fingers in salute. 'Well, let's do our bit, shall we? We should meet day after tomorrow and see if the agitation has begun. Who knows, they could just be bluffing.'

'Who knows,' I echoed.

Kulbhushan and Harshvardhan left together and with everyone gone I fell upon Nagina. I grabbed hold of her and cupping her breasts kissed her deeply right there in Hariyali, in her father's house. 'Nagina,' I said breathlessly. God, we were a demented pair.

'Anmol, who was on the roof yesterday?'

'Don't worry about yesterday. Nobody knows you came to my room.' I spoke quickly to reassure her.

'How do you know for sure?'

'Trust me,' I said deliberately erasing Somu from my mind and signalled her to come along. I didn't want to talk to her in Hariyali because Vimla Singh lurked in the corners, though she never revealed herself because I offended her sense of social hierarchy. 'Will Rai Sahab go to Lucknow?' I said walking out of the room.

'He has an appointment with the chief minister tomorrow. Those were his ideas that Harshvardhan was quoting, not his own,' said Nagina, understanding perfectly.

We were out of the house and walking across the lawns. I spoke urgently and a little wildly. 'Nagina, I have to see you. The memory of last night is driving me crazy!'

'Anmol...'

'We have to meet. Tell me where?'

'Anmol, I...'

'Nagina, please. The time for excuses and games is over. It was you who came to my room first, not me. You cannot play the coquette now.'

'Anmol!'

'*Where?*'

'In my room.' she said hurriedly, looking over her shoulder as though she expected her mother to be following us.

'In Hariyali?' I was shocked.

'Yes,' she whispered. 'Eleven o'clock. Tonight.'

'How do I get in?'

'You know the side door? The one through which we used to escape when the tutor wanted us to learn our tables? Be there at eleven. I'll let you in.'

Does one ever realize the mistakes one is making when one is actually committing them? Does god or fortune or whoever it is out there give us some warning, some foreboding of a coming storm? No. No black cat crossed my path and neither did my left eye flicker to warn me of danger. I had no premonition, no fear. I only felt a rising excitement, an expectation, a feeling of total invincibility. I was on the wheel of fortune and the wheel was only going up, up, up. Life was wonderful and Nagina was glorious.

Nothing could go wrong.

The third of November was a brilliant day. The first chilly winds rolled down from the foothills of the Himalayas. I dressed quickly and had a huge breakfast. I was eating enormous quantities of food and all of it was high fat and high cholesterol. Vidya would kill me if she knew I actually ate a three-egg omelette, four tiny cocktail sausages and heaven knows how much buttered toast. But then, she didn't know that I needed to keep up my energy. I was handling the sangharsh by day and making love to Nagina by night. When the bearer gave me freshly brewed coffee, my cup of happiness really overflowed. I'm a simple man with simple needs. Good food, good whisky and Nagina, that's all I ask for.

The launching of the agitation had been delayed by endless preparations and even though I had spent the entire time with Somu and Imtiaz Khan, neither of them budged an inch. I told Rai Sahab to be patient. Once Imtiaz Khan had gained mileage and become the local hero, he would change his tactics. The farmers could not afford more losses. They would want the factory to run. Today was the day the agitation was to be officially launched, today was D-day.

When I reached the chowk everyone was in a tremendous mood. The place was overflowing with people, banners, streamers, gulal and hawkers selling everything under the sun to the gullible crowd. The crowd was excited and raring to go. Pushing, jostling, raising slogans, almost as if they had come to a fair. I think the real agitators were missing. I mean the fellows who had given their mandate for the agitation.They were nowhere to be seen. Probably sitting at home and contemplating the horrors in store for them. Instead the netas and their sideys had taken over the agitation. I spotted Somu near the makeshift platform from where the speeches were to be given and went to speak to him. He was wearing a new white kurta-pajama with a smart, black Nehru jacket. His hair had been freshly cut and his beard shaved. He looked and smelled clean. 'Vah, Somu, you look like a bridegroom,' I said, pointing to the red tilak on his forehead.

'I'm getting cold feet, Bhaiyyaji. What if this agitation does not succeed?' He glanced pointedly at Imtiaz Khan. 'If things go wrong, he will slink off and I will get all the brickbats.' That was true of course.

'You wanted this moment of glory,' I said. 'Make the best of it.'

'Ah, man is a vainglorious creature,' said Somu. 'This creature of blood and bones who screams at the slightest prick of a needle thinks himself capable of great deeds. But he is only a pawn in the hands of fate. Truly do our scriptures say that even a leaf does not fall without god's will. It falls because it was destined to fall.' He walked away, leaving me staring after him. What did he mean?

'Malhotra Sahab.' I turned to find Imtiaz Khan standing before me resplendent in a black embroidered topi. A black achkan and a white pajama completed his outfit.

'Adaab,' I greeted him. 'You look great.'

'So the day of the agitation has arrived. You see us all ready for every sacrifice.' Imtiaz Khan smiled showing brilliant white teeth.

'Haan,' I said. 'But not compromise.'

'It's too late for that Malhotra Sahab. Hear that?'

'Kisan Morcha Zindabad!

Imtiaz Khan Zindabad!

Somu Bihari Zindabad!'

Slogans rent the air. Dust and enthusiasm mingled with the gulal settled on everything. Marigold flowers were everywhere and many were crushed underfoot. Imtiaz Khan and Somu wore what looked like a dozen garlands each. Small children carried streamers and balloons. Everywhere there was excitement. I watched the struggle to get the crowd organized into a procession and start moving. It would take them ages to reach the factory gates considering the speed at which they were moving. Pamphlets were being distributed. I could see hundreds of fists punching the air as the marchers shouted slogans. It almost seemed like Somu had won an election and this was a victory procession for him. The procession went past me with Somu in front, along with the haji and the pradhan, Ras Bihari, Bhanu and other enthusiasts.

Imtiaz Khan stood beside me and watched. He had donned a pair of dark glasses now and as he watched he stroked his beard. 'Why aren't you in the front?' I asked him.

'I've done my bit,' he said. 'It's Somu's show from here.'

'Somu says that if he loses this gamble he will resign from the secretaryship.'

'Somu is an emotional lad. Every battle doesn't have to be won. You gain in stature even when you have fought and lost. It is the fighting of the battle that is important. This will make a neta of Somu.'

'He will gain respectability,' I said.

'He will,' agreed Imtiaz Khan, echoing my sentiments. 'He could stand for elections if he wins this round against the Rai Sahabs.'

The procession was almost out of sight now and thankfully the dust and noise levels had decreased. One of Imtiaz Khan's flunkies brought us a couple of chairs and glasses of steaming tea which I didn't have the heart to refuse. I took a sip of the tea and grimaced in distaste. It was so thick and syrupy it coated my tongue. Imtiaz, who still wore three garlands of marigold around his throat, slurped his tea noisily. 'Somu is made, I tell you. He has a bright political career. Politics is a nasha. When you win and you feel the power of public adulation, it's like achieving nirvana. There are no more doubts, no pain, no fear. You forget everything but the euphoria of success. It's wonderful! Once politics gets into your bloodstream, you can never get rid of it.'

'I don't think Somu visualizes himself as a politician,' I said.

'You will see that everything that I have said is true. Wait and see, the difference in Somu will be almost tangible.'

'Hmm,' I said. 'I hope he doesn't become a politician. Politicians have a way of losing touch with reality once they get into the race for self-perpetuation.'

'That's not true! Look at me. Am I not worried sick over the farmers of Majhauli?' His eyes almost pierced into me.

'True,' I said hastily. 'The juloos must have reached the factory gates by now. Don't you think we should join it?' I could see that I had offended him. Luckily he didn't say any more but got up in a huff.

We got into a jeep and went to the pandal that had been erected outside the factory, right next to the main gate of Rai Bahadur Hukam Singh Sugar Mills. The arrival of the jeep was greeted with renewed enthusiasm and cheering. A temporary platform had been erected next to a big double tent. The road in front of the platform was covered with huge durries. There were people everywhere and I estimated that there were almost as many people now as there had been in the pradhan's village. I stayed inside the jeep and watched the show. One by one everyone made speeches that were on the same lines as those made in the pradhan's village. Photographers were busy clicking and it seemed as though the enthusiasm of the people would never end. Their hand clapping and slogan shouting went on and on and on. In contrast, the factory behind the gate was as silent as a graveyard. No one came to see the agitators or listen to their speeches, not even children or stray dogs. They too seemed to have been locked away. The guards who manned the gates stood watching the show with impassive faces. Somu had ensured that the agitators were not on the mill's property. He had also ensured that the road was not in any way obstructed.

Hukam Singh Mills...
Hai Hai!
Band karo! Band karo!
Yeh atiachar band karo!'
Nahin chalegi, nahin chalegi,
Dhandle baazi nahin chalegi!

A cavalcade of three official-looking Mahindra jeeps suddenly drew up and came to a screeching halt, raising a cloud of dust. A number of uniformed officers stepped out of the jeeps and

Somu shouted: '*Arré* Bhaiyya, Ras Bihari, sprinkle some water around otherwise I will surely be asphyxiated by all this VIP dust!'

Thunderous laughter followed this remark. I got off the jeep and walked to the centre to hear what was happening. 'Sit down everybody,' shouted Ras Bihari. In the days leading to the preparation of today's tamasha, Ras Bihari, Somu's cousin, had emerged as Somu's chief organizer and factotum. 'Sit down and keep quiet. The Sahabs have come to look us up.'

More laughter but everyone went down on their haunches until the only ones standing were the heroes of the day – Somu, Ras Bihari, the haji, Imtiaz Khan; and the visitors – SDO, Amar Nath, a young PCS officer, the DSP, Lal Singh, and about twenty constables armed with twelve-bore rifles but totally harmless, more in a picnic mood than a militant one. Still, the DSP wasn't taking any chances. He ordered fifteen of the constables to take positions behind the crowd and felt obliged to unglue his hands from his huge stomach and pat his service revolver threateningly. It was a ludicrous warning from a cop who had such a huge paunch that he looked as though he was about to drop twins there and then. Beside him, the young slim PCS officer of medium height looked like a schoolboy.

'Namaste, Khan Sahab,' Amar Nath greeted the MLA. 'Nice show you people have put up.'

'Clear the road! Clear the road at once!' shouted Lal Singh, waving his baton around importantly.

'I'm sure they will clear the road, Lal Singhji,' said Amar Nath quietly waving down the crowd that had begun to rise. He turned to Somu. 'Well, Som Dutt, I heard that you got hit by a truck yesterday. Did you file a report?'

'No, Sahab,' replied Somu grinning widely. 'The truck disappeared, and I could not take the number either.' He dismissed the matter and looked at me. 'Sir, let me introduce to you a very old friend, and the son of a former employee of the mill, Anmol Malhotra.' I shook hands with both the officers.

'What's all this about, Bihari?' Amar Nath turned back to Somu. 'Khan Sahab? Would you like to explain?'

'I'll be glad to,' said Imtiaz Khan. 'But first, chairs for our honoured guests. Please be seated.' Imtiaz Khan smiled at Amar Nath, like Dracula, showing sharp white incisors. 'The factory will run only when we give cane and we will give cane only when we are paid.' Delivering this fait accompli, he sat back with the air of a guy whose business is satisfactorily over. Amar Nath and the DSP looked at him in perplexity, not realizing that Imtiaz Khan had really said everything that was to be said in the matter.

'This is blackmail!' said Lal Singh belligerently when he realized that the MLA had said what he had to say.

'Blackmail!' shouted Imtiaz Khan. 'DSP Sahab, are you accusing *me* of blackmail?'

The crowd moved restlessly as Imtiaz Khan's voice rose. Amar Nath frowned at Lal Singh and put a hand on Imtiaz Khan's arm. 'Khan Sahab, what he means is that today is the third of November and the factory is to begin crushing on the fifteenth of November. You should have raised your demands and sat on dharna much earlier. That was the time to protest, now is the time to run the factory.'

'Look, Nath Sahab, I understand the law. It is not blackmail to take what belongs to you. I'm not extracting blood money. I'm only asking for what is legitimately mine, or in this case, ours. And as for timing, it is not as though we suddenly decided to sit on dharna. We have tried to negotiate with everyone. Somu, tell the SDO Sahab what all you have done.'

'He knows,' mumbled Somu.

'Tell him anyway. Speak up, Somu, there's nothing to be afraid of.'

'We have been speaking to Rai Sahab for at least two months prior to this dharna. After the farmers started complaining we drew up a petition and gave copies to the owners, to the collector of Meerut, to you, Sir, to everybody. We pleaded about our poverty and our children, but our pleas fell on deaf ears. When the cane commissioner Sahab came here we told him too, as well as the deputy cane commissioner who came here for inspections. Everyone knows that Rai Bahadur Hukam Singh Sugar Mills Pvt. Ltd. has not paid us money for the cane they crushed and made sugar out of. Everybody. Even the newspapers have been writing about it. When all our pleas fell on deaf ears we had no choice but to agitate.'

'When we were begging they were ignoring us, now that we insist on being heard they have brought the police upon us!' shouted Ras Bihari, the volatile one.

'That's not true,' Amar Nath cut in emphatically. 'You have brought the police upon yourself. This,' he pointed at the crowd and the tent, 'this is a potential law and order situation. Five thousand of you have gathered here and you expect that the police will not come? How is that possible? I have a job to do. You know that.' Amar Nath, though a reed-slim boy, had dignity and a calm personality that invited attention. He didn't raise his voice but people listened to him.

'I suppose so,' mumbled Ras Bihari.

'You bet it's so. And I have a duty to resolve the situation.'

'Sir, you are a sensible man,' said Imtiaz Khan. 'I want to ask you a question. If the government fails to pay you your salary for one year, what will you do?' He sat back and waited for a reply.

'You know better than to ask such a question,' said Amar Nath. 'The way to solve a problem is not through strikes and dharnas. You must find a more peaceful way to resolve them.'

'But, Sir, *this is the peaceful way!* The father of the nation himself taught us that strikes and dharnas are a peaceful form of protest. We are doing nothing that isn't peaceful. We are not breaking the law in any way. All we are doing is to protest peacefully and let the world know that we have been treated badly.' Imtiaz Khan spoke loudly and emphatically. The crowd edged closer sensing a confrontation.

'We will protest till our last breath!' shouted Ras Bihari. 'We will plead with the collector, we will beg before the chief minister and if there is no response we will go to the prime minister, but we will not give up!' Ras Bihari was a short man with a shorter fuse and he had a loud voice and the ability to ignite a crowd to fever pitch.

'And if the prime minister does not listen, will you set fire to the factory?' asked Lal Singh, scratching his belly and expertly squirting an orange stream of spit avoiding everyone's shoes and clothes.

'I'm sure that situation will not arise,' said Somu while Imtiaz waved down Ras Bihari who had jumped up in anger. He was like a porcupine, always bristling with anger.

'This is a potential law and order situation, Sir,' said Lal Singh pompously. 'I think we need to take serious action here.' He was twirling his baton as though he was just itching to bring it down on someone's head. Amar Nath was silent.

'Come now, don't you get carried away by the fiery slogans of young blood? They are the ones who still have some idealism left, let them keep their illusions.' Imtiaz Khan spoke almost patronizingly.

Lal Singh turned and spat on the ground. 'They are rascals, Sir, don't you believe any of them. This Somu and his cousin brother are history-sheeters. I have a list as long as my arm of cases against them. We will have to remove these fellows otherwise there is bound to be trouble. Let the bastards feel the lathis on their backsides and I can bet they will forget all about the agitation in a second!'

'Hmm,' said Amar Nath while the crowd seethed at the words of the uncouth police officer. They kept quiet only because both Somu and Imtiaz Khan gestured for peace.

'What will happen to the standing cane if the factory does not run?' asked Amar Nath.

'Whatever has to happen will happen,' said Somu, arms crossed over his chest.

'We will set fire to our fields but will not give any cane to the bloodsuckers!' yelled Rai Bihari, and the crowed cheered in reply.

Amar Nath turned around suddenly, causing the crowd to move back a step. The DSP hurried after him and the two of them held a hurried consultation near Amar Nath's jeep after which the SDO drove off in a cloud of dust.

The moment he left, Lal Singh was back in form. He stopped holding his stomach in and ordered the constables to get him a chair and some paan and chewing tobacco. This was going to be a long drawn out affair and there was no point getting all worked up about it. He knew from experience that the bastards would tire in a day or two and slowly drift away. Maybe the Rai Sahabs would slip a little something to him for all the trouble he was taking. He settled down and told the constables what he wanted for lunch.

The dharna settled down in a couple of days and lost its novelty. The fluttering shamiana in front of Rai Bahadur Hukam Singh Sugar Mills Pvt. Ltd became a familiar sight. The hangers-on disappeared and only the core group, led by Somu and Imtiaz Khan, hung on, shouting slogans and raising clenched fists every time a car entered or left the factory. The police force dwindled and even Lal Singh stopped bothering to come. He was bored with the sameness of the food and the sameness of the speeches.

The sugar industry began in India in the year 1933. Most factories were situated in very remote areas. Cane supplies fluctuated widely during those days, and factories exploited the farmers. So, in 1938, came the first Cane Unions in Uttar Pradesh, which is the second largest manufacturer of white sugar in India. These were set up to organize a regular supply of cane, to curb malpractice in payment and to develop cane and its varieties. Over the years these purposes developed and expanded and legislative enactments were made and more institutions were created. The most important of these bodies is the Cane Growers' Union, whose job it is to take care of the interests of the growers, and to coordinate the development programmes of the sugar mill.

The secretary of the Cane Growers' Union is actually nominated by the government and is a very important functionary because of the elected nature of the rest of the union's structure. The Cane Growers' Union became a hotbed of politics and earned a regular income in the form of commission from factories. This commission began at a fixed price of fifty paisa and went up to five per cent of the cane price. The union is important to the extent that it is the union that prepares the calendar and decides the bonding policy of the farmers. The bond is calculated every year and an agreement is signed between the farmer and the union. The union, which has to ensure supply of cane to the mills, issues parchis to the farmers. These parchis tell the farmer when he is to supply what quantity of cane and to which centre. Every day the factory gives an indent of the quantity of cane that is required and on that basis parchis are given to the farmers three days in advance to ensure that the requisite quantity of cane arrives at the purchase centres daily. When he gets the parchi, the farmer cuts the cane and delivers it and it is the union that pays the farmers, not the factory. The factory pays the union by cheque but the union pays the farmers cash. It's interesting how the union makes money on the side. The legitimate sources of funds include the factory's commissions to the union, income from interest, and government funds that are given for seed, fertilizers, pesticides, etc. Then, of course, there are the illegal means of making money, of which there are many. First, even though the union gets a delivery of money from the bank every week, it never has enough small change. If a farmer is to be paid Rs. 452.50, he actually gets paid only 450.00 and the union pockets the change. It might seem a small amount, but it gets multiplied so many times that the union ends up with a sizeable packet. Second, there exists, with the blessings of the union secretary, a system of casual loans. This means that if a fellow needs extra cash he is given the cash, but the union takes twenty rupees per hundred as its cut for being so generous to the farmers. Then there are farmers who are not members of the union but who have cane. The union is able to slip them in by rotating the parchis for a commission. This is possible because the union does more bonding than is required. Further, these farmers, because they are being slipped in, are paid at a lesser rate than what the union has received from the factory. Even a difference of ten rupees can multiply the figures astronomically. Next, the union has to keep a fellow at the weighing centres to ensure that there is no under-weighing and the farmers are not being cheated. Actually the union 'sells' a centre to the clerks. This is much like the 'selling' of good or bad police stations (read: police stations that have the potential to make money and those that don't). Somu told me that a good centre is sold for as much as Rs.1000 a month and there are as many as fifty such centres in Majhauli. It gets more interesting now: under-weighing helps the factory and over-weighing helps the farmer's union. The weight of the cane is 100 kilos, but the union representative is willing to give the farmer a parchi of 120 kilos and make a killing. Lastly, the factory pays 'peace of mind' money to the union secretary. It is not money for services rendered, it is money paid to reduce the union secretary's nuisance value, and to ensure a quick and timely supply of cane.

All this and much more I learned in the early days of the agitation when I sat with Somu in the tent and talked and whiled away the endless hours. Talking to Somu I also learned valuable lessons about the important role of the secretary of the Cane Growers' Union. The secretary can create infinite trouble for the factory. Since it is he who pays the farmers and not the factory directly, he can withhold the money and incite the farmers by saying that payments have not been coming regularly from the factory. The factory is dependent on the union for its day-to-day supplies of cane and a two-day loss of cane could amount to a loss of crores to the factory. The union secretary could stop distribution of the parchis, delay supplies of cane, send less supply to the factory, make a totally false calendar, send farmers to the factory to create a nuisance and, as in the present case, start a strike and ruin the factory. He could make life hell for the factory by the simple method of collecting more cane, jamming the gates, creating a hue and cry and giving the factory stale and dry cane.

Union leaders are often criminals, or at least bad guys who know how to use threats to suit their purpose. They can terrorize the population and become very powerful, and they are nearly always affiliated to party politics. Somu himself was an ex-criminal, though he pretended otherwise. He had been tried for murder and he had an army of goons whose leader was Ras Bihari. These goons would even commit murder if he, Somu, wanted them to. Beatings and threats were weapons often used by the union to intimidate farmers. The police is more often on the side of the unions than of the owners, and the politicians are, of course, entirely with the union. The daily presence of Imtiaz Khan at the dharna more than proved that.

Somu did not admit it, but after our talk I realized that between the auction of centres and the commissions from such centres, the blood money received from the factory, his salary from the union, and other sources, Somu made a cool ten lakh every season – maybe more. And I'm talking net income made by Somu alone! The money given to the other members of the union and the politicians was all extra!

The dharna carried on. I spent half the day with Somu and the other half with the Rai Sahabs. As the days went by, restlessness increased in both camps. In the Rai Sahab camp there was something akin to desperation. Rai Sahab had made two visits to

Lucknow, one on his own initiative, and one at the behest of the chief minister.

The chief minister had told him in no uncertain terms that he was not happy with the situation and that Rai Sahab was to find the money somehow and pay the farmers. If the so-called peaceful agitation turned violent there would be trouble and the chief minister would support the farmers, not Rai Sahab.

Rai Sahab ran from pillar to post. No one was willing to give him one crore, leave alone the five crores that he needed. He asked the government for a loan but the amount was too much and the Majhauli case was too much in the press for the chief minister to make a deal with Rai Sahab and give him money, (though he might have been inclined to if he got to keep some of it). Banks were not even giving Rai Sahab an appointment and Satya Pal, the one person who could have helped Rai Sahab, continued to holiday on the magnificent beaches of Bali. He did not reply to Nagina's letter or telegrams and refused to take her calls.

There was talk of mortgaging Hariyali, but how much could they get against it? Not even a crore of rupees. The house might be huge and full of artifacts but it had little site value, situated as it was in the middle of nowhere. Going to the market for that kind of money was out of the question. Every mill in UP was caught in a similar situation. They all had huge amounts as cane arrears and nowhere to raise the money from. Majhauli was much worse off because of the deteriorating relations between the mill and the farmers. It was the only mill in Uttar Pradesh to face an agitation and the chief minister was very upset with all the adverse publicity. He had ticked off Rai Sahab quite sharply the last time they had met.

The agitation which had begun on the third of November now settled into a routine. The gates of Rai Bahadur Hukam Singh Sugar Mills remained closed. The factory was silent and the inmates of Hariyali were invisible. Nothing much seemed to be happening. But all the apparent calm was only surface deep. Faces in Hariyali were stark and yellow, nostrils were pinched and tempers were short. Every day there were arguments between Kulbhushan and Nagina, between Nagina and her mother, between Kulbhushan and Rai Sahab and even between Rai Sahab and Vimla Singh. Rai Sahab and Nagina blamed Kulbhushan for his too-hasty modernization and expansion. Kulbhushan accused Rai Sahab of being senile and short-sighted. The management and staff of the factory took sides too and Harshvardhan became the beating stick for giving Kulbhushan a bad time. It began at breakfast and continued till dinner. There was nothing to do, nowhere to go and no solution in sight.

I got my share of brickbats because I had been especially called in to handle the situation and I had been a total failure. The tension and the waiting were beginning to get to me too.

I was getting repeated phone calls from Bhaskar who was in a panic because that fellow from Andhra from whom we had taken an advance wanted to know how soon he would get his liquor licence. I called Mathur and reminded him of the photographs and received the licence soon enough. After that I was happy to receive Bhaskar's calls for it gave me a chance to tell him how indispensable I was to Goodwork Consultants. I gave him speeches on how he could not carry on Goodwork Consultants on his own and how I was the more important partner. If he wanted me to come back then he needed to pay me seventy-five per cent of the money. In future that would be the sharing pattern: whoever did the major work in a case got seventy-five per cent of the payment. I think all the talk about easy money that I had with Somu probably had something to do with the way I spoke to Bhaskar. Naturally Bhaskar was incensed and called me names. So I called him some more names and the quarrel reached new dimensions in which Nagina was dragged in as the vamp and the real reason for my change in behaviour.

'It is her!' screamed Bhaskar. 'That Nagina woman you ran off with to Majhauli! What about Vidya? That poor woman is in her father's house in Ambala waiting every day for your phone call while you are sitting in Majhauli and doing it with that nagin!'

'Bhaskar, for the last time, leave Nagina out of this. She has nothing to do with my decision of changing the basis on which we share the commission.'

'Like hell she doesn't! You sit in her pocket the whole day sniffing around like a dog! You abandon me! You abandon Vidya and the children!'

I cut the line before he could say anything else and sat on the bed with my head in my hands. It was more than a month since I had come to Majhauli and there was no solution in sight. But I was too deeply involved with Nagina and the mill's affairs. I couldn't leave things at the inconclusive stage they were in. Besides, the truth of the matter was I didn't want to go back to Delhi and I didn't want to go to Ambala and fetch Vidya. I didn't want to think of her homely face and her mundane problems. I didn't want to make love to her.

Every night Nagina and I made love, exploring each other's bodies with endless curiosity and energy. After we had made love we lay together in the dark and I listened to Nagina talk about herself and what she wanted. She was sure of what she wanted. She wanted the agitation to stop, she wanted to get her hands on enough money to start a distillery. She spoke about how she would manufacture new varieties of liquor and package and market her products. She was brilliant, animated, full of energy and ideas. Nothing mattered to her more than her work in Hukam Singh Mills. She hated her mother and accused her of poisoning Rai Sahab's mind against his own daughter and denying her a legitimate right in the property. Legally Nagina was in the right. The mill, the distillery, Hariyali and everything else could be half hers. And she was not going to be deprived of her rights. She would fight tooth and nail for Majhauli and Hariyali.

I would lie there listening silently as she spoke of her dreams and deepest fears to me. Her drinking, her endless pills (amphetamines for a high, Calmpose to control anger),the hysterical weeping over Nishant, her anger and frustration against the agitating farmers, SP's tight-fistedness, her ambitiousness and selfishness – moved me. I was passionately, obsessively in love with her. It was a madness, a junoon, and I had no control over it.

At the site of the agitation, the waiting was wearing everyone down. Somu himself was calm and patient but Ras Bihari was growing restless and irritable. Bhanu, whose college had reopened but who refused to go back, hung around moodily with a pack of other youngsters, all of whom had a stake in the strike. These boys played endless games of cards beneath the neem tree. When they got bored with cards they spent hours hitting an empty beer bottle with stones and chalking up points in the dust with a stick.

People complained about the racket, but they refused to stop. I noticed an increased aggression in their demeanour. Their language was getting rougher, their actions more hostile. These boys also developed an antipathy towards Imtiaz Khan, whom they blamed for taking less interest than he should. They felt that it was Imtiaz Khan who had got them into the situation and who was now was backing out of the affair when it seemed to be in danger of blowing up in their faces.

The fact was that since the agitation seemed to be lingering on without an end in sight, Imtiaz Khan had grown bored and pushed off to Lucknow. I didn't blame the old fellow but the agitators were less charitable. Also the agitation was now in danger of dividing into two camps. The farmers who looked at their crops every day had begun to waver from their resolve. Their new refrain was that if the mill began crushing it would at least pay them for this year's cane and they could carry on with the business of living. Every evening there were heated discussions on whether the dharna should continue or not.

On the fourteenth of November, exactly a day before the factory boilers should have been fired, Harshvardhan paid the agitators a visit. I don't know why he was chosen by Rai Sahab to be an emissary but my guess is that he was probably sent inspite of Rai Sahab's opposition. Well, Harshvardhan came in the afternoon dressed in black trousers, a khaki shirt and a black sleeveless leather jacket. He stepped out of a gleaming Contessa looking debonair and striking and walked up to Somu who lay on a wooden diwan in the tent. Somu had not shaved in three days and wore a dirty pajama-kurta. He was smoking a beedi and playing cards with me when Harshvardhan arrived. I was struck by the contrast between Harshvardhan's mean, ugly face and the studied elegance of his clothes and manner. He took out a cigar from his pocket and took his time lighting it. The rich aroma of the Havana cigar floated through the air disdainfully. He blew smoke at least four times and kept everyone watching and waiting.

'Well, Somu,' he finally said, 'glad to see you look so well.' Somu cleared his throat in reply. 'Are you feeling okay?'

'Yes,' said Somu shortly.

'Good, for I have come to tell you that the boilers are to be fired tomorrow as you very well know. I do hope the farmers have got their calendars and parchis. Like every year, we would like you to come to the puja and the meal that is served after that. In fact,' Harshvardhan spread his hands and grinned wolfishly, 'bring your friends.' The son of a bitch was behaving as though he was the owner of the mill.

'Thank you for the invitation,' said Somu gravely. 'I would love to come but I am waiting for a money order. We all are,' he pointed to himself and the others. 'As you can see we are not dressed for a party and we don't have proper clothes. If the money comes and we can buy new clothes, we will be glad to attend.' He folded his hands courteously.

'Listen!' Harshvardhan turned to the crowd and shouted, 'This is to let you know that Hukam Singh Mills is firing its boilers tomorrow. Everyone is invited to puja and lunch. Just be sure that the carts start lining up tomorrow!'

'Hukam Singh Mills *hai hai!*' shouted Bhanu. The people, who had been taken aback by Harshvardhan's words, now looked at Bhanu. The boy's face was red with anger and he punched the air with his fist. A wave of anger went through the agitators. The chant was taken up by the boys who stood up and shouted vigorously along with Bhanu and soon the entire congregation, all thirty-forty of them shouted, 'Hukam Singh Mills, *hai hai!*'

With the exception of Somu and I, everyone was screaming. I could see the anger on Harshvardhan's face. Then it took on a cunning expression and he played dirty. He lifted a hand for silence and added in a voice loud enough for everyone to hear: 'For your information, Imtiaz Khan Sahab, who as you all know is the MLA of the region, has consented to be the chief guest at the function tomorrow. Let me repeat that we will be happy to have all of you with us!' Saying this he turned on his heel and began walking towards his car.

There was a moment of stunned silence. Imtiaz Khan had let down the agitators and joined the sahab log! Then the buzz started as everyone asked everyone else how this could have happened.

'He's a liar!' screamed Somu. 'Don't listen to him.'

'I told you, Bhaiyya, Imtiaz Khan is a traitor!' Bhanu shouted at the top of his voice.

'Traitor!' screamed the other boys.

'Betrayer!' shouted Ras Bihari.

'Maro!' said a voice and in seconds the peaceful crowd transformed into a violent mob led by the boys. The people lunged after Harshvardhan. Harshvardhan was walking with rapid strides and was almost in the car when a stone came whizzing from behind and hit him on the shoulder. He was wearing a jacket and it couldn't have hurt him but he suddenly whipped around and faced the crowd with a gun in his hands. His face was ugly and ferocious but he was smiling. The crowd fell back in shocked surprise. 'All right, you bastards! Come on! Who wants to be the first target!' He was crouching and had a finger on the trigger and his arm was outstretched. The crowd, which was increasing very rapidly, was inflamed with anger. But the sight of the gun stopped them.

'Cowards!' screamed Bhanu. 'Frightened of this faggot! This gay who sleeps with a man! Go for him! Hukam Singh Mills, *hai hai!*'

'*Hai hai!*' screamed the crowd.

Bhanu lunged at Harshvardhan, one hand on his collar and one hand on his face. He must have drawn blood because there was a scream of rage from Harshvardhan. Both of them fell down with a mighty thud and the gun went off. *Bang*. There were screams all around. Everything after that seemed to happen in slow motion. Bhanu was thrown back by the impact and landed in the middle of the road. The crowd, frightened by the gun, hung back but it was still screaming for Harshvardhan's blood. Bhanu in the meantime struggled to get up as his feet slipped in the loose earth. The bullet had caught him in the shoulder. He managed to get to his feet and was lurching across the road, urging the crowd against Harshvardhan. I could see him then, his face all dusty and tear-streaked, his hair plastered with sweat and his bloodied shirt torn and hanging loose from his shoulders. Bhanu's face was distorted with anger and hatred and I could see his wildly swinging eyes. He was running towards Harshvardhan's car which had started and was reversing in double quick time to get out. As the car swung on to the road, it almost collided with an oncoming truck which swerved violently to avoid collision. The truck swung to the opposite side to avoid the car and there stood Bhanu, still screaming and pointing at the retreating car. He did not see the truck, and the truck driver could not see him. On a road with barely a vehicle or two, this truck was travelling at a high speed, and rammed straight into Som Dutt's kid brother. Like a rag doll, Bhanu's body landed half on the road, half in the dust, and the truck driver, fearing for his life, pressed down on the accelerator and fled.

It was Somu who flew across the space to where Bhanu lay. Slowly we gathered around Bhanu and Somu. Somu howled like an animal in pain, every breath he took was a scream of anguish.

Bhanu was dead.

Somu began raving and shouting, tearing at his clothes and hitting his head on the road with grief. I watched with tear-filled eyes as poor Somu, who had always looked upon Bhanu as his son, cracked under the grief of his sudden demise. 'Oh cruel Yama! If you needed a soul so badly why didn't you take mine? Bring him back to life! Bring him back to me, I beseech you! Take me instead. Enter in your records. . . received one sinner, one black soul beyond hope of redemption. Torture me! Boil me in oil! But bring back Bhanu to life!' Somu screamed and clutched the bloodied Bhanu to his chest.

'Somu, leave him, we need a doctor.'

'Somu, step aside.'

'Somu, let us take him to the doctor.' The people tried to make Somu give up Bhanu's body but he bared his teeth at anyone who dared to come too close. 'Don't touch him,' he roared. 'Don't touch him.' Somu began picking up stones and throwing them at the people who were coming too close, giving vent to the lava of grief that was welling up inside him. He screamed abuse at everyone, wiping his streaming eyes and nose on his kurta sleeve and the people watched from a safe distance as they might watch a mad dog, trying to assess which way he would turn. Finally he sank down beside Bhanu's body and pulled his head on his lap.

I stayed for a very long time and watched as Somu sat on the road hugging Bhanu's crushed and broken body. When he could scream no more, he began crooning to the boy. He seemed to be speaking to him and stroking his cheeks, maybe even trying to breathe life into his cold body. By now the entire town had gathered around and not an eye was dry. The sound of their wailing and weeping must have reached Somu but he still would not let anyone approach. He even chased his own wife away with a stick when I knew, because he had told me, that it was she who had brought up Bhanu like her own son. I stayed till the police arrived and then I left. The police would handle him now. They would need the body for the post-mortem and other formalities, they would take care of Somu.

I went straight to Hariyali. I found the Rai Sahabs and Harshvardhan sitting around in a semi-circle as though waiting for a performance to begin. I looked at their painted and polished faces, nourished with creams and lotions, and felt a deep visceral disgust well up inside me. They were all there: Rai Sahab, Vimla Singh, Kulbhushan, Harshvardhan and Nagina: self-absorbed, devious, rich and influential. Tragedy didn't seem to touch them as much as money and power did. They didn't want to hear details of Somu's grief, they wanted to know what to do now. How to salvage the situation. Perfectly understandable, I suppose, but for once I was disgusted with myself for being on their side.

'Whose idea was it to send Harshvardhan?' I snarled the moment I entered. I was in no mood to be trifled with.

'Now look here, Anmol,' began Kulbhushan. 'This has nothing to do with Harshvardhan.' Like a good Hindu wife he couldn't bear to hear anything against his swami.

'No? Then whose fault is it? Was it your idea to send him there with a gun?' I whirled upon Kulbhushan in anger.

'Gun?' said Rai Sahab. 'What gun?'

'The gun that your precious Harshvardhan pulled out and fired at the crowd. He almost killed Bhanu with the gun the first time and the second time he did kill him by driving like a maniac.' I passed a hand over my eyes. The image of the broken body of young Bhanu was fixed in my mind.

'It was an accident,' muttered Harshvardhan.

'It was an accident,' repeated Kulbhushan.

'It was an accident but an avoidable accident. You, Kulbhushan, did not listen to me or anyone who spoke a word against Harshvardhan. Now this death is going to be chalked up against you. You are the murderer. The moral responsibility of bringing this, this vile criminal, this bastard, into Majhauli is yours and yours alone.' I shook an accusing finger at Kulbhushan. With my bloodshot eyes and dirty clothes, I must have looked like a portender of things to come for I seemed to frighten everyone into a moment of silence.

'Aren't you being a little overdramatic?' said Vimla Singh finally with a slight curl of her upper lip which I found most offensive. Vimla Singh treated me like a cockroach.

'I don't think so,' I said harshly. 'The boy who has been killed is Bhanu Dutt, the younger brother of Som Dutt Bihari, the leader of the agitation. Not only was the boy barely twenty years old and studying for a B.A. in Meerut, he belonged to the backward community and I need hardly point out to you that in the days of the Mandal Commission this is enough to incite everyone into violence. For your information, Somu loved the boy as his own son. He had brought him up and was very proud of him.'

'I'm sorry he's dead but where is the need for you to play such an emotional and dramatic role?' Vimla Singh was at her nastiest.

'Perhaps you have difficulty in understanding,' I said angrily. 'The peaceful agitation is over! The people, the farmers, are all going to scream for your blood now. You as good as murdered him!'

'I think Anmol is tired and needs rest,' whispered Harshvardhan, digging in his pocket for his musical lighter and cigar.

'Don't you patronize me, you faggot!' I screamed and in an instant I had his collar in my fist. I would have hit him a solid blow on the nose if Nagina hadn't intervened. She caught my hand in both her little ones. 'Anmol, please,' she pleaded.

'Call the police! Anmol is violent!' screamed Kulbhushan.

'Yes, call the police!' I shouted. 'This man should be in jail. He's a criminal and I will not stay in the same room as him a minute longer.'

'Harshvardhan Gupta, leave us please,' said Rai Sahab getting up and holding my arm to prevent me from leaving.

'Why should he leave?' began Kulbhushan in a high whining voice.

'Kulbhushan, you may leave too if you like but Anmol stays.' Rai Sahab turned on Kulbhushan in anger.

'You should mind what...' began Vimla Singh.

'That's enough, Vimla!' Rai Sahab snapped at his wife. He remained standing until Harshvardhan Gupta left the room and Kulbhushan decided to sit down. Then he closed the door, made me sit down, and went himself to the liquor cabinet and poured me a neat brandy. 'Drink this and tell us exactly what happened and what we should now do.'

What happened? What had happened was that one young, innocent, backward boy was dead. That's all. What was the big deal? In this country where lakhs die every day of hunger, disease, dirty water and accidents, one more was dead, that was all. Yesterday he was young, passionate, idealistic; today he was dead; tomorrow he would be a handful of ash; and the day after, not even a memory. I felt a deep searing grief. I sat with my hands clasped between my knees and tried to remove the image of Somu clasping Bhanu's broken body to his chest from my mind. I wanted to cry. Instead I let the glass slip from my fingers and watched it shatter as it hit the floor. Immediately Rai Sahab sprang up to call in the servants to wipe and clear the mess before it ruined the carpet, reacting true to form. Another callous, rich seth unaffected by want and poverty. I felt suffocated by the accoutrements of wealth and yet, perversely, I wanted to shake off the smell of tragedy that clung to me. The real tragedy was that I was becoming like them. Yes, I was becoming like them.

Amar Nath, the SDO, and Lal Singh, the fat DSP, entered the room.

'How's the situation, Nath Sahab?' I asked.

'Well, we've sent the body to Meerut for post-mortem. For the present the problem has shifted to Meerut because everyone has gone there, but I'm not sure about tomorrow.'

'Will you hand over the body to the family tomorrow?'

'Yes, but I'm not sure what time. You, I understand, are an eyewitness to the whole affair.'

'Yes,' I said.

'Tell me exactly what happened.'

I repeated my story with many interruptions as Amar Nath kept asking for details. He was taking down notes.

'Now, Rai Sahab, let us not mince matters,' said Amar Nath. 'I am afraid that tomorrow is not going to be a very easy day. I fear we will have to take measures for the safety of the factory and you personally.'

'Why me personally?'

'Well, you are perceived as the villain, you know. It was your man who went there and it was your truck that ran over the boy.'

'I'm so sorry it had to happen like this. Do what you think is best,' said Rai Sahab with dignity.

'I plan to ask for more forces from the district headquarters for tomorrow and the day after when the funeral will be held. Collector Sahab himself will be here tomorrow but I must cover all the possibilities. Rai Sahab, will your office be open tomorrow?'

'Do you want me to close it?'

'I don't think Rai Sahab should close office,' I intervened. 'We should keep things as normal as possible.'

'I agree,' said Amar Nath briskly. 'Besides, half your staff is local. If the office remains open at least some of them will remain out of trouble. Rai Sahab, do you think that the agitation has supporters within your office?'

'Maybe.' Rai Sahab looked helpless.

'Now, for Mr Harshvardhan Gupta. Where is he?' Amar Nath looked around as though he expected Harshvardhan to be crouching behind a sofa or a plant.

'Why do you want him?' Kulbhushan spoke for the first time.

'Inciting the crowd! Shooting at people! Rash and negligent driving! Do you want to hear more, Mr Kulbhushan?' Amar Nath looked at Kulbhushan with narrowed eyes.

'He is also responsible for almost getting Imtiaz Khan killed,' said Lal Singh, scowling. 'Some of the boys went to the MLA's house and tried to lynch him just because Gupta told a lie about the MLA Sahab being the chief guest at the factory function.'

'But...'

'Sir!' A constable came running in. 'Collector Sahab wants to speak to you.'

'I'll be back,' said Amar Nath and he went outside to talk to the collector from the wireless in the car.

As soon as he left, Lal Singh stopped sucking in his belly and gave a huge sigh of relief. 'Bastards! If I were given my way I would have strung the motherfuckers by their feet from the nearest tree at the first hint of an agitation.' He spoke softly so that only Kulbhushan and I could hear him. Lal Singh continued his denunciation of the agitators: 'Ungrateful lot, history-sheeters all of them.They need a bamboo up their backsides, that's all!'

He was such a buffoon. God help this country if this was the country's police.

'One piece of good news,' said Amar Nath, coming back. 'We've caught the driver of the vehicle. But they have a problem in Meerut already. The crowd outside the hospital is huge. We can be sure that they are going to make a big tamasha out of the funeral. Collector Sahab is very worried.'

'I want to give my condolences to Somu,' said Rai Sahab.

'I don't know whether you should go to the Dutt household,' Amar Nath sounded hesitant. 'But I'll talk to Collector Sahab. Has Gupta come?' he asked the constable.

'Yes, Sir.'

'Where are you taking Harshvardhan?' squeaked Kulbhushan.

'Meerut.'

'Why? Is he under arrest?' Kulbhushan was almost in tears.

Amar Nath ignored him and spoke to Rai Sahab. 'No. I'm taking him away to Meerut for his own security, Rai Sahab. I'm not arresting him – yet. Also, I'm going to put a twenty-four hour surveillance on the factory. Please ask your security chaps to be vigilant too.'

'Do you think they could harm the factory?' Rai Sahab sounded incredulous.

'I don't know anything. I'm taking all precautions. Now, has anyone seen the cremation ground? I suggest we take a round of that too so that we know the route the procession will take and how big it is.'

'This is Majhauli, Nath Sahab, nothing ever happens here. We have never even had a communal incident here,' protested Rai Sahab.

'Maybe, but I'm not taking any chances.'

'We should go for section 144 Cr. P.C.' said Lal Singh, heaving his bulk out of the chair.

'What's Section 144 Cr. P.C.?' I asked.

'Preventive Section. People are not allowed to move, assemble or even stand in groups. Prevents people forming processions and protesting,' Amar Nath spoke absently.

'We must go in for Section 144, Sir,' repeated Lal Singh.

'I know, Singh Sahab,' said Amar Nath wearily. 'According to you we should beat up the entire town. But we are not going to. There is going to be a funeral procession. They are entitled to mourn their dead and cremate them with honour. We can't have Section 144, that's just asking for trouble.'

'If you have this Section, whatever it is, then people can't take out a funeral procession?' I asked.

'Precisely. And that will surely lead to trouble. The public is already very agitated. If we prevent them from forming a funeral procession they will very probably burn Majhauli.'

'Yes, Sir.'

'I think I will now go to the cremation ground. If there is anything else, please let me know, Rai Sahab. And Mr Malhotra, I want you to go to Meerut and make a statement.' Amar Nath patted me on the shoulder.

I didn't get back from Meerut until late. The tension in Meerut was palpable. The government machinery was worried, Lucknow was monitoring the situation and the delay in handing over the body had made the situation worse. The post-mortem had not started. The collector appealed to the people to go home and come back the next morning but no one was listening. When I left Meerut, the collector, the SP, the SDO, the DSP and scores of other officials were still around discussing, planning and anticipating tomorrow's event. The crowd outside the hospital was huge and seething. Every face was dark with anger. Sullen, and unnaturally quiet, they sat in the dirt and waited.

I met Somu at the police station where he had been called by the collector to discuss the funeral arrangements. He told the collector that as soon as the hospital authorities released the body after the post-mortem, they would take the body to Majhauli in an ambulance and keep the body at home for the rest of the day for people to pay their respects. The cremation would take place the next morning.

Somu's eyes were glazed and unfocused, he looked drugged, numbed with shock and strain. I tried to convey my sympathies to him but he wasn't listening.

The post-mortem and other formalities took a very long time and it wasn't until three in the afternoon that the flower-bedecked ambulance left Meerut for Majhauli. Bhanu's body reached Majhauli around four o'clock and about five-thirty we went to pay our respects to the deceased. I went with Rai Sahab and Kulbhushan. We were accompanied by the collector and the DSP.

Somu lived near the main crossing of the town, a fairly wide road. That day the entire road and crossing was jam-packed with people. There were people on the roof tops, in the surrounding houses, in the streets, on top of poles, just about everywhere. The car could not reach the house and we were forced to get off and walk part of the way. Even though gun-toting policemen surrounded us, we were surrounded by a hostile crowd in seconds. I was terrified; the slightest word or gesture would incite these people to violence and then we would all be dead, killed by the grief-stricken, bare hands of the furious mourners.

By the time we entered the house and saw the white-shrouded body I realized it would be difficult to get out of there. I dared not meet anyone's eyes. We sat in silence for about fifteen minutes while a priest chanted hymns. There was no wailing and crying, only the smell of incense, the chanting of mantras and the terrible anger kept in check by sheer willpower. I sensed that one false move and we would all be butchered by this crowd of people who hated us with passion.

'Somu,' Rai Sahab went and put an arm around Somu's shoulders. 'Please accept my heartfelt condolences on this painful occasion. I am totally bereft of words. I can only pray that god grants you the strength to come out of this stronger and more self-sufficient.' Somu sat like a stone. He said nothing, did nothing. It was as though he wasn't even aware that someone had touched him. The atmosphere of the place, the animosity, the pulsating, brooding silent anger was frightening. I touched Rai Sahab on the shoulder. The sooner we got out of this place the better. Our presence wasn't helping matters. All of us walked out of the house into the blinding sunshine. Was it my imagination or was the crowd bigger? More hostile?

'Let us leave quickly but without showing any haste,' said the collector almost pushing us out of there. So he felt it too. He was concerned for the safety of Rai Sahab. He kept his hand on the small of Rai Sahab's back and nodded right and left at the crowd to keep up a semblance of normalcy. Somehow we reached the car. As soon as we were seated, the driver asked us to lock the car. 'Start the car and move. Slowly now,' the collector advised the driver, trying to look calm though rivulets of sweat soaked into his collar. He spoke through closed lips. 'Slowly but steadily. Drive now, keep moving but carefully. Don't touch anyone. Don't even touch anyone's pajama. Good lad. Easy does it, easy. Almost there, keep going.' Sweat was pouring down the face of the terrified driver too. I was seated in front, next to him. The collector, Rai Sahab and Kulbhushan were squeezed in at the back. Hundreds of dark, furious faces surrounded us. We were the despicable symbols of arrogant wealth.

Slowly the driver manoeuvred the car through the crowd, guided and encouraged by the collector. Somehow we made it to the Meerut road where Rai Sahab's car was parked and the crowd was firmly behind us. The collector sighed in relief and mopped his face with a handkerchief. 'All right, Rai Sahab, you can go home now.'

We went back to our vigil in Hariyali. It was mid-November and getting to be chilly. The dark was thick and the quiet deathly. There was really nothing to do but wait for morning and the cremation. Kulbhushan and I went on a round of the factory and the boundary walls checking on the guards to see whether they were awake and alert. Everything seemed to be normal. The office staff had left and the gates were locked. There was no sign of any crowd or any tension but we knew that trouble was just a heartbeat away.

It was almost eleven o'clock in the night when Durga Das the collector and the DSP along with some officers, came in for a meal and some rest. Since I too was staying at the guest house, I ate with the officers.

'What's the situation like?' I asked the collector.

'Tense but under control, as they say,' he laughed, eating his food with a healthy appetite. He was an experienced man, reliable in an emergency. Amar Nath, the SDO, had told me that the chief minister thought highly of Durga Das. 'But you guys need to do something drastic about your public relations, you know. I am surprised at the animosity against the family. Everyone is against the Rai Sahabs.'

'Hmm,' grunted the DSP. 'I thought that anger was only against the son, but it's against Rai Sahab too.'

'That's because he is perceived as weak and ineffective as far as controlling his son is concerned,' said the collector, as he helped himself liberally to the mutton biryani and accepted two kebabs from the hovering bearer. 'The recent firing of old and trusted people has really brought his stock down. Hiring a thug like Harshvardhan Gupta was a very stupid move. I am surprised he did a thing like that. Everyone has always spoken very highly of Rai Sahab's administrative abilities.'

'Yeah,' said the DSP. 'I suppose it is old age coupled with love for his son. And the engineer fellow, what's his name?'

'Gupta,' I volunteered. 'Harshvardhan Gupta.'

'As I said, Gupta is a third-rater,' said the collector.

'Yes. I'm told he defrauded the company he was working for earlier. And Rai Sahab hired him!' The DSP helped himself to more rice and chicken curry.

'Rai Sahab has abdicated power. Kulbhushan takes the decisions and Rai Sahab does nothing about them.' The collector was a more frugal and discriminatory diner. He ate the biryani and the curd but avoided the heavy curries.

'What are the Rai Sahabs going to do now?' The DSP sounded almost plaintive.

'Search me,' said the collector accepting a small helping of the pineapple cake and ice-cream which had come from Hariyali. In fact, the entire dinner had come from Hariyali. 'You should know, Mr Malhotra. Tell us.' He looked pointedly at the three gulabjamuns which I had served myself.

'Actually, Sir, I am in the dark too. I don't work here, you know.' I quickly swallowed one of the gulabjamuns.

'Yes, so I heard.' Was it my imagination or did his voice sound ironical? 'But you are close to the family.'

'I suppose so, but they don't confide in me.'

'Still, you've been here for almost a month and you have been intervening in the agitation on their behalf.'

'True, Sir, but who can say what the malik-log actually think?' I tried to avoid the issue. The collector was ruining my dinner.

'As far as I can see, there isn't much that they can do except pay up.' The collector got up from the dining table and lit a cigarette. I had been dying to smoke and promptly lit up too. The first lungful of smoke made me gasp with relief.

'They don't have the money, or so they say,' said the DSP loosening his belt.

'What's the solution then?' The collector accepted a cup of coffee from the waiter.

'Sell the factory and pay up.' The DSP had now sprawled on the sofa. He was obviously in discomfort and longing to get into chappals and a pajama-kurta. But since the collector, a younger man, was not in the mood to retire, he had no choice but to keep sitting.

'If they cannot handle it the state government can take over the factory,' said the collector.

'Oh no!' I was shocked. 'I'm sure it won't come to that. They are bound to work out some solution.' Was the fellow serious, I wondered?

'Well, let's get over this crisis first. After that we will talk about the future.' The collector stubbed out his cigarette and dug a toothpick in his teeth. 'Tell me, Mr Malhotra, is it true that Kulbhushan's sexual preferences are for men?' Before I could answer, he continued, 'Hmm, well, like it or not, he is facing the social consequences of being so open about it. This is not America, you know, where gays even have marital rights. This is India where we pretend we don't even fuck our wives!' He flicked the toothpick into the ashtray.

'From what I hear, the daughter is the more capable of the two,' said the DSP.

'Well then, Rai Sahab should have chosen the daughter as his successor. What's wrong in that? This is a country that had a woman prime minister for years.'

'True,' sighed the DSP.

'What do you say, shall we go back? Kyon, DSP Sahab?' Asking this question the collector ruined whatever happiness the food had brought into the DSP's life.

However, he responded quickly enough, 'Yes. And we can send Amar Nath and the others to eat. I hope there is food for them?'

'Yes, Sir,' assured the mill's public relations man who had been hovering in the background. 'We can feed an army.'

I walked out with the officers. 'Has the crowd reduced or not?' I asked.

'They are going home now to rest so that they can gather fully reinforced tomorrow. That's the news on the wireless. You take your rest too, Mr Malhotra, and do not worry. We are here to handle all situations.'

In spite of his reassurances, the law, as it happened, was not able to take care of all situations. But that was the next day. For the first time since coming to Majhauli, I slept that night without thinking about Nagina. But my rest was not peaceful. I was disturbed by nightmares about the accident in which sometimes it was me who was killed by the truck, and sometimes Bhanu came back to life just as they were about to light the funeral pyre. He laughed ghoulishly as he sat on top of the logs of wood and said that they were burning the wrong person and the person who needed to be burned was Anmol Bhaiyyaji. Perhaps it was my guilty conscience, though why I felt guilty about Bhanu's death I cannot answer.

It was twelve noon and the funeral march had begun. It was the second huge march undertaken in less than a month's time and the same people were present. But what a difference there was! This time there was no gulal, no elation, no hope, no new clothes. And there was no Bhanu. No, that's not correct, there was Bhanu, but he was now a lifeless, white-shrouded, putrefying body that everyone wanted to get rid of. I went early in the morning to try and talk to Somu again but he wouldn't talk to me. Ras Bihari was at his belligerent best. He caught my arm in a vice-like grip and told me to go before he or anyone else lost their temper and hurt me.

'But what are you planning, Ras Bihari?' I put an arm around him and pulled him outside. 'Please don't do anything foolish. Majhauli is full of policemen. If you try something, they will shoot,' I pleaded with him.

'That's what the police and the rich always do, kill the poor man. You do your job, we will do ours.' Ras Bihari stank of sweat and liquor. I think he hadn't taken a bath since Bhanu's death and his eyes were bloodshot with grief and weariness.

'What is your job?'

'Revenge!'

'Revenge!' I echoed in dismay. 'Bhanu died in an accident, Ras Bihari. How can you avenge that? No one was to blame except the driver and he too has been arrested.'

'The driver wasn't to blame, Rai Sahab was! You've treated us like scum for too long. No more! You killed an innocent college-going boy and with him you killed our feelings of remorse and guilt. Why should we go around feeling guilty? For what? For being alive? Don't we have the same right to life as you? Look at the way you people have taken the Mandal issue. Why does it kill you guys that someone finally wants to treat us with respect? Go away, Bhaiyyaji. You are not to blame and I don't want you to be hurt in this battle.'

'What battle? There's no battle.'

'Somu is in pain. Last night after you people left he tried to cut his wrists. Can you understand what it means for him to lose Bhanu like this? Can you?' Ras Bihari thrust out his chin at me.

'I think I can understand, Ras Bihari. But more violence and more deaths will not make him feel better.'

'They might.'

'Ras Bihari...' I stared at him in despair.

'Leave, Bhaiyyaji.'

I tried reasoning with him some more but he just walked away. I was desperately worried now. I knew in my gut that something awful was about to happen. I racked my brains and only one name came up. Imtiaz Khan, MLA.

Imtiaz Khan didn't talk of revenge, thankfully, but he did say that the Rai Sahabs were to blame and they would have to face the consequences. He was having a hard enough time trying to undo the harm done to his reputation by Harshvardhan and other gossip-mongers and he didn't have time to worry about us. And, he added, he was going to recommend to the chief minister that the factory be taken over immediately by the government because the Rai Sahabs had proved themselves thoroughly incompetent to handle the factory and the situation. If the Rai Sahabs had anything to say, it would be best if they spoke to the chief minister since he was the only person listening.

It was obvious that the tension had got to Imtiaz Khan too and he was in no mood to cooperate. Next I went to the police station where the collector and other officers were encamped and told them what I had heard and what I feared.

'Thank you for the good news,' said the collector. 'We are aware of it.'

'But the MLA can't talk in this irresponsible way.' Talk of the factory being taken over by the government had shaken me.

'Sir.' A constable came in and saluted smartly. 'At least six truck loads of pro-reservationists are coming from Delhi.'

'What about additional force?'

'They are here. And more truckloads of people are coming from Lucknow too, Sir.'

'The fact that this boy is from the backward classes has complicated matters. Where's the route map which they have given?' asked the DSP.

'Here, Sir. They have decided not to go anywhere near the factory.'

'Are they to be trusted?' asked the collector who had been listening.

'Who knows, Sir.'

'What do you think, DSP Sahab?' The collector asked again.

'We'll have to make arrangements.'

'Okay then, move our fellows now. It's almost nine o'clock. Everyone has helmets, lathis?'

'Sir.'

'Everyone knows where he is deployed?'

'Sir.'

'How many armed men?'

'Two platoons, Sir. One is going to be with us and one with Amar Nath. One in the front and one in the middle. We hope the back will take care of itself.'

'Where is Amar Nath?'

'He's briefing his men, Sir.'

'Good. The boy is smart,' said the collector.

*

That was that then. I had done my duty, the rest was up to them. The sun was high up in the sky and shadows non-existent by the time the procession actually started. Bhanu's body was covered with white, orange and red flowers. The mourners' faces were hard and stony but the procession was strangely peaceful and orderly. The mood of the funeral procession was scary. It would have been more natural if there had been weeping and wailing and beating of breasts. I joined the procession immediately behind the bier. A huge contingent of police virtually surrounded the procession. Security was really tight. The funeral procession wound its way through the entire town, stopping four times for speeches and condolences. Most speeches were short and to the point and no effort was made to inflame the crowd or play on emotions. It was obvious, though no one was being named, that Bhanu had not died an accidental death. Bhanu had been killed almost as surely as someone had taken a knife to him.The leaders of the procession were taking great pains to let the authorities know that they were not going to create trouble. The crowd followed the body through the day quietly, patiently. Round and round went the procession, covering the same ground at least three times and tiring out everyone. Finally, at almost four in the afternoon, the procession reached the cremation ground. As Bhanu's closest living relative, Somu lit the funeral pyre.

Back in the guest house I splashed my face with cold water and sat down on the edge of my bed. I needed a glass of something straight and strong. It would revive me and take the ache away from my muscles. I took a bottle of whisky and drank straight from it. Then I got up to report the day's events to the bosses of Hariyali.

On my way down I noticed the lights on in Dhai Din Ka Dera. A gust of night breeze blew the curtains aside just then and I saw that bastard Harshvardhan in the drawing room. So he was still around. And he wasn't alone. Kulbhushan was with him.

I stood in the garden and watched Harshvardhan and Kulbhushan in a tight embrace. Thighs, heads, shoulders, arms, hips and hands clinging together like they were physically one. With their free hands they held their glasses to each other's mouths. Harshvardhan tilted Kulbhushan's head back and poured the entire contents down his throat. Kulbhushan leered at him coquettishly and then giggled as Harshvardhan's beefy hand closed on his crotch.

'You bastard! If you don't clear out by tomorrow I'll call the police and have you thrown out,' I shouted from where I stood, trembling in rage.

The window crashed open and Harshvardhan stuck his neck out of the window. 'Well, well, well. Nagina Aggarwal's hero,' he drawled. 'I thought you'd be in the factory staving off the backlash.'

'Anmol, what are you doing here?' squeaked Kulbhushan.

'You filthy bastard. If the house is not empty by tomorrow I will come and shoot you, ' I shouted at Harshvardhan. 'And as for you, Kulbhushan, if you don't keep this prize shit away from me I'll...I'll shoot you too!'

I was still shaking with anger as I rang the doorbell of Hariyali. When I entered the lobby I heard the phone ring. 'Ji Sahab, yes, Sahab, I will tell Nagina Memsahab.' The bearer's voice rang loud and clear in the room. 'Nagina Memsahab, phone from Delhi. It is Aggarwal Sahab. He is back from *phoren* and says you should call him.' I turned around quietly and walked straight out of the house and back to my room.

I sat on the edge of the bed and pulled off my shoes and tried to relax but found myself unable to. There was no point in staying on now. My role here was over. Nagina would probably go back to SP. No question of the factory starting either. I was missing the kids. I should go to Delhi and then to Ambala to talk some sense into Vidya. I would come back after a week maybe and carry on from there. Or maybe I would not. Was my role that of chief troubleshooter in the day and prince consort at night? What if Nagina went back to SP now that the factory seemed out of reach? What if she tired of me and found a new boyfriend who screwed better than me? What if after all this Harshvardhan stayed on? Thinking of that bastard made me even more frustrated. I was moody and restless. Then I remembered what Harshvardhan had said about trouble brewing in the factory. Was he on to something? What if Somu's sympathizers tried to foment trouble there?

Immediately I got up, put on my shoes and went to the drawing room of the guest house. There I found Sen, the public relations man. I borrowed a torch from him and told him that I was going for a round of the factory.

I entered Hukam Singh Sugar Mills through one of the minor gates, jumping over it, in fact. Where were the guards? I found three of them behind the godowns, sitting on their haunches, gossiping. They scrambled to their feet the moment they saw me and ran for their beats. I let them go without reprimanding them. That wasn't my job. I checked the godowns, the office building, and the shiny new molasses tanks. All was quiet and normal. I turned back and walked towards the main factory which was a huge structure of corrugated iron sheets. I began from one end, testing all the doors as I went along taking care to keep in the shadows. All the doors seemed locked. There was no way of getting inside unless one went in through the front, where the cane was fed into the crushers. Ever since the factory had been renovated and converted into the continuous pan process, the romance had gone out of making sugar. Some of the old men even said the sugar tasted different, though that was obviously not true. The factory was totally sealed off. All you saw from the outside was this mammoth structure and this huge hand with four steel fingers that picked up the cane and dropped it into the moving chute. The chute went into a hole in the wall almost forty feet above the ground and delivered the cane straight into the crushers. Then I remembered Kulbhushan talking about some repairs that had called for a part of the wall being pulled down so that the chute could be refitted. The repairs had been made but because of everyone's pre-occupation with the strike, the wall had not been rebuilt. There was a gaping hole high in the wall, at least thirty feet above the ground. It was possible to climb up the chute on the rungs set in the wall. On an impulse I climbed up and cautiously walked along the chute, thinking to myself that if someone started the machinery now I could be carried along the chute and fed into the crushers.

I stepped into the chute and shone my flashlight into the gaping hole. Nothing. I switched off the torch and was turning to go when I stopped short. Was that a footprint on the chute? Yes. I shone my torch again and examined the chute carefully. Hadn't Kulbhushan said that the repairs were complete almost a week ago? Could that footprint be a week old? I stuck the torch inside my waistband and decided I was going to investigate further. I was thirty feet above the ground, on the chute and at the point where the cane disappeared from sight. The only way to get inside the factory was to climb down the crushers. I proceeded to do so, cursing as I slipped on the oily, dirty machinery and lost my footing several times. Somehow I hung on and jumped the last ten feet, landing safely inside the cavernous factory.

It was pitch dark inside. The huge solid machinery of the crushers and the boilers was all around me. I had walked almost through the entire factory and was near the centrifugal drums when I heard a strange noise and glimpsed a white light. It was an acetylene torch!

'Who's there?' I shouted. In the huge, empty factory, my voice sounded loud and reverberated all around. The blow torch was switched off immediately and there was a sound of running feet. I ran towards the sound and tripped over something on the floor. My torch flew out of my hand and rolled away. I groped around in the dark and my fingers closed around... a rope? I felt it again and realized that it was wire. Wire? What the hell was wire doing in the middle of the floor? I gave it a small tug and found that it would not yield. It was either tied or fixed on both sides. In the meantime the blow torch had been switched on again. 'What's going on? Who is there?' I shouted, and getting up I again ran towards the sound. Against the light of the blow torch I saw two men. They were cutting open a hole in the wall of corrugated iron.

'*Jaldi karo!*' one of them shouted. 'Quick, he's coming.'

I was upon them and swung a fist at the fellow who was nearest. I got him in the side of the neck and both of us went down. 'Who are you and what are you doing here?' I shouted.

The guy I was fighting hit me on the head with a hard object. I staggered but steadied myself and hit him again. I could see a little now and was able to give him a good, solid blow. He fell back with a grunt of pain and I put my knee on his stomach.

'Help!' he shouted to the other fellow who swung around at me, the blow torch flaring in my face. The heat was so intense that I screamed and fell back as the flame seared my face and eyes. The fellow whom I was fighting slipped away and ran towards the opening that they had cut out.

'Leave him, let's go,' he shouted to the guy who had the acetylene torch. But the guy with the torch had learned the strength of his weapon and he came after me. I turned to flee as soon as his intention became clear to me. But he was quicker and the blow torch got me in my back full blast for a few seconds even as I ran forward. I screamed in pain as my clothes caught fire.

'Forget him!' shouted the guy who didn't have the torch. 'Come on, let's go. Leave him alone! Let's go, let's go!' I was writhing in agony on the floor trying to put out the flames. I heard my assailant throw down the torch and run. They were gone. Somehow I struggled to my feet and half crawled, half walked out of the hole which they had cut into the wall and dragged myself to the office. In front of the office I met the chowkidar. 'Quick, call the police and other security guys. I think someone has sabotaged the factory!' I gasped and sank to the floor.

He ran for the phone while I leaned against the wall and gasped for breath. My back was scorched. I was thinking of Rajiv Goswami. 'Quickly, quickly!' I shouted after him in a feeble voice as I staggered towards the gate. It was then that the world came to an end, or so it seemed to me. There was a mighty blast from inside the factory. I turned to look and saw angry orange flames shoot up into the sky and turn into a mass of thick, black smoke. There were screams, shouts, bells ringing, the mighty roar of the fire and smoke everywhere. It was like we were in the middle of a battlefield! Or maybe we were in hell. My face and back were burned and there, in front of me, Rai Bahadur Sugar Mills had blown up. So much for our security precautions and so much for the police's bandobast and information.

The police spies, or informers, as they are called, had said that nothing was being planned. Obviously they knew shit all. The saboteurs had played their cards right. While all attention was on Bhanu's funeral procession, they'd crept into the factory and planted a bomb. The timing was right and the operation was a success. Full marks to them and a failing grade to all the district officials who were right there, on the factory premises, sleeping in the factory guest house!

We should never have relied on them, I thought, just before I passed out.

nagina

Papa and I reached the factory with the collector Durga Das, Amar Nath, Lal Singh, Kulbhushan and an army of flunkies. We stood in the ashes and greasy stinking muck of spilled sugar juice, holding hankies to our noses. I was horrified by the extent of the damage. Papa was almost in tears. He stood in the middle of the debris and slush holding a charred piece of metal. The expression on his face said everything. He kept twisting the piece of metal in his hands and looking at his shoes. 'My shoes are ruined,' he said finally as though the ruining of his shoes was the bigger tragedy.

'Mine are spoiled too,' squealed Kulbhushan. 'And they are Gucci.'

'What are we going to do, Nagina?' Papa's eyes were wet. He was looking at the destruction of a lifetime's work.

'It's a dastardly act,' muttered the collector.

'How can the bastards destroy the factory,' wondered the SDO. 'It feeds them!'

Amazingly, the bomb achieved in an instant what we Rai Sahabs could not have achieved in months of negotiation and intrigue. Uptil now the whole world, including the press, had been accusing my father of being a blood-sucking Shylock. When Bhanu died, the entire district machinery called a press conference in Lucknow and painted my family black. It was that pansy, Harshvardhan Gupta, and the clever and conniving Som Dutt Bihari, alias Somu, who'd made us sound like some medieval tyrants. But now, from villains, the Rai Sahabs had become victims. Suddenly everyone thought that while Bhanu's death was unfortunate; it was not because of the Rai Sahabs, and that they, certainly, had not wanted him to die.

Everything changed with the explosion in the factory. Suddenly the chief minister was ringing up Papa. The collector began to hunt for Ras Bihari who had disappeared without trace and Somu was hauled in for questioning.

Financially the company lost nothing. The insurance company paid up quickly and I recalled the old engineer, Vikasji, to repair the damage and take Harshvardhan's place. It was amazing how quickly it was fixed. Not only was the damage to the factory minimal, Vikasji repaired the damaged portion in next to no time. The factory was functional in less than a month.

Of course, the biggest advantage was that the agitation was finished. Officially it was not called off, but with Imtiaz Khan being forced to give a strong statement against the sabotage in Rai Bahadur Hukam Singh Mills, Somu being hauled off to the police station and Ras Bihari absconding, the agitation was doomed.

Anmol was something of a hero. The newspapers wrote extensively about the sabotage in Rai Bahadur Mills, the damage done and the exemplary courage displayed by Anmol Malhotra, friend of the family.

Anmol lay on his stomach in one of the Hariyali bedrooms. All the drugs in the world could not dull the searing pain in his back. The doctors – experts I had specially brought in from Delhi – treated the burns and declared them to be third degree. Luckily his face was less of a wreck though the pain was exruciating. I rang Vidya and told her not to tell his parents. I didn't want them all to come rushing to Majhauli.

I was sitting with Anmol, watching him drift in and out of an uneasy sleep when Amar Nath came to visit me. He looked tired and his clothes were crumpled but his eyes were alert and bright. He told me that I was brave and that the administration had failed to anticipate the situation. All their intelligence had failed. I told him that it required courage to say that, true courage. He smiled cynically and said that was why he said it when there were no witnesses. Then he looked at me closely and said that it was strange how the Rai Sahabs had won a potentially lost situation.

'What do you mean?' I asked.

'Look at it,' he said. 'Today you are the heroes and the CM has asked Imtiaz Khan to explain how the sabotage took place. The tables have turned.'

'So?'

'So, it's strange, is it not, how no one else had a whiff of what was going to happen except Anmol?'

'You would have too if you had your ear to the ground,' I said shortly.

Amar Nath looked me directly in the eye and said, 'You will tell me though, won't you, what Ras Bihari could possibly gain from sabotaging the agitation?'

The next day Vidya arrived in Majhauli with her father and brother in tow and announced she was taking Anmol back to Delhi immediately. She arrived looking like a mad woman – hair all over the place, no make up, her face broken into a million wrinkles of grief. She had lost a great deal of weight and looked dark and hollow-cheeked. She wore a brown and yellow printed salwar-kameez of a colour and print that didn't suit her at all with a crushed and trailing yellow dupatta looped around her throat.

Her long thick hair was plaited simply and severely. She refused all refreshment, all requests to stay the night. She said she had come to take her husband home and she was going to do it immediately. She was the picture of self-righteous anger; making everyone shrivel with guilt.

Vidya strode into Anmol's room with me trailing behind. 'Anmol, I have just one question,' Vidya said, oblivious to my presence in the room. Her eyes were over-bright and burning. It was obvious she was controlling herself with great difficulty. 'What does Nagina mean to you? I mean,' she said her voice breaking, 'what's there between the two of you?'

Anmol exhaled slowly and inadvertently his eyes met mine. 'Let things be, Vidya. It might be better that way,' he said uneasily.

'No, I want to know.' The demon of jealousy was tearing at her vitals.

'What?'

'What is my status vis-à-vis Nagina?'

'You are my wife.'

'And she?'

'She's a friend.'

'Anmol, don't you think it's time you were honest with me? I know from Mataji that you had an affair with her when you were young. It is continuing, isn't it? *Isn't it*?' Her voice rose hysterically.

'Yes,' Anmol said. There was no point in lying.

'*Anmol!*' Vidya clasped a hand over her mouth as though she feared she was going to vomit.

'You wanted to hear it. Yes, I have had an affair with Nagina.' Anmol closed his eyes.

I did not want to see Vidya's betrayed face, so I looked the other way. I could hear her ragged breathing. Like a drowning person coming up for air. Slowly I opened my eyes and stretched my hand to touch her half turned away shoulder. She recoiled from me in horror and began shaking her head as though she wanted to deny me, deny the affair, deny everything.

'Vidya,' I whispered. 'Please...'

'Leave me alone, you bitch.'

'Vidya...'

'Leave me alone! Leave me *alone*!' And then the tears and the accusations came. She sobbed and wailed and gave vent to everything that was inside her. It was as if she'd plunged a knife inside herself and was twisting it around violently. She opened her hurt for us to see; her huge gaping wounds of betrayal.

Vidya fell on the ground and banged her fists on the floor. She abused Anmol and me. She even knocked her head on the floor many times. I was scared, scared she might hurt herself and scared that someone might come in and see all this. Strangely enough nobody came in. As she continued to keen and knock her head, Anmol struggled to get out of bed and reach her. In trying to get up he grazed his back and let out a tiny scream of pain, loud enough to be heard by Vidya. Immediately her demeanour changed. She was all concern for him.

'Anmol!' Vidya was up in a trice and easing her husband back on the pillow, crying all the while. 'Anmol, why did you do this to me? Why? What did I do wrong? Tell me and I will try to improve myself.' She threw herself on his chest and wept. 'She's more beautiful than me, I know. But, Anmol, *I'm* your wife, the mother of your children and I love you. You want me to be more glamorous? Okay, I'll cut my hair and perm it. I'll give up fighting against Mandal and all my other socialist activities. I will, I promise you. I'll go to parties with you. Please don't leave me. Don't leave me and the kids. Please.'

Anmol gathered his wife in his arms and held her while she sobbed out her heart. I knew that even though she was torn and devastated inside, Vidya would never bring up the subject of Anmol's infidelity again. She had taken a beating. The assurance of the activist had been ripped off her face. She was abject in her desire to please Anmol. I knew that when they went home she would never once fling his indiscretions in his face, she would behave with great stoicism and make a great effort to remain cheerful and keep the children from irritating her husband.

Like all Indian wives, Vidya would be so anxious to make amends that it would seem as if she, and not her errant husband, was the guilty party.

Anmol went away with Vidya but I wasn't worried; I was happy not to have him around till he recovered and I knew I would have him back when I wanted.

The factory restarted and the familiar sight of carts lining up at the factory's gate was deeply satisfying to me. Business picked up – cane rolled in and sacks of sugar went out. Farmers looked happy as money started to flow to them and there was food to go around. For me, personally, there were two victories. First, it was I who broke the coconut and lit the lamp when the factory restarted. Papa was happy to hand over the reins to me because I had proved my capability when it was most required. I could see the anger and helplessness in my mother's eyes as she took in my growing influence and strength. But what could she do?

Kulbhushan withdrew from the factory and work. He did not visit even once to see how the repairs were coming along. He was nowhere to be seen when the insurance people visited and he was certainly not there when the factory restarted.

In fact, the deterioration in Kulbhushan's mental condition was sudden and severe. I think the breakdown began when the police first arrested Harshvardhan. The panic and fear in him was so intense that he just lost interest in everything, except the desire to hold on to his gay lover, clearly the dominant partner in their relationship. For a short while, from within the sanctity of his room, he made perfunctory noises about how the factory should be handled which no one heard or cared about and soon even the pretence of working stopped. He took – I still can't believe it, of all things – to wood carving! He began whittling in his spare time, which, considering the minimum time he spent on actual work, seemed like all day.

How far Kulbhushan had drifted became clear when he chose to shun my second victory: The opening of the distillery and the launch of Somras Distilleries and Breweries Pvt. Ltd.

The idea of opening my own distillery and brewery came to me after Anmol left. One evening, about a month after Anmol's accident, the family gathered for dinner in the drawing room of Hariyali. The evening began politely enough. In fact, it was one of those rare evenings when the four of us, Mummy, Papa, Kulbhushan and I, were alone for our old pre-dinner drinks ceremony. There was no Harshvardhan around to distract Kulbhushan any more and, showing a rare glimpse of his earlier charm and courtesy, he opened a bottle of red wine and poured us each a glass. We sat in silent harmony, happy to listen again to the drone of the factory and waiting for the whoosh of let-off steam, a sound that was music to my ears.

Then my mother struck. 'Nagina,' she said in a soft, insidious voice. 'Don't you miss your son?'

I had a mental vision of Nishant lying in bed with his arms and legs splayed and a thin streak of saliva dripping into the pillow from his open mouth. 'No,' I said decidedly.

'That's strange,' she said. 'I *adored* my children and my husband. I couldn't bear to live a day without them.' She pursed her lips and looked at me obliquely.

'Good for you,' I muttered feeling an old sense of impending humiliation. Was Mummy going to ruin my happiness like she always did?

'I mean, you continue to live here in your maika and…'

'She is working for us now, Vimla,' Papa interrupted. 'Have you forgotten all that she has done to get the factory running again?'

'True. But now that the factory is running what is she going to do here?'

'I'm going to set up a distillery and run it,' I announced suddenly. 'I'm going to make my own liquor and market it.'

Until that moment I had never consciously thought about setting up a distillery and here I was shooting off my mouth about marketing liquor! SP would divorce me if he got so much as a hint of what I was up to. Stunned silence greeted my pronouncement.

'Nagina, what a wonderful idea,' Papa was the first to find his voice.

'*Wonderful?* What's wonderful about it? It's the most bogus idea I've ever heard,' my dear brother spluttered.

'You stay out of this, Kulbhushan,' I growled. 'I know exactly how much business sense you have.'

The earlier Kulbhushan would have pounced on that jibe, but the new one merely fished out a thin chisel from his pocket and began cleaning his nails.

'You can make Kulbhushan shut up but what about SP? He hates the idea of your working and now if he hears about you manufacturing liquor, he'll probably divorce you!' Mummy's face and voice spat venom. 'Besides, where will you live? You can't continue to live in Hariyali all your life.'

'Vimla…' began Papa.

'Mummy,' –I cut Papa short – 'for once you are absolutely right. I will not live in Hariyali, I will live in Dhai Din Ka Dera and I will divorce SP,' I drained my glass of wine and put it on the table.

'*Nagina!*'

'Nagina…?'

'What Nagina? It's been staring me in the face all this while and I didn't see it. SP and I don't have a marriage. We don't have a life together. Never did. And besides, I'm going to float a new company, Somras Breweries and Distilleries. I am going to make the best desi liquor in the whole of Uttar Pradesh, the best desi liquor in the whole of India!'

Nobody said anything to my sensational announcement. Kulbhushan had already lost interest and was huddled in a corner of the sofa, lost in contemplation of his nails. Mummy looked aghast and furious, and as for Papa, I'm not sure what thoughts were racing through his head.

'Divorce SP, live in Dhai Din Ka Dera, manufacture and sell liquor? You are crazy! Mad! I will not allow you to behave in this irresponsible manner!' Mummy sat up, her cheeks burning with anger, her pallu falling off her shoulder on to her lap.

'I, I and I! That's all you can think of – ' I turned on my mother in fury but Papa cut me short –

'Where will you get the money from?'

'From where you got it, Papa, for the expansion of the mill – from government coffers. I'll take a government loan. As for the rest, SP will give it me.'

'Why would…?' Mummy's voice was high-pitched and screechy.

'Don't be naïve, Mummy. SP will gladly pay to get rid of me,' I laughed. 'To get rid of both me and Nishant. SP has so much money that if I took a truckload of it away he would not miss it.' I dismissed SP and thought of what I would do. 'We have loads of our own molasses and we do nothing with them. We will sell it to liquor manufacturers. I'll use it to start making industrial alcohol and liquor. I'll open a separate company, my own company. And in five years, if all goes well, I'll go public, collect money from the market and set up my own co-generation and paper unit!' I was exultant. The ideas were tumbling out of me at breakneck speed and I was beside myself with excitement. I got up and began striding up and down the room.

'Nagina,' Papa was looking at me amazed. 'I didn't know you were so ambitious. You really have it all planned out.'

'Yeah,' said Mummy sourly. 'You have really planned out everything. It's as though you are going to take over everything.'

I laughed. My heart swelled with a sudden boost of confidence. 'For the moment I'm going to take over Dhai Din Ka Dera. I hope that freak, Harshvardhan has removed his stuff from the house, otherwise I will just throw it out.'

'Harshvardhan will stay with me when he comes back,' said Kulbhushan suddenly. 'And I don't want to have dinner with you, Nagina,' Kulbhushan got up in a huff. 'I will eat in my room.'

'I think I will eat in my room too. I'm not too hungry,' Mummy got up and looked pointedly at Papa waiting for him to follow suit. Papa stared at his shoes and said nothing. Finally Mummy left the room.

It was my first victory over my mother. I came and sat opposite Papa. 'I think we both understand that if any decisions are to be taken, they have to be taken by you and me, Papa.'

'Yes.'

'I mean any decisions. I mean decisions about Rai Sahab Incorporated. That means sugar, alcohol, paper, co-generation, expansion, everything.'

'Yes.'

'Also you have to now play a larger role. You have to run for President of the Indian Sugar Manufacturers' Association, Papa.'

'Hmm.'

'The MLA, Imtiaz Khan needs us. He will support us. Pay him double what you are paying him. And you have to go again to Lucknow, Papa, and press your advantage with the CM. Now that we have the upper hand, if you became the President of ISMA you can ensure that only Hukam Singh Mills gets a licence for further expansion in the area and no one else. We don't want others cutting into our cane area.'

'Yes, yes, you're right. I will go to Lucknow.'

I took a deep breath and steadied myself. I had made my decision, and I had made it easily. I felt my mind beginning to relax. I had done the right thing, the only thing. If there was anyone who could take over Rai Sahab Incorporated, it was I.

And I would make the company grow. Now I needed to go to Delhi for a last meeting with SP and two visits to my lawyers. One to discuss my divorce, the other to draw up the papers of Somras Breweries and Distilleries Pvt. Ltd.

I lived through a period of extreme crises in the next few months. First there was SP and the divorce. I went back to Sundernagar and waited for him in Nishant's room. I confronted my spouse across the bed of our sleeping child, our child who did not grow up, our child who could not bind his parents together.

I sat on the bed and smoothed Nishant's hair off his brow while SP sat in cross-legged elegance on a chair on the other side of the bed. His cream trousers had a razor sharp crease and he'd matched these with a deep mustard shirt of Italian silk and Italian shoes in brown. His left hand beat a tattoo on the arm of the chair as he waited impatiently for me to say my piece. If he was surprised at my request for an audience in Nishant's room he did not say so. I looked at the suave picture he cut and felt a rising anger in me that I didn't try to curb. The sight of SP, who had never worked in his life and spent entire days grooming himself, had always irritated me. But there was no denying that, with his impeccable clothes and manners, he was one handsome bastard, if a totally unemotional one.

Well, I wasn't about to shed tears over him when I knew that he shed no tears over either me or Nishant. As long as he had Radhika and his air-hostesses and his sacks of money he wasn't bothered about anything or anyone else. 'SP,' I said, taking the direct route, 'I want a divorce.'

He looked at me calmly. 'Why?'

'What do you mean *why*? You know *why*, because nothing is working out.'

'Things haven't been working out around here for a long time. Why do you need a divorce now?' There was nothing in SP's face except polite interest.

'I need a divorce because I am shifting to Majhauli and I am starting my own distillery and liquor business, besides looking after sugar, of course. I need money.'

'So are you divorcing me because there is no real marriage left or because you need the money, or' – SP paused, pursed his lips and sneered – 'because you have found a new love interest?'

'It could be one or all these reasons,' I said shortly.

'So I was right. It is a new boyfriend and money. And Kulbhushan? What does he have to say to all this?'

'Kulbhushan no longer comes for work. He carves. He gets wooden blocks, teak, mahagony, Burma teak, white wood from Canada and I don't know what else.'

'But why?' SP looked bewildered.

'He says he has found his vocation,' I stated matter-of-factly.

'You don't seem too worried.'

'Of course I am worried,' I snapped. 'Hariyali and Majhauli need me. I saved the mill! I, not Papa, and not Kulbhushan. It's now up to me to continue the family business!'

'Of course,' SP murmured and stood up. He stared at Nishant whose arms and legs had been neatly arranged on the bed. Had it not been for the grotesque angle of his head he would have looked normal. A shadow of distaste crossed SP's face as he abruptly turned away and walked to the window. 'Who's the boyfriend, Nagina?'

'There isn't any,' I said shortly.

The silence between us grew. I stared at my lovely child, my Nishant who was supposed to have ended the darkness between us and bring light and happiness into my marriage. Things never happen the way you want, do they? The trick is to accept what happens and make the most of it. Like Baba said, if you live in a flood, don't fight the current, go with the flow. I came out of my trance at the sound of the bedroom door opening. 'Where are you going?' I stared at SP with antagonism.

'Out, for dinner.' He stood with his back to me, caught in the act of leaving the room.

'But I told you I wanted a divorce and a settlement.'

SP made no reply and stepped out of the room.

'Stop!' I screamed.

He stopped and turned to look at me with raised eyebrows.

'I hate it when you leave things unfinished. Stay here, damm you, and talk to me.'

'There's nothing to say. You want a divorce, you want a divorce. Full stop.'

'It's not a full stop. I want a settlement too. And I want a big settlement. I'm not going to give you your freedom so easily!'

'I don't remember asking for any freedom.'

'No, you wouldn't. Why would you? You do no work, take no responsibility. You spend your days beautifying yourself and you spend your nights whoring. You are not a family man and I have put up with this lifestyle of yours for far too long. In fact, I've taken enough shit from you and I'm not prepared to do it anymore. I'm going to take my son and leave and live my life on my own terms now.'

'Good for you,' said SP and closed the door on my face.

'You bastard!' I screamed picking up my shoe and throwing it at the door in fury. 'Come back and finish this quarrel!' I was in a towering rage and strode after him into his bedroom. 'Don't you leave me like this! I am not your bloody servant, I am your wife and I want to be treated with dignity.'

'Leave, Nagina,' said SP 'I have things to do.'

'What things do you have to do, SP? Haan? Haan? Manicure your nails and pedicure your toes? Wax your non-existent chest hair? Weave your hair piece? Or is it that you have to select your condom for the night? Ribbed or scented? Pink or purple?'

'You disgust me.'

'I disgust you? I?' I physically launched myself at him, ready to gouge out his eyes. We got into a very undignified brawl that ended in one of the few satisfying bouts of sex that SP and I had ever had. When I finally left him I made it very clear that the question of the settlement was not yet settled and as far as I was concerned the figure would not go below ten crores. And I left him to chew on that.

I got the divorce and I got the settlement and I shifted into Dhai Din Ka Dera with Nishant and my servants. Apart from ten crores I also got a house in Jor Bagh in a nice quiet lane which I made my base in Delhi. I called Anmol from there, told him I needed him back immediately, and he came without asking any questions, without a word of disapproval from his chastened wife.

Back in Majhauli, Papa became chairman of Somras, I was the managing director and Anmol was my manager. Kulbhushan had by now stopped coming to office entirely. Papa and Mummy watched his growing withdrawal in horror while I restrained myself from saying I told you so. Mummy was so traumatized by

Kulbhushan's seclusion and apathy that she didn't even comment on Anmol's return into my life and work.

The distillery in Majhauli was big and modern and had a licence to manufacture desi liquor, IMFL as well as beer. Anmol kept asking me how I had managed the licences. Apparently, the government had stopped giving licences for the manufacture of potable liquor. Well, he didn't know the Rai Sahabs as well as he thought he did and he certainly had a lot to learn about me. I not only got the licence, but Somras Distilleries and Breweries Pvt. Ltd had the capacity to produce thirty thousand kilolitres of rectified spirit of ninety-six per cent purity per day! But I was not happy. The distillery was under-utilized. Not only was the manufacture of rectified spirit nowhere near thirty thousand kilolitres per day, but of the quantity of rectified spirit manufactured, as much as thirty to forty per cent was being sold as industrial alcohol. As for the rest, it was being sold to small districts for manufacture of country liquor by local manufacturers. The liquor contractors of these districts bought my pure alcohol, mixed and blended it to their taste, then pouched and sold it under their own label. I didn't understand it. Actually I did understand it and I was furious because the profits that should rightfully have been mine went into the pockets of these oily guys. These fellows took tons of my pure, good, undiluted liquor at a fixed rate, added water, caramel and colour to it, and converted one kilolitre of pure alcohol into three kilolitres of potable country liquor. They made crores of rupees, the bastards! As if that was not enough, the government exercised no control over the retail price of country liquor pouches. And so my brand new spanking distillery was losing money. I couldn't bear to watch the trucks of industrial alcohol and trucks of pure alcohol leave the premises daily and hated the sight of the near empty stills and vats of an under-utilized distillery.

I stood at the window of the office staring alternately at the monstrous round containers of molasses and at the line of tankers moving out of the mill. I had wanted to set up a distillery and I had set it up, but what had I achieved? Instead of trucks of molasses, trucks of rectified spirit left the factory. My profits remained low and the vats stood empty. It was all the fault of that wretched Dippy Singh, the so-called expert liquor manufacturer.

Dippy Singh had been to UK to study different ways of aging, mixing and packaging liquor and I was paying him a packet to come up with something new for me to market and sell. But all Dippy was doing was dipping into my till while the stills remained half empty.

'What's the matter, Nagina?' Anmol asked, staring at me with his moonstruck expression. The burn scars on his face and hands had healed into ugly lueucodermal patches.

'It's that idiot, Dippy Singh! He's supposed to be the best liquor guy in UP and England and wherever and he can't come up with anything!' I was so frustrated I felt like breaking something. 'He was supposed to come up with a new concoction better than anything else in the market. But he has come up with nothing, nothing!'

'He's trying.'

'What trying? He's doing shit all! What has he come up with? Just a mishmash of what was already there. That's crap. I want something new, a new colour, a new flavour, a new name, something sensational! I want a new desi liquor, something that hasn't been tried before. Something that people will try and say, ah this is good, this has been made by Somras.'

'You chose the wrong man.'

I felt like throwing the heavy paperweight in my hand at Anmol who stood with his arms crossed, a smug expression on his face. 'What do you mean wrong man? I chose the best. He's the only guy who's been educated in the liquor business. Nobody else has a professional on their rolls. Perhaps you know of a better person,' I smiled sarcastically at him.

'Actually I do,' Anmol uncrossed his arms and grinned back. 'Of course, I'll do much better if I am paid better... and I don't mean in money.'

His ravaged body and his stupid sexual innuendo was getting on my nerves. 'What can you do? Can you create a new liquor?'

'No, but I know someone who can.'

I stared at him. 'What do you mean?'

'I know Nagaraj Rao the liquor baron. I helped him get a licence once. I'm sure he knows someone who can help us.'

'Anmol,' I looked warningly at him. 'I hope you are not making a fool of me.'

'Nope.'

'Do you think he can help with a formula? A formula for desi liquor?'

'Yup.'

'Okay, then, let's talk to the guy.'

Anmol called Nagaraj Rao and the rest, as they say, is history. Not only did he have a new formula but it was good and very simple too. He had a new flavour: sort of pineapply and smelling of pines. It masked the strong alcohol smell and attracted the drinkers. The colour was a very attractive pale gold. I loved it and decided that since Majhauli was in the foothills of the Himalayas something that smelled of the conifers would be liked by the people. Dippy Singh loved it too and with the candour of the very young shrugged off his own failure. He adopted the Andhraite's formula whole-heartedly and got to work refining it. When we were totally satisfied that one could not improve it further we decided to manufacture it and test it on our own workers. The workers loved it and like Oliver, asked for more. Anmol wasn't convinced though and said who wouldn't love free liquor and suggested that before we marketed it we should test it further. Dippy was told to take it to a neighbouring district and sell it through a few liquor vendors. He was to dress locally and gauge the reaction of the drinkers. I was so impatient that I went along every time we introduced it to a drinking shack and sat in the car and counted the number of people who bought it. It seemed to me that everyone and their uncle loved it. I was convinced it was a winner and I couldn't wait to launch it.

Production speeded up and there came the day when it was time to launch my new liquor and we debated who should do the honours. I decided who better than our tried and tested friend, Imtiaz Khan, the MLA. I hate to dilly-dally when I have taken a decision and immediately contacted him. Imtiaz Khan, his bristling beard shining and black as ever agreed to do the honours for a gently persuasive fee of five lakh rupees.

It was on a cold blustery day – more than a year after Imtiaz Khan, Somu and the others had led the strike against Hukam Singh Mills, that the new liquor was launched. Ice-cold winds blew down from the Himalayan foothills. The sky was blue and clear of the tiniest speck of cloud, and the sunshine was brilliant. Imtiaz Khan and Papa did the honours while I stood in the wings and watched. I had done it. My hard work had paid off. The desi liquor which I manufactured tasted different, looked different and was even packaged differently. It didn't look like any of the other liquor pouches of the area. The colour of the liquor was golden and the colour of the pouch a pale copper with writing in black. It shone in the sunlight and it danced tantalizingly on the palate and it was an instant success.

I called it Rasila.

Two things happened after the launch of Rasila. One of course was the phenomenal success of and demand for Rasila. Everyone loved it and everyone wanted it. The demand for Rasila rose and we began to step up the manufacture of it. The second thing that happened was the result of the first. The success and increasing demand for Rasila meant that I needed my own liquor contractor or supplier, someone with a large number of drinking outlets so that he could pick up my stock on a daily basis and leave me free from marketing hassles. I also needed a liquor contractor big and influential enough to handle the opposition that had started to come from manufacturers of hitherto successful brands of desi liquor. While I checked on this, success brought another problem. Almost overnight I began to get nasty feedback and hate mails from everyone. Liquor and sugar manufacturers were beginning to hate my guts. Not only was I a woman, I was successfully running the sugar mill and I had hurled myself into the liquor business without so much as a by-your-leave. The priority was identifying the right liquor contractor and ensuring that production did not slag.

The problem of manufacture I handed over to Anmol. He had become somewhat surly of late, quite unhappy with the fact that I didn't get to spend much time with him. I figured the challenge of running the distillery efficiently would occupy him. He didn't really have the brain or the vision to think ahead, to scheme, to plan, to plot. Anyway I needed him to follow instructions and do what I asked. I could do the thinking, thank you very much.

'We have crossed fifty thousand pouches today,' said Anmol.

We sat in the huge living room of Dhai Din Ka Dera. It was raining outside and so cold that I had asked the servants to light a fire. I sat on by the fire, a balloon glass of brandy on the table beside me. Anmol sat sprawled on the opposite couch wearing a huge Pakistani salwar-kameez. For some reason he loved this parachute-like dress with the massive legs and the shirt reaching down to six inches below his knees. I swear it took nine metres of cloth to make.

Nishant lolled contentedly on the carpet in front of the fire surrounded by all kinds of toys with twinkling lights and clanging sounds. Occasionally a few guttural sounds escaped his throat, sounds that I knew indicated laughter and happiness. Nishant was happy in Majhauli. I had stopped keeping him under wraps and introduced the world to him. I got his attendant to wheel him around the factory and the workers' colony every day. He seemed to like watching the kids playing cricket and marbles and catch. I looked at his fingers as they moved as though trying to catch the rotating wings of the helicopter with alternating red and blue lights. 'He looks happy, doesn't he?'

Talking about Nishant or looking at him always made Anmol uncomfortable. He didn't know how to deal with him. 'Who?' Anmol looked fleetingly at Nishant and said nothing.

'Did you know that the production of Rasila is going up? Soon we will reach our target figure of one lakh. But the pouches are not moving, only the stock is piling up,' I said.

'Nagina, everybody loves Rasila. In fact, if you had not introduced me to Scotch whisky I would be drinking it myself,' Anmol held up his glass in salute and winked at me.

'Well, if everybody loves Rasila why isn't the stock moving?'

'Should start moving soon, I guess,' said Anmol spreading his long legs out and crossing his fingers over his protruding stomach. The plate on the floor near him was littered with chicken bones. No matter what the day of the week Anmol needed his tandoori chicken and butter naan. He picked his teeth with the nail of his little finger.

'Don't do that!'

'What?' Anmol looked at me uncomprehendingly.

Anmol had always been a big guy but now he looked like a lala fast going to seed. His burnt face had coarsened and bloated, hiding his biggest asset, his bronze eyes. 'Anmol, if the stock is not moving at least you should try to understand why it's not moving.' I was getting really frustrated. 'Nathu,' I yelled. 'Come and take Nishant Baba away and put him to sleep! Nobody does anything on their own around here. Everyone needs somebody to give them instructions.'

Anmol patted his thigh: 'Let me give you some instructions on how to make me happy, come to me, baby!'

I looked at his huge head and fast disappearing neck and exploded in anger. I called him a dehati, a gigolo, a duffer, a slow top, a fool. I said he had no brain in his head only an endless supply of semen which was why he could think of nothing but sex. Well, life was more than a hard-on and when was he going to realize that? If he spent his entire time just romping in bed then Somras would soon go down the drain. Then I said I wonder what had made me bring him to Majhauli when his sole qualification was a voracious appetite for sex, food and drink in that order. I could have got myself a gigolo for the first purpose and saved myself a great deal of trouble and expense!

Anmol did not move an inch. He sat quietly, sprawled on the sofa, his legs spread out in front of him. The glass of whisky was still balanced on his bulging stomach, and moved up and down with each breath he took. Only his eyes, those deep bronze-coloured eyes looked wounded. 'I didn't mean it, Anmol, honestly, I didn't. It's just that I desperately want Rasila to succeed and Somras to succeed and become big. You see, this is my idea, my venture. Somras has to be big. Rai Sahab Incorporated has to be big.' I took a deep breath and steadied myself. 'Actually what has been troubling me all day is that I've learned that the other liquor manufacturers have decided to form a cartel against me and that they are going to prevent the contractors from picking up Rasila. They are going to reduce the prices of their liquor so that Rasila is more expensive. People won't buy it and contractors won't lift Rasila. They will kill Rasila!'

'Who's doing this?'

'Shakil and Sons. The biggest liquor manufacturers in north India.'

'Where did you hear this?' asked Anmol. 'I haven't heard any such thing.'

'You would have if you had your ear to the ground, Anmol. That's what I mean when I say that you are not paying attention to your work. You are not involved in Rasila with your heart and soul. I think you worked harder for sugar.'

'That's not fair, Nagina. I left my work, my wife, my kids and I came for you because I love you.'

'Yes, you came and yes, you love me. But you don't love liquor the way you love sugar. You have to be totally involved with the business of liquor, a part of everything. You must know what sells and what does not, who's ahead and who's behind, who's planning what, who's going to undercut you and who's going to outbid you. Liquor is not simple business. It's a job for goondas and dons. By now you should have created an army of your own goons and spies.' I looked at him in exasperation. 'Instead I am having to do all the thinking and running around.'

'Army of goondas?'

'Yes, an army of goondas, Anmol. It's not enough to manufacture liquor, you have to sell it and you have to take care of the opposition.'

'You should never have come into liquor, Nagina. It's a bad business. Sugar is cleaner.'

'No business is clean, Anmol, you should know that by now. God, I don't understand how you continue to remain this, this teddy bear kind of person, totally unaware of the real world. It's not enough to create Rasila. We have to make it succeed.'

'It will succeed, Nagina, just relax. Why can't you think of anything else? You can think of nothing but Rasila. We are together, sharing a meal as a family, and we should enjoy our time together.'

'We could never be family,' I whispered looking at him in anger and despair.

'What?'

'Nothing. Let's eat.'

'You know, for someone who eats so little you are putting on weight. If you have to become fat you might as well eat. What do you say?'

I turned and left the room without answering. There was a reason why I was becoming fat. I was pregnant. That it was a boy and normal I had already confirmed on my last visit to Delhi. It was the most wonderful news I had received in a long time. Even though the baby was Anmol's I would tell the world it was SP's . All I wanted now was for Rasila to get going so that I could announce my pregnancy to the world and enjoy impending motherhood provided, of course, that Anmol would stop driving me crazy. I had not told him about the pregnancy and I had no intention of letting him know he was the father. I had a feeling he wouldn't be able to cope with the news.

I got into bed and lay in the warmed room hugging a cushion to my chest. The rain continued to drum outside and I could see rivulets streaming down the window pane. There is something about rain in the winter that makes you appreciate the comforts of home and hearth. I thought of the baby in my womb and how my planning and scheming had worked. Even SP could not deny the baby was his because of our last encounter. In fact, I was toying with the idea of getting more money out of him for the child's education! And Papa would finally get the heir to his millions that he so dearly craved. My new son would be Rai Sahab. But first I had to find a solution to the cartel problem. And I had to find the man who would defy the cartel and take on Shakil on the one hand and sell Rasila on the other.

Papa became president of ISMA, the Indian Sugar Mills Association and the ceremony of passing on the baton took place at the Taj Mahal Hotel on Man Singh Road in Delhi. Everyone went to see Papa's moment of glory. Mummy, Kulbhushan, Anmol and I and the senior management of Hukam Singh Mills. I was dressed to kill in a long black skirt, black patent leather shoes and a black and gold halter neck blouse that left my shoulders exposed.

I knew that the women in the room hated my looks and the men couldn't take their eyes off me.

The union minister for food and civil supplies was the chief guest along with the chief minister of Uttar Pradesh, who had come especially for Papa. A phalanx of secretaries and joint secretaries and, god knows who else, crawled out of the woodwork of Krishi Bhavan to partake of the free drinks and food. Why is it that all bureaucrats wear white shirts and white bush shirts and horrendous sweaters knitted by their wives and mothers? Not one of them shows any style. And they clutch at food as though they'll never get it again. I have no qualms in saying that all bureaucrats are freeloaders and parasites. I hate them.

'Hello. You are Nagina Singh, are you not?'

'Yes,' I shook the proffered hand.

'I'm Priyadarshan Singh.' I looked at the tall thin figure in a denim shirt. He had an untidy white-streaked beard and long hair which he had tied in a ponytail. Who was the guy? 'I'm the cane commissioner of UP. Congratulations on your father's success. It's a deserved one.' Well, well a bureaucrat with a difference. He smiled widely at me. Another mark to him, I thought. According to Anmol, bureaucrats never smile; they look like constipated old files. This one didn't look like an old file, he looked the NGO type.

'Thank you,' I smiled.

'Can I get you a drink?'

'What are you drinking?'

'I am a whisky man.'

'Okay, red wine for me.'

'Stay right here. I'll be back in thirty seconds.'

He was back in probably less time. He handed me a brimming glass. 'Cheers! Sorry for the overflowing glass. I am only saving myself the bother of having to run for seconds. The service is notoriously poor in this place, don't you think?'

'Are you an IAS officer?' I asked watching him light an expensive cigarette.

'Yes, salt of the earth and a rod in the steel frame. I am a blue-blooded bureaucrat.'

'Blue-blooded?' I stared at him a bit stupidly.

'I am what was called royalty in the olden days.'

'Oh, you mean one of those thakur types,' I said finding my tongue. 'The sort who leave their own wives at home and devour other men's wives?'

He threw back his head and laughed loudly. I noticed a number of people looking at us. In a room full of rich and powerful sugar barons this bohemian cane commissioner – whom everyone present in the room was trying to court – was spending time with me. The situation was bound to lead to some heartburn.

The speeches began and I left Priyadarshan Singh to sit at the high table with my family and the family of last year's president. It was a wonderful moment and I glowed with happiness at Papa's triumph. Papa looked very distinguished in his white bandgala and white trousers.

'That was well done, wasn't it?' It was the ubiquitous cane commissioner back by my side as soon as the ceremony was over.

'Do you dress like this in office too? And why do you have a ponytail?'

'I dress to please myself. And I think I look handsome in a ponytail.'

'You look like a bureaucrat posing as a poet.'

'My dear Gina – can I call you Gina?– Nagina sounds like a courtesan's name. My dear Gina, I am both a poet and bureaucrat. I don't need to pose as either.' He laughed again. 'And incidentally that dig about wives was not fair. I have no wife to leave behind.'

I was furious at the temerity of the man. He dared to call me, Nagina Singh Aggarwal, one of the wealthiest and most powerful women in Delhi, a courtesan! It was too much. I turned upon him in fury, my shoulders heaving and the light of battle glittering in my eyes. 'You look magnificent when you're angry,' he whispered, holding my arm tightly as though he feared I might slap him.

My breath was coming fast but I didn't pull away. I was glad I had dressed with care for the evening. CC's interest in me had been registered by many. The sugar barons, already wary of my growing influence and my fast growing distillery were watching us in apprehension. I caught Shakil – the largest liquor manufacturer in UP and the prime mover behind the cartel that had formed against me – staring at the both of us. I smiled at him. The glimmer of an idea had come to me.

I turned and gave CC a brilliant smile even as I flicked my long mane of hair back over my shoulder in a gesture calculated to draw attention to its length and lustre. 'The wine is beginning to pall, don't you think? And the company is beginning to bore me. What do you say to going to Ghungroo? The champagne there is genuine and guaranteed not to give you a headache,' I said referring to a hip and happening nightclub.

CC looked at me speculatively. 'I can't agree more but there are two things. One, I can leave only after the chief minister leaves and two, I can't afford five-star hotels. I can only take you to *Kake da Dhaba*.'

Laughter exploded from my throat. 'I'll sell my diamond anklet and buy you dinner!' I said loudly. We left together in full view of everyone except the chief minister, who had already left in my car.

Papa and I met in the round room of Hariyali. By now it was clear what Shakil was doing. He, being the biggest liquor manufacturer in UP, had the monopoly of liquor all over the state but in the west he was virtual king. Most of the other manufacturers sold in the south and in Madhya Pradesh and Orissa. They did not stray into his turf. And now that I had started to sell Rasila in the districts of the west he didn't like it and was doing everything to keep me out of the area. He got both the liquor manufacturers and contractors to form a cartel against me. He pressurized the liquor contractors to pick up all the desi liquor in the region except Rasila. The pricing was such that everyone else was selling liquor cheaper than we were. So the stocks of Rasila began to pile up and the movement of trucks outside Somras came to a virtual standstill. Sugar cane entered and sugar left, but liquor remained where it was. Anmol, the idiot, had stepped up the production of Rasila and in no time the godowns were overflowing. If Rasila did not start moving soon I would have to stop production.

'What did Priyadarshan Singh have to say?' asked Papa without beating around the bush.

I sat on the elaborate carved jhoola with my legs in track pants folded under me and a strong cup of coffee in my hands. I looked straight at Papa.Our relationship had changed. Papa no longer asked me what I was doing with Anmol or how I'd got the information out of Priyadarshan Singh. We were equals now.

'I've learned the way to tackle this problem, Papa. I'll handle CC, you handle the chief minister.'

'CC?'

'The cane commissioner, your Priyadarshan Singh, the guy with the ponytail.'

'What is the way to tackle the problem?'

'It is clear that Shakil is preventing anyone from lifting Rasila. He is too big, too ruthless and too organized to be defied. Small contractors are afraid of him.'

'Hmmm.'

'CC suggested we get the state government to change its liquor policy. Instead of the present policy where bidding is done by contractors or suppliers district-wise, we must ask the chief minister to auction area-wise. We should then bid for western UP and become both the manufacturers and suppliers of the area. That way we keep everyone out of the region, including Shakil.'

'It's a good idea but you will make an enemy of Shakil and he will fight hard and dirty.'

'I know,' I drained my coffee cup. 'He already hates my guts. If I get the policy changed, he will probably have me murdered!' I laughed uneasily.

'It also means that you will have to keep an army of goons to keep Shakil and company outside the area. Otherwise, Shakil will capture the liquor shacks and the kalaris and ensure that they don't sell Rasila. That way Rasila still doesn't get sold and other people's liquor, that has been illegally smuggled into the district, gets sold. So you need the chief minister and Priyadarshan Singh to manage the policy change, then you need to outbid everyone else in the auction and you need to either be your own supplier, or ensure that the supplier/contractor is your man.'

'You mean become a liquor supplier?'

'Well, Shakil is his own supplier in many districts. But I think it would be better if you found someone good and dependable. And one last thing – you need your own army of goons. You cannot survive in liquor without it. It's a dirty, highly competitive business.' Papa echoed Anmol's sentiments. 'But I am convinced you can do it. You have the two essential qualities: brains and ruthlessness.'

'Yes, Papa.' I was content.

'So? What do you propose? What is your role and what is mine?'

'I propose you buy the chief minister and I buy CC. This is Plan A which culminates in our getting the liquor policy changed and ensuring that in the auction we invite the bid for the western region. Simultaneously we work on Plan B, which is identifying the right supplier and getting him on our side. Plan C is creating and managing our own army of goons.'

'Success will depend on Plan B, that is identifying the right supplier.'

'Not on Plan A?'

'I have a feeling we can manage Plan A too. This is a greedy chief minister. Also the main protagonists of Plan A will be you and me. We will do it.' Papa got up and stared out of the window. 'I have been thinking about the supplier and the more I think the same name comes up – Sita Ram Jat. He is the liquor contractor for Meerut, Muzaffarnagar and Bulandshahar. He also covers Ghaziabad and Dehradun through tie-ups and associates. And yes, Saharanpur too. We are already there in Bijnore. To begin with that's a very respectable area, don't you think? Once Rasila gets established here it will be much easier to move it further inland.'

'Isn't Sita Ram Jat the fellow who dresses in white and wears hundreds of gold chains?'

'Yes.'

'I don't like Sita Ram Jat. He's a very oily character,' I declared petulantly.

Papa smiled indulgently. 'He is an oily character all right and he's not even a Jat. He is actually a refugee who came from Pakistan during Partition. He doesn't drink or smoke and tries to cultivate the image of a god-fearing man who lavishly supports all public religious functions like Durga Puja, Ramleela, Janamashtmi and what have you. But he is actually the cleverest, shrewdest, most ruthless don in the area.'

'Sounds like a pleasant man,' I commented.

'He's into everything – liquor, drugs, prostitution, extortion, kidnapping. He can use the knife, gun and lathi with equal dexterity. But my informers tell me that now he's interested in turning respectable. He only wants to deal in liquor and money-lending.'

'Hmmm.'

'He is, or was, Shakil's man. But now they have fallen out and Sita Ram Jat hates Shakil and has vowed to finish him. He will work with anyone who is against Shakil.'

'Okay, I'll send Anmol to contact him,' I said.

'No, not Anmol,' said Papa emphatically. 'Do this yourself.'

'But...'

'Beta, remember one thing, your employees should not know what you are thinking or doing. Play your cards close to your chest. Use different people for different jobs and keep everyone guessing. Like you did to end the strike in the mill. That was a master stroke.'

'But, Anmol...'

'Anmol is good and loyal but he lacks initiative and he lacks drive. He will always follow, never lead. He cannot take decisions.'

I wondered for a moment whether I should tell Papa that I was pregnant but kept quiet. It was early days yet and this was not the best time.

'I don't think Anmol is suited to build the army of gooms either, Papa,' I said reflectively. 'He is a bit of a simpleton.'

'No, he is definitely not suitable. For that Ras Bihari is best.'

'Ras Bihari is in Dubai. After Amar Nath hinted at his involvement on the night of the explosion, I had to send him away.'

'Bring him back. He is clever and aggressive and he knows the area and the people. And he is a fugitive, dependent on you. He will be loyal to you and will always fear you because you can get him arrested.'

I looked at Papa with new respect. He was right, I had to be clever. In business there was no place for sentiment. And in all this Anmol was of no use. He was way too trusting. I had to manage everything, like I had managed the strike. I thought about it and wondered what Anmol would say if he knew I had caused the explosion in the factory? How would he react to the fact that I had been able to buy off Ras Bihari, that Ras Bihari planted the bomb that almost killed Anmol under my instructions? Well, the less Anmol knew the better for him. It was better too if he never found out that the baby I carried was his. He would strut around like a proud peacock and tell everyone. Or it could be worse. His conscience might plague him and push him to do the right thing and marry me. God forbid!

'What are you thinking?' Papa asked.

'Nothing,' I smiled grimly. 'Just how to get Ras Bihari back and use him.'

'You will work it out, I know. I have faith in you.'

I looked out of the window at the gardens of Hariyali. They were in full bloom and the lawns were lush, green and rolling just like the English downs. I lived in Dhai Din Ka Dera with Nishant but I had breakfast with Papa every day. That was our time together. We discussed the day's work and I took advice from him about problems. Mummy had tried to come to these meetings and take charge but Papa had told her not to.

'Changing the liquor policy is going to cost us a packet,' I mused. 'How much do you think the CM and CC will want?'

'I was thinking about that. Shakil is a very clever guy. He would have understood what we are planning. You see, he too would have done the same if he were in our place. So he too will try to reach the CM. He may have already done so. In fact he may have already given the CM money.' Papa stared unseeingly at me.

'But why would Shakil give the CM money?' I was bewildered. 'He's not interested in changing the liquor policy. The present policy suits him.'

'To prevent the liquor policy being changed, what else?' Papa said impatiently.

'Oh,' I digested that.

'I know just the person to give me this information,' Papa said and smiled diabolically. I hadn't seen him smile like that in a long time. First the agitation and then Kulbhushan's condition had almost broken his spirit. 'For a long time now I have been nursing a mole in the chief minister's office. It's payback time for him now. I will get the information about Shakil, the liquor policy, everything –'

I interrupted him happily, 'Meanwhile, I will contact CC and Sita Ram Jat in Lucknow and I will arrange to bring Ras Bihari back from Dubai.'

'Right. And don't discuss your plans with Anmol. You shouldn't need to.'

As it happened, I didn't need CC to reach Sita Ram Jat. No sooner had I reached the mill's palatial guest house in Lucknow I received a phone call from someone who called himself Munshiji and said that Sita Ram Jat was on his way to meet me. Before I could protest that it was ten in the night and I was dog tired, he had hung up. Angrily, I put off changing my clothes and sat down to wait. The cheek of the man! Had nobody told him that he couldn't call on a lady alone at ten in the night, least of all in backward Lucknow? Ten became eleven thirty and I was at bursting point when the bearer came in and said Munshiji had come to see me. Munshiji? I thought the Jat guy was to come.

'Namaste, Madamji,' said a voice behind me and I whirled around to face a tall, fat, imposing guy clothed from head to toe in pristine white. A tiny weasel-like character followed him and immediately ran to the windows to draw the curtains and shut and latch the door.

'What the hell…?' I was so startled by the sudden intrusion that my heart began to thud.

'It's okay, Madamji, we must take all precautions. I am Sita Ram Jat.' He sat down uninvited and did not introduce the weasel-like character who came and sat on the floor at his feet. I stared at the strange pair in astonishment and a little fear.

'Why have you locked the doors and windows?' I squeaked.

'We don't want the entire sugar and liquor world to know that we are meeting,' he smiled at me. I disliked him even more on sight than I did by reputation. He wore at least three thick gold chains around his neck and solid bracelets on his wrists, not to mention several flashy rings on all his fingers.

'If this is a secret meeting why is he here?' I pointed to the guy on the floor.

'Oh, Munshiji, ignore him.'

I stared at him, beginning to feel more than a little intimidated. I was in my own guest house and had at least three servants hovering outside. To gain time I got up and went to the cabinet to get a drink. I had stopped drinking now that I was pregnant but I really needed the brandy. Sita Ram Jat refused a drink saying he was a teetotaler, the sanctimonious bastard. I took a huge gulp of the brandy, almost choked on it, and sat down with a red face and increased nervousness. Sita Ram bloody Jat had caught me on the wrong foot on my own turf. And that was not all. When he began to speak I grew smaller and smaller as he deftly revealed every aspect of what I thought was *my* game plan.

'Madamji, I know that you and Rai Sahab are trying to get the liquor policy changed. That's a very good move. Let me also tell you that you will succeed in this move of yours. The CM feels that if an area-wise auction takes place there is less maara-maari among the liquor manufacturers and suppliers. But Shakil doesn't know this. He thinks the CM is on his side. But this crafty CM is on no one's side. He will take money from both Shakil and you and do what I tell him.'

'And what will you tell him to do?' I stared at him, bristling at his arrogance.

'I will tell him to change the liquor policy and arrange the auction area-wise. And further, I will help you to win the bid for the western region and I will sell Rasila and make it the most popular brand in UP.'

'Presuming you can do that…' I began.

'What do you mean presuming I can do that? Of course I can do that.'

'The question is, why would you do it?'

'I have my reasons.'

I digested this as I sipped my brandy. Was this man to be trusted? Would he do what he said he would do? And what were his reasons? While I ruminated over his motivations he sat calmly like Buddha, allowing me to study him, making no move to explain himself. Munshiji sat so quietly on the floor he had become part of the furniture. I got up to refill my glass reminding myself mentally that I shouldn't be drinking. Ten minutes passed while I debated what to do.

'Madamji,' Sita Ram Jat whispered suddenly so close to me that I jumped. He had got up and now stood behind me. 'You and I have a common enemy, Shakil Miyan. There is no better bond for friendship than a common enemy.' Having delivered this master statement he went and sat down again. We stared at one another while Munshiji stared at Sita Ram Jat's feet. Another five minutes went by while I absorbed what he had said.

Then Sita Ram, the fraud Jat, spoke again. 'I can lift twenty thousand kilolitres of Rasila or one lakh pouches per day. You have to do nothing. Just manufacture and pouch, I will lift your stock, pay the excise and sell the liquor. Together we will wipe out Shakil from this area. Isn't that what you want?'

'Yes,' I said immediately.

'Good. Now that the basics are clear, all we have to do is decide on the price to be paid for Rasila.'

'Now?' I squeaked. Things were going too fast for me. I wasn't exactly prepared to negotiate the price of Rasila, and certainly not at this time of the night when I was alone and without advisers. I looked at my watch. It was well past midnight. Was this man insane?

'Now is as good a time as any other. Besides it would be good if we did not meet too often. After today we will communicate only through Munshiji and whomever you appoint as your representative.'

'Give me a few minutes, I'll be back. Meanwhile what will you have to drink?' I was buying time.

'Tea. Hot, strong and very sweet tea in a tall glass please.'

I escaped from the room. Telling the bearer to send in tea and whatever else he could rustle up I made one quick call to Papa who was in Delhi and another to Anmol in Majhauli. After consulting them I came back into the room and took some time to collect my thoughts as we ate sandwiches and finger chips with our tea.

Then, as Sita Ram Jat bit into a kachori I spoke: 'My price is sixteen rupees a pouch,' I announced. My cost of manufacture of one pouch of two hundred millilitres of Rasila was ten rupees and I knew that the retail price of Rasila in the kalaris was sixteen or eighteen rupees so I started at the top. Sita Ram Jat laughed so hard that he dropped his plate and broke it. We finally settled at twelve rupees and fifty paise. We drank more tea on that note and Munshiji also consented to a glass of tea and a laddoo.

'You just ensure an uninterrupted supply of Rasila and I will make Rasila the queen of Uttar Pradesh. No one will trouble you, Madamji, not the excise people, not the police, no one.'

'You could have given me a better price. I think you have treated me like a helpless woman and taken me for a ride,' I giggled a little. It was the brandy topped with the tea that was making me drunk.

'A woman who is capable of bombing her own factory is more capable than a lot of men I know.' Sita Ram Jat spoke softly. I felt my heart stop before starting to thud again. How did he know? No one knew of this except me, Papa and Ras Bihari, whom we had bought out after Bhanu's death, and who had done the actual planting of the bomb.

'Let Ras Bihari be your representative. He has worked for you before,' said Sita Ram Jat with a mocking smile as he got up to leave.

A deep terror took grip of me.

Papa had told me that Sita Ram Jat was a monster who killed people right and left like other people kill mosquitoes, that he was like a poisonous snake whose touch alone was enough kill you.Well not only had he touched me, he had me totally surrounded and embroiled in his nefarious activities. He was going to be my sole supplier. He could destroy me just by refusing to pick up my stocks. And the biggest horror was that he knew about the bomb and Ras Bihari. He had me in the small of his palm and could crush me like an insect. Forget Ras Bihari going to jail, I could go to jail if it became known that I had paid Ras Bihari five lakhs to sabotage my own factory and the strike. It was I who had got him his passport and sent him to Dubai. I was truly frightened. I opened my bag and took two Calmposes quickly and then had another panic attack. What was I doing? Here I was, close to three months pregnant, drinking brandy and popping pills all in the course of one evening. When I could no longer handle the tension I phoned Papa.

'Don't panic, Nagina. I would take this whole encounter as a victory. We have won a major ally and if he knows about your weakness, so what? I know enough about Sita Ram Jat's activities. I think we are equally balanced.' Papa was sanguine when I blurted out the whole story.

'But what I don't understand is why me? Why has he chosen me to be his ally?'

'It's logical. He's UP's biggest liquor contractor and you are moving towards becoming the biggest manufacturer. Besides, he has an axe to grind with Shakil.'

'What axe?'

'It's some personal insult or injury, I don't know the details. He wants to destroy Shakil. He is using you.'

'But that will make Shakil my enemy,' I protested.

'Yes, it will. It is inevitable and not to be feared. Business battles are not girl fights. You are in the real world now.'

'But…'

'Sita Ram Jat is using you to destroy Shakil, just like you used Anmol and Ras Bihari to destroy Somu and the strike. What was ethical about what you did then? Just think of keeping up your end of the bargain. And get your army and armoury ready. Shakil will use every means to hit back at you. Remember that. He won't give in easily.'

Papa and I succeeded. We got the liquor policy changed, we outbid everyone and got the right to supply only our own desi liquor in ten districts of western UP. I signed a contract with Sita Ram Jat to supply one lakh pouches of Rasila per day. And I smuggled Ras Bihari back to Majhauli with the help of Sita Ram Jat.

*

Somras Distilleries and Breweries went into overdrive mode. I cracked the whip on Anmol's head and drove everyone crazy. From dawn to dusk we worked to bring the production of Rasila to one lakh pouches per day while simultaneously maintaining quality. Everything had to be streamlined and perfect, from the colour, the look and the potency to the packaging and production. I was in the distillery every day with Anmol and the workers, allowing no compromises anywhere. But the one thing I could not control was the drinking in the distillery. We got alcohol of ninety-four per cent purity from the stills and it was from here that the robbery began. When I first learnt of the quantities of liquor actually drunk on the premises I was shocked. Security and checking were strict enough to ensure that alcohol in pouches could not be carried away. But it could be drunk. The workers had their mouths to the still almost all the time! We passed off two per cent of the production as incidental losses and most of it was drunk on the premises! It was a wonder that the workers managed to work at all. No one could hope to drink so much potent liquor and have a life expectancy longer than ten years.

Strangely, Anmol stopped drinking when the heat was on. There was also a marked change in his relationship with me. He resented the fact that I had joined hands with Sita Ram Jat. He had no idea that Ras Bihari was working for me. He would have gone ballistic if he did. Luckily, he virtually stopped coming to Dhai Din Ka Dera. I knew he was disturbed but I really had no time to worry about Anmol's feelings because in whatever spare time I had, I worked clandestinely with Ras Bihari and Sita Ram Jat.

Ras Bihari's job was to map each and every shop and each and every kalari and drinking shack in the ten districts of our area and keep a record of the pouches supplied and consumed there. His job was also to post one or two men in every kalari to ensure that nothing but Rasila was either sold or consumed in the shacks. If anyone so much as mentioned another brand they were beaten up, arms fractured and skulls broken open. Ras Bihari's men combined with Sita Ram Jat's men to keep all other brands away.

Naturally there were clashes, major clashes. Shakil's men tried all kinds of tricks to sneak in their liquor into our area. They beat up the shack owners and the kalari owners. Every day there were pitched battles at different spots where both sides clashed. Country-made guns and knives were used and in a couple of places there were even a few killings. Naturally the police and excise department came down heavily but there was nothing they could do. It was a turf war, a do-or-die situation especially for me and Somras. If I showed fear I would be finished. I kept Anmol totally out of this game and grimly fought on.

'Nagina,' Anmol popped his head through the door and looked at me, a question in his eyes.

'Come in, Anmol,' I sighed. 'What is it now? Supply of packages delayed? Quality issues? Really, Anmol, you should deal with day-to-day problems of production on your own.'

'What's wrong with you, Nagina? I have not said a word and here you have accused, tried and sentenced me! Sometimes you really make me angry.'

'Okay,' I said shortly. 'What is it?'

'There are complaints about Rasila.'

'What nonsense are you talking!'

'The complaints say Rasila is not of thirty-six per cent purity. It is diluted and tastes bad.'

'Impossible,' I snapped.

'That's not all – two men have died and it is said they died after drinking substandard Rasila in Samariya village.'

'You're crazy. They must have drunk some rubbishy hooch! No one can die from drinking Rasila.' I was beginning to get really angry and could feel the blood pounding in my temples. I should get my blood pressure checked, I reminded myself. The stress was not helping my pregnancy. If only Rasila would settle down I would go to Delhi and get all my check-ups done.

'Two people have died, Nagina, and forty others are sick. There will be more dead by the evening. And it's due to Rasila. You forget, no other booze is allowed in the region except ours. We have the contract for the area. There's no way we can escape this one. I am afraid Shakil has really dealt a huge blow this time. I don't know if we can survive.'

'Don't talk rubbish! If you are scared you can run away with your tail between your legs. How dare you even think that Rasila will not survive!' I went on in this vein taking out my anger and frustration on him. But the truth was the clash between Shakil and me was getting worse. Durga Das the district magistrate had telephoned me and warned me that the warring had to stop and that if we did nothing to resolve matters he would be forced to take stronger action. This, translated, meant if we didn't sort out our differences he would recommend suspension, even cancellation, of the licence. He was right. Both Shakil and I were losing people and business. In the last clash three of my trucks had been set on fire and one of the drivers had died of severe burns. Ras Bihari, ever the avenging angel, was dreaming up a suitable reply to this. It would mean more deaths and loss and damage to property and growing insecurity all around. I had listened to the district magistrate but said nothing. I had to do something. Was it time to talk to Shakil? If I initiated the move towards reconciliation I would reveal my fear and would lose the battle. Shakil would say, see this area-wise auction is not working and that the old policy was better and he would prevail upon the CM to reverse his decision. I would lose everything that I had gained. When Anmol told me about the spurious Rasila it was the last straw. But I calmed down a bit and told him to give me all the details. It seemed that the only liquor drunk in the drinking shack was Rasila. The police had recovered and captured both empty and full pouches of Rasila and sent them to the lab for examination. All the recorded evidence seemed to suggest that no other brand of liquor had ever been drunk there since the time Rasila had gained monopoly in the area. This was very serious indeed. If only Papa were there to guide and help me. But he was in the South of France, holidaying with Mummy.

'Somebody filled poisonous stuff into Rasila packets and introduced it into the shacks to discredit Somras.'

'That much is obvious,' I snapped before turning to stare at Anmol. An idea had struck me. 'If this is true then how did they get Rasila pouches? We make our own pouches.' I narrowed my eyes. 'Go to the supply unit and check the stock register to see how many plastic sheets we have and how many pouches we manufactured. I am hundred per cent sure there will be a mismatch.' I stood up. 'I think we have a traitor in our own home. Someone from Somras has helped Shakil. Someone supplied him pouches with Rasila stamped on them. It could not have happened any other way.'

I was right. Fifteen sheets of plastic with Rasila stamped on them were missing. But before I could react to this and take action I had to face another problem. The excise department mounted a raid on our factory, coming down on us full strength, destroying this and sealing that. I had to use all my ingenuity, an overly generous amount of money and my influence with CC to extract Somras out of the mess. But I knew it was only a temporary reprieve.

I called up Papa long distance in France. 'Papa, there is a problem,' I said without bothering to apologize for waking him up. I had not kept the time difference in mind when I called him.

'Tell me,' said Papa promptly. A long minute of silence ticked by as Papa thought over what I told him. 'There is only one thing to do... sabotage Shakil's factory.'

'Sabotage Shakil's factory?' I squeaked.

'Yes. It will take too much time to identify who stole the sheets, and it will take longer to locate where the hooch is being made and pouched. Besides, I don't think he will repeat the trick of packaging hooch in Rasila pouches again so actually there is little point in pressing that line of action except to catch and punish the culprits. I bet you, they will turn out to be people totally unconnected with Shakil. On the other hand, if you target his distillery he will be caught totally unawares, because he will not expect you to go that way. I mean, he will expect you to make an issue about the missing sheets and he will try to mislead you. Pretend to go along. In fact, put Anmol in charge of this investigation and tell him to follow each lead scrupulously and discuss all details within hearing distance of everyone. Ensure that Shakil knows you are falling into his trap. He will lead you a bit of a dance before finally bringing you up to some deserted shack with an antique distilling unit which nobody has used for centuries. As I said, fall for it and tell Anmol to follow every lead and so on. In the meantime, plant a bomb in his distillery. Shakil has a rather respectable old Sikh gentleman as his adviser. He can be easily linked with Punjab terrorism and made the fall guy.'

'Papa!' I could scarcely talk.

'Do it, Nagina! This is your litmus test.' Papa put down the phone without saying goodbye.

I sat for a long time digesting what Papa had said. It was brazen, diabolical and totally unethical. But the more I thought about it the more it made sense. Everyone knew Anmol was my right-hand man. They would expect me to use him and listen to him and follow his advice. And Anmol, poor innocent, would go by every word of mine and end up exactly as Papa said he would – angry and flustered at having been made a fool of. Nothing would be lost except maybe some pride and self-esteem that could easily be salvaged. In the meantime I had to use Ras Bihari to target Shakil!

And so I immediately started an elaborate drama. I called Anmol and the head of purchase and stocks and I threw this major fit and told everyone to find out who was behind the whole mess and warned them that if I did not get results in twenty-four hours I would ensure that heads rolled. I called up CC and made the right noises. I hauled in the excise guys and screamed at them telling them to catch the guys who had made the hooch and asking them to round up the culprits. In short, I made everyone's life hell. Sure enough, in thirty-six hours we had a confession, an FIR and an arrest. It was a junior clerk in my office. I told the SDO that I wanted to be present at the questioning and landed in triumph at the thana with Anmol and sundry other Somras flunkies in tow.

'So this is the criminal,' I thundered at the poor bastard who probably just wanted a new TV for his children and had been bought off for a minor amount. I was right. He confessed that he had given a guy fifteen sheets of plastic for the measley sum of fifteen thousand rupees. But he couldn't or wouldn't name the guy he gave the sheets to. I arranged his bail and sent Anmol to his house with another fifteen thousand rupees to get the name. Another twenty- four hours later I had both the name and the guy to whom the plastic sheets had been given. I gave Anmol permission to use any means to make the man speak and dusted my hands off this matter. Now Anmol would follow the leads while I took care of other things.

It was Friday evening and I was all packed to leave for Delhi early the next morning. Tomorrow was the night, the night when that bastard Shakil's factory, distillery and molasses tanks, would be wired and blown up. Everything of his would be destroyed; everything. It was going to be quite different from the cosmetic bomb I had planted in Hukam Singh Mills. This one would really destroy. Targeting the molasses tanks was my master stroke. The destruction of the molasses tanks would set him back by at least two years. It wouldn't destroy the man because he was too big, but it would be a major setback. By the time he recovered, he would voluntarily be seeking other areas to sell his liquor. Of course the cleverest move was to frame his Sikh manager. I would destroy Shakil while at the same time showing him how to save face. By the end of it Shakil would himself be condemning Karamjit Singh. All it took was the strategic placement of a couple of witnesses and the sending of a letter pointing to Karamjit Singh who, foolishly, had made a few noises against Operation

Blue Star and had stated in the gurdwara that the demand for Khalistan was a justified demand. It was all very innocent and innocuous actually but it could be easily twisted to sound dangerous, especially if linked with the bombing and the clues I was going to plant.

I opened the liquor cabinet and stared at the array of bottles there debating with myself that a little nip of Bailley's coffee liquor did no one any harm and that I really needed to relax tonight. I rang for the bearer and asked him to get me my dinner. I was suddenly starved. I ate a huge helping of a very cheesy lasagne with big chunks of chicken in it. With it I had a salad with vinegar dressing and thick slices of bread dipped in olive oil and covered with shredded mozzarella cheese. As if that was not enough I finished the meal with a huge slice of cheese cake. Who cared about the calories anyway. It was not everyday that one was pregnant and free to eat anything and in any quantity too! When I felt I didn't even have room to breathe, I poured myself another generous helping of Irish crème and relaxed, my hands folded on my stomach.

There was definitely no hiding the fact that I was pregnant. It wouldn't be long before people started asking me when the baby was due. It struck me that I could also use my pregnancy to generate some sympathy for myself as well as declare my innocence. After all you cannot expect a defenceless, pregnant woman to do anything against the law, can you now?

'Madamji?'

I jumped the moment I heard that familiar oily voice. The door had opened silently and Sita Ram Jat stood there hands folded, a smirk on his face, his clothes spotlessly white.

'How did you come in?' I demanded my heart pounding. I started to call to the servants when he stopped me by raising a hand.

'Don't call anyone. Munshiji!' He ordered and Munshiji immediately darted in and drew the curtains across the windows and locked the door while I watched in mounting fear. What was the fellow up to now? I thought he had said we would not meet except through seconds, like dueling partners. 'Sit down, Madamji.'

I backed into the sofa. My legs were wobbly and I was glad to sit down. 'How did you come in?' I repeated.

'Madamji, I came to congratulate you in advance. What you have planned for tomorrow is brilliant, a masterstroke, a strategy worthy of Chanakya. Wah, wah! I salute you.' He clapped twice.

'What do you mean?'

'I am talking about your three-way strategy. Wonderful! Brilliant! Work of the genius that you are.' I had turned pale with fright. 'What an idea. Here, Anmol mounts a raid into a silly non-existent distillery and still, supported by police and district administration. Flashing red lights, wailing sirens and excited Anmol, burning with righteous energy to right a wrong done to Somras. Alas, when they arrive there they find that they have been misled, in fact they have been made a fool of! They come back full of anger and injured pride to you, the malkin, but you are unwell and in Delhi. You are pregnant and have to take care of your health so that the coming baby is healthy.' Sita Ram Jat smiled at me thinly. Gold gleamed in his mouth and around his neck while his eyes remained flat and staring. 'And there, in Bijnore, in Shakil and Sons, four different bombs go off one after the other – boom, boom, boom and boom! There will be fireworks, atishbaazi! Wah, wah! Shakil will be destroyed and no one from Somras will be anywhere near. In fact, Rai Sahab himself will also be in Vilayat! Brilliant!'

I could feel the reverberations of his voice in the room like outwardly moving sound waves that actually seemed to touch me with a clamminess that made my skin crawl. After a long silence I felt, not saw, because I could not look at him anymore, I felt, Sita Ram Jat come up behind me. He spoke softly but every word hit me like the blow of a hammer. 'And that's not all is it, Madamji? In the bombing of Shakil's factory you have arranged for the death of Ras Bihari and in the raid at the abandoned hooch still you have arranged for the encounter of Anmol, your lover and friend and the father of your child! Ma Durga, creator and destroyer, I salute, you!' He folded his hands and bent deep before me. 'I bow to thee a thousand times!'

'Nagina!' It was a mingled scream of horror, terror and grief. 'Is this true, Nagina?' Anmol stood in the door that Munshiji had failed to bolt, the door that led to my bedroom. Anmol stood there like a crazed Neanderthal giant.

'No, no, Anmol…' I pleaded. 'Don't listen to him. He's lying, the unscrupulous bastard!'

'Nagina, Nagina, Nagina,' Anmol moaned hitting the wall with clenched fists. 'How could you be so ruthless?'

'No, Anmol, please listen,' I pulled at his arms.

'Don't touch me!'

'Tut, tut, tut. All this unnecessary display of grief and histrionics. How Ras Bihari will laugh.' Sita Ram Jat delicately lifted up the ends of his white trousers and sat down.

'Ras Bihari? What about Ras Bihari?' Anmol asked lifting a tear-stained face from the wall. 'What has that bastard done now?'

'Ras Bihari is Madamji's new lieutenant,' explained Sita Ram Jat. 'He bombed Hukam Singh Mills and now he will bomb Shakil and Sons. Bas. Seems, Anmol ji, that you have been replaced.'

'You son of a bitch!' Anmol screamed and hurled himself at Sita Ram Jat. But before he could reach Sita Ram Jat, the tiny weasel-like Munshiji jumped up with the speed of lightning and plunged a knife into Anmol's side. Anmol didn't scream. Nobody screamed. Anmol just fell over with a huge crash as I ran to open the window. Putting my head out I vomited the huge meal I had just eaten.

When Anmol fell he pushed the knife deeper inside him. I vaguely registered Sita Ram's pronouncement that Anmol was dead.

The bombing in Shakil's factory took place as scheduled. Sita Ram Jat and Munshiji moved quickly and placed Anmol's body in the abandoned hooch factory and made it appear like an accidental death during the raid. It did not do to ask how they managed to convince the police that Anmol had died there, six hours later, and not at midnight in Hariyali as had actually happened.

Fourteen hours after Anmol's body was secreted out of Hariyali it was brought back and laid out with due ceremony in the veranda. I sat down beside the body of my dead lover with Kulbhushan who looked a bit dazed but appropriately dignified in a carefully chosen white kurta-pajama. Papa and Mummy were still away in the South of France. It was up to Kulbhushan and me to arrange the final ceremonies. I asked Vikasji, my engineer, to call Vidya and inform her about what had happened. Then I sat back and waited for Anmol's family to reclaim him.

From where I sat Anmol's body looked grey and shrunken. I thought of what Siddh Baba had said. The more you want from life, the more you pay. But Anmol had paid the heavier price. Did that mean his passion was truer than mine? Though I wore my dark glasses I did not shed any tears behind them. The Rai Sahabs do not display their grief in public.

As the news of Anmol's death spread, the villagers and factory workers started trickling in from all around. They stood in silent clusters in the Hariyali lawns, for once totally unfazed by the grandeur of the place. In the space of two hours there were more than a thousand people. They trampled the flowerbeds and flattened the lawns and ground their beedis into the garden but refused to budge from where they stood. I was amazed and a little scared to see the outpouring of sorrow for him. The pandits chanted hymns as the people stood vigil through the night, waiting for Anmol's family to arrive and decide where the cremation should take place. At one point I got up to ring the police fearing that the crowd would turn violent.

Vidya reached in the wee hours of the morning with her parents and Anmol's parents, Anmol's brother Guddu and two distraught and bewildered children whose names Anmol had never mentioned to me. Anmol's father, thin and ramrod straight, refused even the glass of water we offered him and taking his cue, the whole family refused to partake of any refreshment. Kulbhushan and I put up stoically with their disregard. After about a half hour, Anmol's father announced that he thought it was only fitting that Anmol's last rites were performed in Majhauli — the town that was both his birthplace and his karmabhoomi.

At seven the next morning we went to the burning ghat in the centre of the city. A crowd of a thousand followed. Anmol's father lit the funeral-pyre of his first-born son and then we sat in the shade of a tin-shed waiting for the flames to devour Anmol.

'I told him not to go to Majhauli, Bhabhi, but he would not listen.' A tall, thin man came and knelt beside Vidya.

'Bhaskar Bhaiyya, what will I do now?' Vidya's eyes swam with tears.

It was Bhaskar, Anmol's business partner in his consulting firm.

'I told him to stay away from her,' he indicated me with his chin. 'But Anmol was like one obsessed. She took him away from you, Vidya. She's a nagin, a churail. She used him and destroyed him.'

'Shhh,' Anmol's father looked at Kulbhushan and me in consternation. Even after losing his son, even though he no longer worked for us, even though we were only the children of the man he had once worked for, he was still somehow indebted to us. Still beholden to a family he had served all his life. Still scared to incur the displeasure of the Rai Sahabs.

'What's there to shhh, Pitaji? Anmol has gone and he has gone only because of her.' Again Bhaskar indicated me. He was shouting loudly now and all of Majhauli was listening in. 'Take a good look at Naginaji, Vidya. She is the enemy you should have been battling, not some faceless Mandal ...'

' Vidya,' Kulbhushan stood up and walked across to her. He folded his hands solicitously in a namaste. His fine-cotton, designer kurta-pajama gleamed white and pure. 'Bhabhi, don't worry, the Rai Sahabs will take care of all your children's needs.'

'No!' Bhaskar shouted. 'We need nothing from the Rai Sahabs. Just stay away from us, you bastard.'

Vidya put a restraining hand on Bhaskar's shoulder. 'It's not their fault, Bhaskar Bhaiyya. The system is so entrenched that repression flows in our blood. Dutiful, unquestioning, servile namak halals, that's what we all are. What Anmol was. What I am. It's not just power or money or caste – our subservience is our failing. What reservation was I fighting? What is one seat when the odds are stacked against you from birth to death? The rich and connected always win. And the poor are effectively silenced by the little scraps thrown to them by the rich. Scraps that make them more grovelling and more subservient.'

I finally looked at Vidya then. I wanted her to understand that I had fought the same battle. That suppression and subservience is a woman's lot irrespective of what caste you belong to or how rich or poor you are. Our eyes met. This was not the Vidya deranged with grief I had seen when she had come for Anmol after his accident. This was a woman in control. She looked at me with eyes full of such hatred that I was silenced. And reassured.

She was as frustrated by her limitations as I had been. Her hatred of me would empower her, I thought. Her hatred of me would give her the strength to live.